More Than You Can Say

Also by Paul Torday

Salmon Fishing in the Yemen
The Irresistible Inheritance of Wilberforce
The Girl on the Landing
The Hopeless Life of Charlie Summers

More Than You Can Say

PAUL TORDAY

Weidenfeld & Nicolson

LONDON

First published in Great Britain in 2011
by Weidenfeld & Nicolson
An imprint of the Orion Publishing Group
Orion House, 5 Upper St Martin's Lane
London WC2H 9EA

An Hachette UK company

1 3 5 7 9 10 8 6 4 2

A CIP catalogue record for this book is available
from the British Library

978 0 297 85824 9 (cased)
978 0 297 85825 6 (trade paperback)

Typeset at Spartan Press Ltd,
Lymington, Hants

Printed and bound in Great Britain by
Clays Ltd, St Ives plc

The Orion Publishing Group's policy is to use papers that
are natural, renewable and recyclable products and made
from wood grown in sustainable forests. The logging and
manufacturing processes are expected to conform to the
environmental regulations of the country of origin.

www.orionbooks.co.uk

'Your story will be laughed to scorn. Of course people will be sorry for you . . . they will say that a meritorious soldier, more notable perhaps for courage than for brains, has gone crazy, and they will comment on the long-drawn-out effects of the War.'

John Buchan, *The Three Hostages*

'A government-commissioned report is recommending that servicemen and women be routinely screened for mental health problems throughout their employment . . . the report also calls for the creation of a specialist mental wellbeing website and online support network, focusing initially on troops returning from operations in Afghanistan.'

ITN News item, 6 October 2010
The UK has had troops in Afghanistan since 2002

One

I had been living on the edge for the last couple of weeks. If I were truthful maybe for the last couple of years. Maybe ever since I had left the army. I had started looking over my shoulder again, mostly at things that weren't there. Camilla, my girlfriend at the time, used to say I had paranoid tendencies. I used to reply that, if she'd been where I'd been, she'd be paranoid too. It was a small thing, but it irritated her. Then at a party we had a falling out. It was one of those arguments like a summer thunderstorm, violent but not serious; at least I hadn't thought it was at first. I can't remember what the particular row was about. We were always having them. Anyway, I walked out of wherever we were at the time – a party, somewhere in Kensington – and went to a pub and had a drink. Then I had another drink.

It turned out it was serious after all – the row with Camilla, I mean. Apparently I'd said I would marry her. I can't remember exactly when I had proposed or whether she had said yes, 'I'll think about it' was more her style, but after I left her she rang me on my mobile several times. Eventually – this must have been after my third or fourth drink – I decided to throw my mobile phone into a bin. Then I decided that was a bad idea, because someone might find it and run up an enormous bill that I would have to pay. So I walked all the way to the Embankment and threw it into the river. No more calls. No more Camilla.

Luckily I don't have the kind of job where you have to show up in the office every morning at eight o'clock. If I did, I would have been fired. I didn't turn up anywhere much before noon for the next fortnight. I drank too much; talked too much when I could find someone to talk to; stayed up too late and then woke in the middle of the morning feeling hung over and sweating. Sometimes I was still wearing the clothes I had put on the previous morning. Then I'd have a shower, tidy myself up a bit – but not too much – and go and have an enormous breakfast in the Greek café on the corner of my street in Camden. Sometimes I would try to take some exercise – go for a walk in Regent's Park, or to the gym. But exercise for its own sake bores me, so if I didn't have any jobs to do for my employer, I usually gave up, went back to the flat and opened a bottle of wine, then read the papers until the sky darkened, the streetlights came on and it was time to go out.

Where I went to depended on my frame of mind. Sometimes I went to the cinema. Occasionally I would call up a friend, from the diminishing list of those who would still speak to me, and try to persuade him or her – usually him, most of the 'hers' had put a line through my name in their address book – to go out for a drink or a cheap supper somewhere. In recent weeks the only invitation I'd received was a gold-edged card inviting me to attend a reception at Lancaster House for veterans of the Afghan Campaign. I don't know why I didn't throw it out. I don't like those sorts of occasions, on the whole, but I suppose it was the thought that I might meet one or two people I had once known. In the end I wrote and said I would come. Maybe it would make me feel better to talk to someone else who knew what it had been like.

If I had nowhere else to go, I would go to the Diplomatic, a private members' club. Why it chose that particular name I do not know as diplomacy was not an obvious quality of most of the membership, either professionally or personally. If there was any common ground shared by the members, apart from a love of card games, backgammon and roulette, it would be hard to say what it was. We had a German Graf, an English marquess, an East End property dealer and a Turkish Cypriot drug dealer on our list. We even had a few bankers who lubricated the club with real cash. Most of us preferred to rely on markers and IOUs in various forms. The stakes were never enormous but, all the same, if you played there regularly, it was quite easy to lose serious amounts of money.

That was one reason why I hadn't been near the club for the last few weeks: I owed quite a lot of money. Several members were carrying my markers for a few hundred pounds each and it was becoming embarrassing. But that's the way cards run. I hadn't held a decent hand for weeks. We play poker mostly, and believe me, you can be a great player – which I am not – but you still need to hold a few good cards if you want to win. The night on which my biographer, if I ever have one, will say I finally lost the plot, I was flush with cash for once. I'd done a couple of jobs and to my surprise my employer had paid me not only for those, but also the considerable amount he owed me in arrears. That was the good news. The bad news was that he fired me.

What he actually said was, 'I think you need to take a nice long holiday. I'll call you some time.'

I said, 'Don't you like the way I work? I thought that was why you hired me.'

My employer – my former employer – said, 'You are showing just a *leetle* too much enthusiasm. You might need more balance in your life, I don't know. I'll be in touch.'

I'd been fired from all sorts of jobs before, for all sorts of reasons, but being fired for being too keen on my work was a first. Anyway, to get to the point, I had over two thousand pounds in cash on me when I went into the Diplomatic that night.

If you don't already know the Diplomatic, I wouldn't recommend you go out of your way to find it. It is down one of those little alleys that still exist in the one or two obscure mews of Mayfair which have not yet been bulldozed to make way for a new office building or a block of service flats for rich non-doms. There is a front door, with no nameplate to indicate what lies behind it, a single lamp burning above it, and a small CCTV camera reminiscent of the entrance to a brothel. Once inside, the rich aroma of cigar smoke – the Diplomatic has not yet caught up with the anti-smoking laws – and the sour smell of stale alcohol immediately dispel this impression. In the tiny hall is a large man squeezed behind a pretty leather-topped desk. This is Eric, the hall porter. Eric checks your name against a list, to see whether you are a member or an invited guest. His orders are to make sure no one is admitted who is not on the list, nor anyone who is not wearing evening dress, so I had put on all the kit. Part of Eric's charm is that, no matter how often he meets you, he will always forget your face, or at least pretend to. If you can get past Eric – and not everybody does – you enter a larger, dimly lit room which is a bar. You can get almost anything you have ever heard of to drink there, and if you want to eat then you can order from the list of bar snacks. I wouldn't recommend the food, but if you want to try a new brand of tequila, or you'd like a glass of Salon champagne, or if you want to drink one of the best dry martinis or whisky sours you can get in London, then Marco the barman will fix you up. Marco's dry martinis give your brain a jolt like an electric shock. I ordered one and sipped the chilly liquid for a second, waiting until the room reoriented itself around me. Then, feeling much better, I took my drink and myself upstairs.

Upstairs there is a large gaming room. There are also a couple of smaller rooms where private games for very high stakes are played. I don't go into those. You wouldn't either, unless you happen to be a Russian oligarch or a Saudi prince. My gang were sitting around a card table playing a variant of poker called Texas Hold 'Em. This particular version doesn't seem to have any rules, with nearly every other card a wild card. I watched for a bit. At the table was Bernie, a heavyset man who owned a lot of rented flats in north-east London; Willi Falkenstein, whose wide estates in southern Bavaria had mostly been mortgaged to pay for his gambling habit; Ed Hartlepool, a man of about my own age who spent most of his time in France to avoid paying too much income tax and then came to London for a couple of days each month in order to lose all the income he had saved. Then there was the mark.

I didn't, of course, know the mark. He was Bernie's guest, so he would be rich and probably stupid. Usually one or other of us would try to bring someone like the mark in order to give the game a fresh injection of cash. He was clearly in awe at being seated at the same table as a German nobleman, which was Willi, and an English one, which was Ed, and I felt sure that when he wrote the enormous cheque at the end of the evening to cover his losses, he would feel a deep sense of gratitude for having been allowed to play with such eminent people. Ed looked up and saw me.

'Well, well – look who's here. It's the Leader of the Pack.'

They had always called me that, after the old song by the Shangri-Las, rather than my proper name, which is Richard. I had been given my nickname because I nearly wrote myself off riding a Ducati around Hyde Park Corner at a hundred miles an hour, which I had done at about three o'clock one morning after a jolly evening at the Diplomatic. It was for a bet.

Everyone turned to look at me except the mark, who blushed and kept his head down, not wanting to appear too familiar with his new friends.

Bernie said, 'Richard, you don't know Gussie here. Say hello to Richard, Gussie.'

The mark gulped and said something. It turned out he wanted to have the pleasure of buying me a drink, so I asked for another dry martini.

'Join us,' suggested Ed. 'But we're playing with cash to-night, Leader. No markers.'

'I have some cash,' I said carelessly. The two thousand pounds was most of the ready I had at that moment and might have to last me God knew how long. I needed at least half of it for rent. For all I knew I might be out on the street within a week if my landlord's patience finally snapped. I was unemployable, or as good as, my parents were unlikely to give me anything, I was broke, close to being homeless, practically destitute. But when had I ever worried about that sort of thing? I wasn't going to start now.

'I might sit in for a couple of hands, if you don't mind me cutting in and then cutting out.'

'The pleasure will be all ours, dear boy,' said Ed. He enjoyed needling me, but was careful never to push his luck. I patted Ed on the back in what I hoped was a patronising way, and pulled up a chair. A waiter handed me my second dry martini. I caught the mark's gaze and raised my glass to him. He blushed again.

The first hand was the best I had been dealt for months. My two hole cards were a pair of kings. Next came the flop: three cards dealt face up. One of them was another king. Then I was dealt a two and a seven. I was up against Ed, who had a pair of sixes showing and I suspected he had a third in his hole cards. He bet hard. I knew he thought I was bluffing when I stayed in and then raised him. At last came the river, the final card that is dealt face down. Mine was another seven, so now I had a full house. I let Ed try to buy the pot, then I called him. What a joy it was to see his expression when I turned over my hole cards to show him my hand.

Half an hour later I was a thousand pounds up. By two in the morning, I had won ten thousand pounds. It was the first time in God knows how long I'd been dealt such good hands. My run of bad luck had gone on for so long no one else at the table – apart from the mark, who hadn't a clue – could bring themselves to believe I held the cards. Time and time again they called my bluff, only to find out that I wasn't bluffing. I didn't need to. It was wonderful, but all the same something inside me kept saying 'Quit while you're ahead.'

Apart from the mark, the other big loser that evening was Ed Hartlepool, and it was beginning to irritate him. He held about a thousand pounds' worth of markers from me and I had made him tear those up. Now he owed me three thousand pounds in cash. The temptation to go on and see whether I could seriously damage Ed's bank balance was strong, but just after two in the morning I yawned loudly and said, 'Well, I think I'm for my bed. Thank you all very much indeed. Is it OK if we settle up now?'

There was general agreement that the game had gone on long enough and, besides, the mark was beginning to show signs of real pain. His losses for the night must have been over eight thousand pounds. There was a general reckoning up at the end of which the mark handed me a cheque for just over five thousand pounds. Ed took out his chequebook, which of course wasn't Barclays or Lloyds or anything like that, but bore the name of some French-sounding private bank. He wrote out the cheque, not looking very happy, then held it up, out of my reach.

'Tell you what, Leader, do you want to double your money?'

'Double or quits?'

'Of course, double or quits. I'm having lunch at the Randolph Hotel in Oxford tomorrow with my uncle. If you can join us by one o'clock sharp, I'll tear up this cheque and write you another for six thousand pounds. And if you don't turn up, or turn up at one minute past, I'll just tear up this cheque.'

I thought about this for a moment. It didn't make sense.

'What's the catch?'

'The catch is,' said Ed, grinning at me, 'that you have to walk there, starting from here, and arrive on time. And you have to produce evidence that you walked all the way.'

There was some discussion around the table about what sort of proof I might have to provide. Road signs collected along the way was one bright suggestion. I ignored my companions and sat and thought about it. Bets of this sort

8

were not uncommon at the Diplomatic. Oxford was about fifty miles from central London, and it was now nearly half past two in the morning. That meant I would have to do four and half – nearer five miles – an hour. I'm a strong walker and I knew I could probably do it. I lifted my head and stared at Ed for a moment, then said, 'Bugger evidence. I'll do it, and I won't cheat. I'll start now and if you want to, you can get in your car and follow me. Otherwise you'll just have to take my word for it. Anyway, it should be fairly obvious when you see me in the dining room at the Randolph whether I've been walking or not.'

Ed looked at me. Then he held out his hand.

'Your word? All right, that's good enough for me.'

It was all very old-fashioned. We shook hands. Willi Falkenstein clapped me on the back and made an unfunny joke about mad dogs and Englishmen.

I said, 'I suppose I'd better get going now.'

A small cheer went up as I headed down the stairs. I heard Ed say, 'Well, that's the quickest I've ever won three thousand pounds back,' and Bernie saying in reply, 'You ain't won your money back yet, Eddie. He's a mad sod. He might surprise you.'

I nodded goodnight to Eric the porter, who ignored me, and left the club. It was raining, but not hard. I set off at a brisk walk in a westerly direction.

I have walked in some difficult places in both violent heat and bitter cold. For the first few miles this walk was, by comparison, a piece of cake. The gentle drizzle soaked through the back of my evening jacket, and my black loafers were becoming rather damp. Although they were quite sturdy, I wondered whether they'd make the distance. I wondered whether I could walk fast enough to collect my six thousand pounds. My biggest worry was being stopped by an inquisitive policeman. I was already attracting some odd glances as I strode rapidly along in my evening clothes. I walked up Park Lane, then at Marble Arch I turned into the Bayswater Road and pounded along that until I reached Notting Hill Gate. From there I thought I'd head west through Shepherd's Bush and up the Uxbridge Road towards the A40.

My plan was to try to find roads that ran parallel to the main roads and motorways, where I would risk being picked up by a passing police car. My other concern was that I might be run over: walking along a road in the middle of the night wearing black clothes wasn't exactly safe, although it would be light by the time I got out of the city.

Somewhere near Shepherd's Bush I found a big all-night supermarket and managed to buy a road atlas and a couple of cans of Red Bull. I swallowed the first of these as I walked, studying the map as best I could under the orange streetlights. A gentleman of the road joined me, a tall, bearded man wearing a long navy blue coat fastened with baler twine and boots stuffed with old newspaper.

'I'm going your way,' he said, exhaling aromatically over me. 'Let's walk together. I'll tell you the story of my life, then you can buy me breakfast. I know a nice little caff not far from here.'

I reached into my coat pocket and peeled a note from the large wedge of cash inside. I had a quick look – it was a tenner. I waved it in front of my new companion, then let go, and it fluttered away in the breeze. He went after it and I increased my pace. I saw no more of him.

As the sky began to lighten, I found myself on a road bridge above the M25, approaching Gerrards Cross. I looked at my watch. It was just after six in the morning. I was beginning to feel quite footsore, and I wondered once again how long my shoes would hold out. For the first time I began to doubt whether I would get to Oxford at all, let alone in the next seven hours. It crossed my mind to go into the next town and find a taxi rank, but I suppressed the thought. In my place, I felt sure Ed Hartlepool would have taken the taxi.

I walked on through Gerrards Cross and along a B road that ran parallel to the A40. I was in the zone now, the way it used to be, my feet pounding the pavement in an endless beat. By now I felt I could go on for ever. The flayed feeling on the soles of my feet belonged to a different person in a different world. My whole body was covered in a thin film of perspiration. The volume of traffic had been steadily increasing and was now a constant roar in both directions. I was becoming increasingly aware of the closeness of trucks thundering past, and cars racing towards me. Occasionally someone would sound his horn as a sign of encouragement or derision, I wasn't sure which. Daylight had crept up on me in the last hour or two without me noticing it. My watch said twenty past eight. I was only just going to make it, as long as I did not slacken my pace. From somewhere a smell of bacon drifted on the air and for a moment I was overwhelmed by the desire to find a café and have an enormous breakfast: a breakfast that would cost me six thousand pounds if I stopped to take it. I kept walking.

Somewhere between Stokenchurch and Wheatley, following a minor road that avoided the heavy traffic, I heard a car behind me and automatically moved closer to the grass verge so that it could pass. It was a bright, clear September morning and I was no longer concerned about being knocked over. All the same I didn't want to take any chances and looked over my shoulder to see where the car was. A black Range Rover was idling along some twenty-five yards behind me. I turned my head to the front again and kept walking. The road ahead was empty.

There was a brief purr as the car accelerated. The next thing I knew it was right alongside me, crowding me into the edge so that I almost stumbled on the grass verge. I shook my head in irritation and again waited for it to pass me. It didn't. It had tinted windows through which only the dimmest outline of its occupants could be seen. Then the nearside front window opened and the driver leaned across the passenger seat.

'Want a lift, old man?' he asked.

The speaker had a pale, narrow face and pale, curly hair. Enormous wraparound sunglasses obscured most of his features.

'No thanks.'

'Good party last night, was it?'

I did not reply, waiting for him to lose interest and drive on.

'Where are you headed?'

This idiot was beginning to annoy me. I could not hold a conversation with him and continue walking at nearly six miles an hour. If I walked any more slowly I'd lose my bet.

'Are you lost, old man? Don't know where you're going? Get in and we'll give you some breakfast and then set you on your way.'

I managed to find enough breath to answer him.

'Would you very kindly fuck off?'

'Oh, if you'd like us to fuck off, then of course that's what we'll do.'

The window of the Range Rover wound up again and

then, instead of overtaking, the car pulled into the verge behind me. I resisted the strong temptation to look over my shoulder again and see what the driver was doing. I could hear the motor running. Half a mile ahead of me was a straggly line of houses marking a small village. Suddenly it seemed important to me to get to that village, where there were other people around, and away from the Range Rover. I tried to speed up a little. Behind me I heard the snarl of the engine as the driver gunned it. I thought, thank God, he's going, whoever he is. There was something about the narrow face of the driver with its enormous aviator sunglasses that had made me feel uneasy.

Suddenly I felt a huge blow to my right side. I was pitched forward into the ditch at the side of the road and my head struck something hard. I was stunned and winded and in so much pain I thought I was going to black out. Then I heard, through the mist of concussion, two car doors being slammed. The next second two sets of hands were lifting me and I was dragged around to the rear of the car, blinking and semi-conscious. The tailgate was opened and then one pair of hands transferred itself to my ankles. With a grunt the two men lifted me up to the height of the tailgate. They must have been strong because I am not a small man, at thirteen stone and six foot two, but they managed it. I was rolled on to the tailgate and then folded up so that I fitted into the rear compartment of the car. Then the tailgate was slammed shut and I was left in complete darkness, the parcel shelf pressing down on me. The car drove off, and I screamed as we went around a corner and I was flung against the side of the car. I remember thinking that I should have looked over my shoulder after all – then I might have seen them coming.

Two

I don't know how long I lay squashed up in the back of the car. Waves of nausea swept over me, accompanied by stabbing pains in my right side. On top of that I started to get violent cramps in my legs because I could not straighten them. Luckily I was not fully conscious; I kept fading in and out. The blow to my head must have given me concussion.

After what seemed like a long time, I sensed the car was slowing down and then heard the scrunch of wheels on gravel. The car stopped, and a moment later the tailgate opened. Somebody yanked me by the legs and I fell out of the car, winding myself again, as well as getting a nice bit of gravel rash on one side of my face.

'You're not going to cause any trouble, are you, old man?' asked Narrow Face.

Another voice said, 'Trouble? I don't think so. Look at him.'

I couldn't see the speaker, but I didn't much care what he was saying because at that point I was sick. I managed to move my head so that I didn't spatter myself and tried to straighten my legs out. They were still screaming with cramp.

'Who's going to clear *that* up, I'd like to know?' said Narrow Face.

'You are,' said the other man unsympathetically. 'But first let's get our guest into the house.'

Our guest? Had I inadvertently won a dream holiday for one at a country house hotel? The two men picked me up, hooking my arms around their shoulders as they half-carried, half-dragged me inside. I did not take in much of my surroundings but was aware of a building in grey stone surrounded by lawns and woods. We were at the rear of a large house. Inside I was dragged along a dark corridor and then up a steep staircase and into another corridor, which was better lit and warmer than the first. We stopped outside a door while one of my new friends unlocked it. I was taken in and dropped on to a bed. After that I don't remember much. I think I slept for a while.

I was woken up by someone asking me my name. I know the answer to that one, I thought. Aloud I said: 'Richard Gaunt.'

'And your date of birth?'

That was a bit harder.

'Third November nineteen seventy-five,' I told the questioner after a moment. I managed to open my eyes. The speaker was not one of the two men who had brought me here. He was short, dark-skinned, had black hair turning grey and wore a dark blue suit. He leaned over me and shone a torch into my eyes. The stethoscope around his neck was a clue.

'You are awake. Good afternoon,' he said. 'I am Dr Ahmed. I want to do some checking up on you, if you don't mind.'

Good afternoon? Suddenly memory flooded back. I had been walking, walking to Oxford for a bet: a six-thousand-pound bet. If it was the afternoon, then I had lost the bet, and the six thousand pounds. I swore.

'Please co-operate,' said Dr Ahmed anxiously. 'It is for your own good.'

'Don't worry, Doctor,' I said. 'Only I've just remembered I'm late for an appointment.'

'Ah. You must rest first and get better. Then we will see.'

He set to work. First of all he produced some cotton wool and alcohol from a black bag he had put down on a chair, and cleaned up the grazes on my face. Then he helped me to unbutton my shirt, and inspected the damage to my right side where the Range Rover must have struck me. He applied some ointment, then prodded and poked me, not unsympathetically, until I winced.

'Unfortunately you may have cracked a rib. I have not the facilities here for an ultrasound scan, but we can be confident it is not broken. You should not exert yourself for a few days. You will have some nasty-looking bruises for a while, but you should heal up as time goes by.'

He checked my heartbeat, took my blood pressure and temperature, and looked again in my eyes and ears with his torch. Then he said, 'Also you have the remains of some mild concussion. Take two of these paracetamol and we will see how you get on. Otherwise, there is not much wrong with you. You are a very fit man.'

He poured me a glass of water to wash down the tablets, then packed his bag and left the room. I heard the key turn in the lock as he closed the door behind him. I sat up on the bed and looked around me.

The room was small, but comfortable and expensively furnished. It was full of those grace notes beloved by interior decorators: blue velvet curtains with yellow silk tie-backs and a fringed and swagged blue velvet pelmet with yellow tassels; a pair of boudoir armchairs opposite a fireplace with an antique fire screen in front of it; a chair and a writing table by the window. The walls were covered in a blue and cream striped paper, and numerous prints and engravings of flowers hung from the picture rail. The bed I lay on was soft and the room was warm.

After a while I swung my legs off the bed and made a careful effort to get to my feet. It hurt, but not as much as I had feared. I went to the window and looked out at a view that consisted mostly of a large blue Atlantic cedar which someone had planted too close to the side of the house. Beyond it I could make out wide, freshly mown lawns and a fringe of woodland. I had no idea where I was.

Turning around, I noticed another door, half open, that led into a bathroom. Inside fluffy white towels hung on a heated towel rail, and a wicker basket contained everything the forgetful guest might need such as a toothbrush and razor. With some discomfort I stripped off my clothes and stepped into the shower. I experienced the glorious relief of needles of hot water massaging my shoulders and back, relieving some of the pain. Once I'd shaved, cleaned my teeth, dried myself and dressed again, I felt a great deal better, relatively speaking.

It was then that I noticed various things were missing. My shoes were nowhere to be seen. Looking around, I realised that my evening jacket was not in the room. Neither was my wallet, nor the envelope I had taken from the Diplomatic with all the cash and cheques from my evening's winnings. I couldn't remember how much money I'd had but it was several thousand pounds, one way or another. My watch, an old Rolex my father had given me, was also gone. It had been an expensive day so far.

I padded across the room to the door that led to the

corridor and tried the handle. I hadn't been wrong: it was locked. What on earth was going on? I appeared to have been kidnapped for no reason at all. Narrow Face and his anonymous friend couldn't have known I was carrying all that cash. And if it was cash they were after, they would have just taken it and left me in the ditch. After the last two years, and the way I'd behaved, I didn't have many friends left – to be accurate, I didn't have any friends at all. But then again, I didn't have any enemies. There might be quite a few people who disliked me, or would not take my phone calls, or who even might cross the street to avoid me if they saw me coming, but I couldn't think of anyone who would bother to go to the trouble these people had gone to. The effort of puzzling through these things was making my head ache, so I decided to do what I did best in difficult circumstances – I gazed at the ceiling and let my mind go blank. I've always believed in not worrying until you know what there is to worry about.

Time passed. Then there was a sound at the door and a man in a dark suit came in. He was carrying a silver tray with a glass of champagne on it, and he had newspapers clasped under his arm. He set the tray down on a small table beside the window.

'Mr Khan sends his apologies for keeping you waiting, sir. He wondered if you might enjoy a glass of champagne, sir, and a chance to read the day's papers. He will ask you to join him presently for a light lunch in the conservatory. I will come back and show you the way as soon as he is free.'

I watched the man leave the room, my mouth open. I suppose I could have mounted an escape attempt, as the butler or whatever he was did not seem especially robust. But at that particular moment, neither was I. Any form of physical exertion seemed like a very bad idea. And trying to escape with no shoes did not appeal to me either. The door closed again, and the key turned. I wandered across to the window and sipped the glass of champagne. It was chilled, and delicious. Then I picked up *The Times*. There didn't seem any point in sulking, so I thought I would make myself comfortable while I could. I sat down in one of the armchairs and began to read the papers. A few minutes later the door opened and the man in the dark suit appeared. In one hand he held my shoes, which, despite being badly scuffed and down at heel, looked quite presentable again, having been buffed and polished to a deep shine. In the other hand he held, on a hanger, my evening jacket, which had been brushed and pressed.

'I'm afraid we couldn't get some of the grass stains out, sir,' he said, 'but you can hardly see them now. If you would be kind enough to follow me downstairs lunch will be ready in a moment.'

I slipped on my jacket and my shoes, and followed the man – servant or secretary – along the corridor, then down a much wider staircase than the one I had been dragged up, and into an entrance hall with a black and white marble floor and oak-panelled walls. Everywhere you looked, the touch of an interior decorator could be seen. Everything – even the older pieces of furniture – looked new, shining with polish, as if they had just been put there.

The servant padded across the hall, then through a large drawing room. This was full of enormous armchairs and sofas, fitted with loose covers in a gold cloth, with yellow corded piping. On the walls hung oils of eighteenth-century ladies and gentlemen, clutching children or muskets. A door had been opened up in the far wall of the drawing room. This led into a vast glass conservatory. At first, all I could see was a profusion of tropical plants and orchids. The hiss of a spray could be heard and I saw an automatic mister travelling along a rail above the beds of plants, showering them in a fine rain. There were two people in the conservatory. One I did not know. The other, stepping from behind a palm tree as I approached, was Narrow Face. A marble table laid for two stood at one end of the room and at the other end was a hotplate, on which various covered dishes had been set out.

The tall, dark-skinned man was dressed in a white shirt and black trousers and he was impressive-looking, in some way I could not at first define. His black hair was slicked back from his forehead with a lotion that gave off a sweet odour of almonds. He had a hawk nose and eyes that seemed very white and clear against his dark skin.

'Good afternoon, Mr Gaunt,' he greeted me. 'My name is Mr Khan. Please come and sit down.'

I looked at him carefully. This was a Pashtun. He might be from the Pakistan side of the border or from the other side, Afghanistan. Either way he came from a difficult part of the world. I stepped forward and shook his hand when he offered it. It was rough and calloused. He waved me towards a chair.

'You must be hungry after your journey,' he said. 'We have some curries here, some lamb, some biryanis. It is nothing much, but I hope it will suffice. I must apologise for the way in which you were brought here. Kevin!'

The smell of the food was so delicious and my hunger suddenly so overpowering that I almost felt inclined to overlook the fact I had been run over by a large car and then kidnapped. Until I had eaten something, at least. But then Narrow Face stepped forward and removed his sunglasses.

The result was not an improvement. Small weak eyes blinked at me as he said, 'Sorry we bumped into you like that, old man. I was trying to park the car and was a bit careless. Do hope you're feeling better.'

He stretched out his hand. I suppose he expected that I would shake it and say 'No hard feelings' or something equally stupid. Instead I stared at him until his hand dropped back to his side and his smile vanished. He was a mean, psychologically damaged-looking man. One day he would be a physically damaged-looking man if I had anything to do with it. Now was not the moment, though, so I just said:

'Where's my money, Kevin? And my watch?'

'What is this?' demanded Mr Khan. 'Do you have some of his belongings, Kevin?'

'Just for safe keeping, Mr Khan, sir,' said Kevin. 'You can't trust the banks these days, can you?' He reached inside his jacket and took out my wallet and the white envelope containing the cash. As he did so I saw he was wearing a shoulder holster under his jacket. He took my watch out of another pocket. The glass was cracked and the watch had stopped.

'We were going to see if we could get the watch fixed for you, old man, but there wasn't time.' Kevin stepped forward, avoiding my eyes, and set my belongings carefully on the table. Then he stepped back and stood at ease.

'Kevin, I am so glad you took these things only for safe keeping,' said Mr Khan. 'Because you know, in my country, if someone takes things that do not belong to them, *we cut off their hands.*'

The last words were spoken softly, but with an emphasis that made Kevin wince.

'Leave us alone, now, while I give our guest some lunch,' said Mr Khan. 'Do not go far away, I may need you later.'

Kevin disappeared in the direction of the hallway. As far as I could tell we were on our own now, unless there was someone else lurking in the undergrowth behind us in the conservatory. The sun had come out and it was warm under the glass. Rich scents of unknown flowers and plants filled the air, mingled with the spicy smells of the food.

Mr Khan started spooning small amounts of delicious-looking saffron rice, and spicy morsels of lamb, on to a plate, which he handed to me. He poured me a glass of iced water from a copper jug.

'Is it to your liking?' he asked, helping himself to a modest amount of rice and a spoonful of curry.

'Delicious, thank you very much.'

We both ate for a moment. Then Mr Khan said, 'But I am forgetting my manners. You must be wondering why you were brought here in such a very extraordinary manner. I must apologise, by the way, for Kevin's carelessness. I hope you are not hurt?'

I drank some water, and said, 'I'm recovering. You seemed very keen to get me here.'

Mr Khan smiled.

'Of course I will tell you why we went to such trouble in a moment. But first, do tell me a little bit about yourself, Mr Gaunt.'

'There's nothing much to tell,' I replied modestly.

'You are an English gentleman? A member of English society? Is that why you were dressed in evening clothes at eight o'clock in the morning?'

This time I was the one who smiled, despite myself. This was the first time I had been called a gentleman and I enjoyed the irony. I wondered why Mr Khan wanted to know about me, and whether there was any reason I should tell him anything. Besides, what was my profession these days? In the last two years I had been a restaurateur for a while; then an ex-restaurateur. After that I had slipped gracefully down the social and economic scale. I had been a barman; a nightclub greeter; a bouncer and a debt-collector. You could take your pick. Few of my trades had lasted more than eight to twelve weeks and the most successful one since our restaurant had gone bust had been helping collect on unpaid or overdue loans. Even that, which was not exactly a gentleman's career, had come to an end. I had been too forceful in my methods with one or two of the clients I considered were having a laugh at my employer's expense.

'No particular profession at present, I'm afraid,' I said. 'My CV is broad, rather than deep.'

'But you were in the army once, were you not?'

'How did you know that?' I asked, in surprise.

'An inspired guess on my part. And now you are a gentleman of means – a man of leisure?'

'I have plenty of leisure at the moment. I don't have a job.'

'And so last night you were at a Dance, perhaps, attended by other Members of Society? Or at a Cocktail Party? I have heard that the English are very fond of Dances and Cocktail Parties.' As Mr Khan spoke he managed to invest each of these imagined jollities with capital letters. I laughed, and then winced as my ribs flared with pain.

'No such luck, I'm afraid. I spent the evening at a club.'

Mr Khan looked very respectful.

'Ah yes, an English club. And this morning you went for a walk to take exercise? The English are fond of taking exercise, I have heard.'

23

'Yes, I decided to go for a walk.'

'All the way from London? That is many miles.'

Mr Khan appeared to be intrigued by my eccentric behaviour but I was becoming restless under his cross-examination. I had waited long enough for an explanation of why I had been kidnapped, and I wouldn't have minded some compensation either. I decided to start asking a few questions of my own.

'You have a wonderful house, Mr Khan, and a very good cook, and a very efficient staff. You must have worked hard to acquire such things around you.'

Mr Khan smiled again. He smiled often but the smiles never quite reached his eyes, with their brown irises surrounded by whites so clear they were almost blue. His eyes remained fixed on me all the time we spoke, scarcely blinking.

'I have been fortunate,' he said. 'I am a trader and a private banker, a rich man back at home, and not a poor man even in this wealthy country. I live here for a few weeks every year and I like to keep the house up to a good standard for my friends and guests.'

'And where is home, Mr Khan?'

'Where indeed, Mr Gaunt? I travel so much I scarcely know where home is, or once was. A long time ago it was a small village in the mountains of my homeland. Now Dubai is my base, but I also have houses in Palermo, Beirut, and here – I am a fortunate fellow.'

Mr Khan was good at not answering questions. I tried again.

'You must do very good business, being a banker,' I said politely.

'Yes, the families I work for support me and I do my best to reward their good faith.'

There was a silence while we both continued to eat. The exchange of career notes seemed to be over. Mr Khan refilled my glass of water, and offered me more lamb, which I refused. He must have pressed a bell push out of sight under the table because the man in the dark suit appeared with a tray containing coffee cups. He set out the coffee things, cleared away the plates and dishes and retreated with his tray.

'Are you a married man, may I ask?' enquired Mr Khan, as we sipped our coffee. The conversation was becoming odder by the minute yet I felt a weird sense of inevitability about it.

'No, as a matter of fact, I'm not,' I admitted.

'Have you ever considered it?' asked Mr Khan. This was such an odd remark, in the circumstances, that I think my mouth dropped open for a moment. I decided to keep talking. Maybe in the end I would find out what this was all about.

'Well, I might have done. But I have never really come close to the married state. Not so far.'

This was not quite accurate, but I felt that the present situation did not warrant too much candour.

'I myself,' said Mr Khan, taking a case from his pocket and offering me a large cigar, 'have several wives. I have found marriage to be a rewarding state of affairs and I thoroughly approve of it. You won't smoke? Do you mind if I do?'

He clipped the end from his cigar, then lit it and drew on it, puffing out a cloud of fragrant smoke. I rather wished I had accepted his offer, it smelled so good.

'God wants men to marry women,' said Mr Khan, continuing his discourse. 'It is our natural state, after all.'

He puffed some more on his cigar. Maybe now was the

moment to ask why his hireling had knocked me down with a car and dragged me here, thereby causing me to lose a six-thousand-pound bet. But before I could assemble the right words, Mr Khan forestalled me.

'How old are you, Mr Gaunt?'

'I'm thirty-three,' I replied. 'Now, Mr Khan, I really must ask you—' But he stopped me again, raising one hand.

'I think it is time you got married.'

'Me? I'm afraid that's not on the cards, Mr Khan. Perhaps you won't mind if I change the subject. Could you explain why I was brought here—'

Again he cut me off, not impolitely, but firmly.

'But that is what we are talking about.'

'I'm sorry?'

'That is why you were brought here. To get married.'

By this stage of the conversation all I could do was stare at him. Mr Khan didn't look like a madman and he didn't sound like one. But the words he spoke were not reasonable.

'Yes,' said Mr Khan, noticing my surprise. 'It is an important step in your life. Unfortunately there has not been much time to consult with you about this. Nevertheless, I feel very certain that you will soon be married and that your marriage will find favour with God.'

'But I don't know anyone I want to marry,' I said feebly. If I had been feeling stronger I would have jumped up and tried to leave this place – and yet there was something oddly compelling about this conversation, even if it repelled me at the same time.

'Fortunately, we have found just the girl for you,' Mr Khan continued. 'I will arrange an introduction in next to no time.'

'Let me get this straight. You want me to get married to

26

some girl you've found and whom I've never met? Is that what I'm hearing?'

'Of course. It is what you British call an arranged marriage. These are so often the most successful marriages. I am a great believer in arranged marriages. All of my wives were arranged for me. They brought money, useful contacts – and, of course, the inestimable pleasures of female company. You too will approve of our arrangements on your behalf, Mr Gaunt, once you know a little bit more.'

Three

There was a silence. I was struggling to understand the situation I found myself in. If I had been writing a report for my superiors when I was in the army it might have read:

'8.30 a.m.: knocked down by large car and kidnapped.
1.30 p.m.: received indirect proposal of marriage from unknown man of Asian origin on behalf of girl, also unknown.'

Mr Khan sensed my confusion.

'You have met Kevin. He is one of my goons. I hired him for qualities other than his ability to think.'

'Oh, good,' I said stupidly.

'His instructions were to find a vagabond – a drifter – a man of no fixed abode. He saw a man in evening dress walking along by the side of the road and concluded, for reasons I cannot comprehend, that you were just such a person. It was *not* part of his instructions to knock you down. But it is so difficult to get good staff these days.'

His assessment of Kevin's abilities was the same as my own.

'I see from talking to you that you are an educated man. A refined, civilised person, who happened to be out for a walk. You still have not mentioned *why* you were walking along the road at that time of the morning in evening dress . . .'

'It's a long story,' I replied.

'That is immaterial. You may tell me later, after you are married. For a little while at least, you should think of me as you would a father-in-law. But perhaps you have a girlfriend at home who is anxious to hear from you?'

'Not at present,' I said.

'Or an employer, wondering why you have not turned up for work?'

'Not at this precise moment.'

'Then I hope that your stay with us will cause you the minimum of inconvenience. Of course, you will be compensated for the use of your time, and for your patience with us, and for the – happily minor – injuries you sustained when Kevin bumped into you with his car. So unnecessary! If you will give us another forty-eight hours I will pay you ten thousand pounds. I hope you will find that acceptable.'

While Mr Khan had been talking I had been thinking. The truth was, no one *was* waiting for me: no girlfriend, employer, friend or dog pined for my return. I had no pressing engagements in my diary, now that I had missed my date at the Randolph Hotel. I had no prospect of employment, and just at that moment, not even the slightest curiosity as to how I might earn my living.

The last two years had been one disaster after another. There had been the restaurant, which had shown so much promise at first. It had failed because its co-owner couldn't do his sums, and had a violent temper that the staff and customers would not put up with – not to mention worse behaviour. Then various jobs, each less glamorous and lower paid than the one before, as I failed to turn up to work or, on turning up to work, quarrelled with someone. It was not an enticing prospect. The thought of my empty flat in Camden with its unmade bed, and unwashed dishes, and scale-stained bath did not tug at my heartstrings. At any moment the landlord was likely to turn up and change the locks, then chuck my few belongings out on to the street: my rent must be at least two months behind. I realised that I had become absorbed in my own thoughts and that Mr Khan was waiting for an answer.

'Another two days here, you say . . . ?'

'Well, another two days of your time. It will be necessary to leave the house for a brief journey to the register office. We have prepared a great deal of paperwork but we will require your co-operation in completing some of the details.'

I thought about all the reasons why I should insist on leaving now. Mr Khan and his servants were at best a bunch of crooks engaged in some sort of scam, which I had yet to understand. At worst, they might be dealing in human trafficking. Almost anything was possible; the only impossibility was that they were pleasant, honest people who wanted to do me a good turn.

But ten thousand pounds! Apart from the cash I had on me I hadn't a penny in the world. Some income from my army pension, but that didn't go far. No capital, no chance of any handouts from my parents after the way I had treated them. But with ten thousand pounds in my pocket, maybe I could start to turn my life around. It would buy me a new suit, a haircut, time to go to the endless job interviews I knew I would have to go to before someone finally employed me. And after all: what were they asking me to do? Put my name on some piece of paper that allowed a woman from India or Pakistan to claim residency and then citizenship. That was what this was all about. Sham marriages were practically an industry these days. One more illegal immigrant wouldn't make any difference, would it? I was vague about the law but I imagined that once I had married the woman I would never have to see her again, and after a certain amount of time I could apply for a divorce.

'Why not?' I said.

'What?'

'I said, OK.'

Mr Khan looked at me and I looked back at him and, for a moment, our gazes locked. Then he said, 'I trust you will not mind if we keep you to your room for some of the time?'

'I would prefer not.'

Mr Khan hesitated for the first time in our conversation. Then he said:

'You may have the use of this conservatory, and the drawing room if you feel the room upstairs is too confining. But you must not go into any of the other rooms. Most of the doors are locked anyway. And you must on no account use the telephone, or go outside. Are these conditions acceptable to you?'

'Yes.'

'And may I have your word as an English gentleman that you will adhere to them?'

Once again, I was amused by the old-fashioned nature of his question.

'Of course.'

In fact, I had decided that for the moment I would not try to leave. I was by now too full of curiosity about the set-up here, and the bizarre arrangements that had been made for my forthcoming nuptials. The house was warm and comfortable and the food was good. Above all there was the matter of the money to be considered, which would more than compensate me for the loss of my bet with Ed Hartlepool –

although nothing could have equalled the pleasure of seeing Ed Hartlepool write me out a large cheque.

Mr Khan stood up. 'I will not detain you any longer. Later this afternoon my assistant David may ask you to sign some forms. I apologise for all the paperwork. At home, matters would be simpler, but we are in England and must obey her laws.'

He must have pressed the bell again, because as he was speaking David arrived.

'Please show Mr Gaunt back to his room,' said Mr Khan. 'But there is no need to lock the door. Mr Gaunt and I have reached an understanding.'

David took me upstairs and as he left me he said, 'I will be back in half an hour or so with some documents for you to complete, Mr Gaunt. I trust that will be in order?'

'I shall be here,' I told him. I went back into my room, lay on the bed and thought about getting married. Would she be thin or fat; fair or dark? My success rate at pulling attractive women was not good. I remembered going out one night, when I was still in the army. We were on a Mountain Warfare Course in the Austrian Alps, which turned out to be a skiing holiday paid for by the grateful taxpayer.

A few of us decided to have a 'grimmie' competition at the local dance hall, to see who could pull the grimmest-looking girl. I won. I don't remember the prize. I do remember how horribly ashamed of myself I felt, as I left the dance hall with a very sweet girl who was, I had to admit, very far from good-looking. The bet didn't require you to sleep with the girl, only to leave the dance hall arm in arm with your partner, and I did that. Outside it was snowing. I turned and looked at my temporary friend, and removed her spectacles and gave her the tenderest kiss I could manage. Then I left her, looking confused but happy, with some mumbled apology and a promise to meet again that I knew I would not keep.

I wondered whether I would draw a 'grimmie' this time. It was quite possible. It didn't matter, in any case. Once we were married I presumed I would never see my new wife again, which was fine by me: I didn't think I was quite ready to settle down and I did not share Mr Khan's faith in arranged marriages. Then again, I had little faith in my own ability to decide which girl to spend the rest of my life with. These days, getting any girl to spend more than a few hours in my company seemed beyond me. I always managed to do something disastrous whenever I met anyone I thought I might like.

There was a gentle knock on the door and David came in.

'If you will follow me, sir, Mr Khan has offered the use of his study for the paperwork.'

I followed David downstairs to the hall. This time we turned right, instead of left. David took a bunch of keys from his pocket and unlocked a door that opened into a small library. There was a mahogany table in the middle of the room on which a few documents had been set out. Two chairs had been pulled up. In the corner of the room was a desk with a flat-screen monitor on it, and a stand-by light glowing on the hard drive underneath.

The room looked like everywhere else in the house: the books were sets of leather-bound volumes bought, it seemed, more for their array of colour than their content. There were no personal touches in the room: no photograph frames, or papers lying about. Mr Khan was either very tidy, or else he rarely came here. We sat at the table, and David picked up a document, which turned out to be my passport. I looked at him.

'We found a door key in your evening jacket, and we took your address from the driving licence in your wallet. Amir, a colleague of ours, has been to your flat to obtain documents which will give us proof that you are a UK citizen, and proof of residence.'

I raised my eyebrows. I did not like the idea that these people had been rummaging through my personal things. It gave me a creepy feeling. That was why Mr Khan had asked me whether I had been in the army. They must have seen something in the flat: perhaps the photograph of me at Sandhurst. It was quick work, and resourceful of them. We sat and filled in a couple of forms. I noticed the name of my intended had not yet been filled in.

'Don't I need to know at least the name of the person I am going to marry?' I asked.

'Don't worry, sir – all in good time. We have already informed the registrar of that name in order to give notice. And we have gained exemption from the normal waiting period. We have told them you have unexpectedly been recalled to active service and want to be married before you return to Afghanistan.'

'I'll have my passport back now, please,' I said, and took it. David made no objection. Instead, he went to the door and called for someone. A small man in a natty suit appeared.

'If you will just stand up for a moment, Mr Gaunt, the tailor will take your measurements. Mr Khan wishes you to look as smart as possible on the great day.'

The tailor produced a tape measure and took a few measurements: inside leg, chest, waist and so on. Then he jotted them down in a little black notebook.

'It'll be a rush job, Mr Gaunt, sir,' he said. 'They say there's no time for a proper fitting. Well, normally I prefer at

34

least two fittings to get the job right. But luckily you're an average shape, sir, so we should be able to cut you something you won't be ashamed to wear. Mr Khan's chosen the cloth: a charcoal bird's-eye for the coat and trousers, and a dove-grey waistcoat. Do you have any preference as to the lining, sir? Only Mr Khan didn't specify.'

'Whatever you think best,' I replied. I realised I was being fitted for a morning coat.

'We have a nice blue silk that would look very good against the charcoal,' suggested the tailor. I nodded my agreement. The fitting over, the man disappeared. David escorted me back to my room.

As I sat there I tried to work out where this house was. I had seen no clues so far as to its name or location: no desk with writing paper on it, no prints of the house, no visitors' book. I could have been anywhere. I tried to recall how long the drive had been after I had been knocked down. I thought it might have lasted for an hour at most. Therefore I was either in Oxfordshire, Gloucestershire, Berkshire, Hampshire, Northamptonshire, Bedfordshire or Hertfordshire. That narrowed it down.

Supper was a more solitary affair than lunch. I dined in the conservatory once more, among the sweet exhalations of the plants and flowers, but there was no Mr Khan to keep me company. I was beginning to feel rather bored. That worried me, because when I get bored my behaviour tends to degenerate. There was nothing to do: no one to talk to, and nothing to read. I'm not much of a book-reader anyway, I don't seem to be able to concentrate these days, so I lingered for a while in the hope that someone would appear: Mr Khan, perhaps, or my future wife. Even Kevin would have been welcome entertainment by this stage. After sitting alone for over an hour, I trudged back upstairs. There was nothing to do except go to bed. I undressed and fell asleep.

I did not wake the next morning until I heard a knock at the door. I sat up, still drowsy, trying to remember where I was. David came into the room carrying a tray on which there was a teapot, a cup and saucer, a small silver milk jug and a newspaper.

'Good morning, Mr Gaunt,' he said. 'I trust you slept well?' He crossed the room and set the tray on the writing table, then opened the curtains.

'Mr Khan told me to say that there is no hurry, but breakfast is ready in the conservatory.'

When I went down Mr Khan was already seated at the marble table. On the hotplate stood a cafetière, a silver teapot and a silver jug full of boiling water. There was a wicker basket full of fresh rolls and croissants, and in another basket, underneath little woolly hats shaped like the heads of chickens, nestled some boiled eggs.

'Mr Gaunt, good morning,' said Mr Khan, rising to greet me. 'I hope you passed a comfortable night? It is a wonderful morning, a real English autumn day. The colours of the trees are changing and the sun is out. In Dubai it is now forty degrees, still very hot. Here it is so cool, so fresh. Autumn is a beautiful time in the English countryside, do you not agree?'

'Season of mists, and mellow fruitfulness,' I replied.

'Ah yes. I do not recognise the reference. Perhaps it is one of your English poets? Here is a glass of fresh orange juice.'

I took the glass and drained it, then tucked into breakfast.

'Do try some of our marmalade,' Mr Khan urged me. 'It is made by Mr Frank Cooper. From Oxford, I believe. We will soon be visiting Oxford. That is where the register office is.'

'Oh yes, I'd forgotten,' I said. 'I'm getting married to-morrow, aren't I?'

'Oh, Mr Gaunt, Mr Gaunt,' Mr Khan chuckled. 'How could you forget such an important occasion? But perhaps it is because you have not yet met your bride? Once you have met her, you will not forget her again, I assure you.'

'And when am I meeting her?'

'Anticipation is the thing!' cried Mr Khan. He seemed to be in a very cheerful mood. 'But you are not dressed to receive a new bride. Finish your breakfast, then go upstairs. You will find your bridal clothes ready for you to wear. Put them on and come back. Then we will make the necessary introductions.'

Mr Khan smiled at me.

After I'd finished eating I went back upstairs to my bedroom. The bed had already been made, and on the bed-spread, in a plastic garment bag, was an immaculate-looking set of morning clothes. Beside it was a selection of cream silk shirts, ties, socks and so on.

I changed into my finery. The charcoal morning tailcoat and trousers fitted me fairly well. The tailor must have worked all night to produce them. I checked myself in the bathroom mirror and adjusted the knot in my tie. I looked all right. In fact, I thought I looked pretty smart. I could have done with a haircut, but the face staring back at me from the mirror reminded me of the younger, more optimistic person who had once inhabited this body, before everything went wrong. I shrugged away the memories.

When I came back to the conservatory, it was empty. Breakfast had been cleared away and now a bronze ice bucket stood on the marble table, along with a couple of glasses. I could see the top of a champagne bottle poking out with a cloth wrapped around it. So there was to be a celebration: I was to drink the bride's health. But where was she? I found to my annoyance that my pulse rate had gone up. I was feeling the sort of apprehension I used to feel when I went skiing, standing at the top of a black run; or on those other expeditions, which had so often begun in the darkness before dawn.

I heard footsteps and went back into the drawing room to see who was coming. A beam of sunlight came through the windows, making the rich patterns and colours of the drawing-room carpet glow as if newly woven. The first into the room was Mr Khan, wearing a dark pinstriped suit and a striped tie. He looked very formal.

'Mr Gaunt,' he said. 'Your new clothes fit you very well. You look, as they say, a million dollars.'

He turned and beckoned to someone lingering out of sight in the hall.

'Mr Gaunt, I am proud to introduce you to your fiancée,' said Mr Khan as she came into the room. 'May I present Adeena, the future Mrs Gaunt?'

My first thought was one of astonishment. For some reason I had imagined I would be meeting a Pakistani or Bangladeshi girl in a sari, with glossy black hair tucked under a headscarf, or else a veiled figure in a hijab. This woman looked like a European: blonde wavy hair curling just at the base of her neck, blue eyes, a honey-coloured complexion, a stunning figure. She was wearing Western clothes, of the sort suitable for a weekend at a country house party: a pale green cardigan over a white blouse and a tweed skirt, with brown suede loafers on her feet. She looked like any other well-bred, well-groomed girl you might expect to meet in such surroundings; and yet, quite unlike too.

But it was her eyes that caught my attention. They were so full of despair and hatred that I almost flinched when she gazed at me. The rest of her face was expressionless as she was introduced.

'I am very pleased to meet you,' I said. Feeling slightly ridiculous, I put out my hand. She took it briefly. Her hand was cool and limp, then she let go.

'Pleased to meet you,' she replied, with only the hint of an accent. Her voice was without inflexion. She looked as if she would, by a long way, prefer martyrdom to marriage. Perhaps she was ill. She did not look unhappy. She looked beyond unhappy.

Mr Khan smiled fondly at us both.

'Ah, the young lovers,' he said. 'I am so happy that God has chosen me to bring you together. I can see that you are wondering about Adeena's fair complexion, Mr Gaunt. I will explain. Her family are from Nuristan, in the north-east corner of Afghanistan, the region you call the Hindu Kush. She is of the Q'ata tribe, and it is said they are descended from Iskander the Great, and his Greek armies, when they passed through the region's wooded valleys on their way to conquer India. She has the blonde hair and blue eyes of her race, so rare in our corner of the world.'

I felt transfixed by the girl's haunted gaze. Whatever powerful emotion lay behind her eyes, it was not unrequited love. There was something so dreadful in her presence it inhibited speech. Mr Khan filled the silence.

'You are dumbstruck. That is very good. I told you she would be worth waiting for. Adeena, Mr Gaunt is a member of English society, no doubt with the most important and interesting connections. Also he is a soldier. Perhaps he has served in Afghanistan. Is that correct, Mr Gaunt?'

'Yes, I was in Afghanistan for a while.'

'Wonderful,' exclaimed Mr Khan. He clapped his hands in delight. 'Then the two of you can share happy memories of that beautiful country. Your bride is a most knowledgeable person, Mr Gaunt. She can tell you everything about the new, modern, democratic and prosperous country of Afghanistan.'

He talked about the girl as if she were a thing, rather than a person. What was her name? Adeena, that was it. Mr Khan walked towards the bronze bucket in the conservatory. We followed him, Adeena moving very slowly as if each step cost her an effort of will. Mr Khan pulled out the champagne bottle from the melting ice, and another, smaller bottle containing what looked like orange juice. After a brief struggle he removed the foil and the wire cage and popped the cork of the champagne. He poured me a glass. Then he unscrewed the top of the other bottle and poured a measure of orange juice into the second glass, which he presented to Adeena.

'You must drink to each other's health,' he said, still playing the part of the proud father-in-law. He lifted both hands as if conducting, enjoining us to raise our glasses.

'Your good health and happiness,' I said, raising the champagne glass in Adeena's direction.

My voice sounded pompous and formal. Adeena raised her orange juice in reply, then opened out her hand in a deliberate gesture and let the glass fall to the ground. It shattered on the tiled floor of the conservatory and the orange juice went everywhere. Then, with one last look of contempt, directed equally at Mr Khan and myself, she turned and walked out of the room.

'Adeena!' Mr Khan shouted after her, but she did not look back. In the silence that followed her gesture, I heard her light footsteps going up the stairs, then the sound of a distant door being slammed with some force.

'She's nervous,' said Mr Khan, rubbing his hands together. 'It is too much excitement for her. First she arrives in a strange country, and now she is meeting a strange man who is to be her husband. She will get used to the idea. She is a frightfully jolly girl, really, when you get to know her. I knew her father. He was a jolly chap too, until he was killed.'

'Well, she doesn't have to like me, does she, Mr Khan?' I said. 'I mean, I don't suppose you plan to keep me around once you have the marriage certificate. Let's be honest, that's what this is all about. I won't tell anyone, don't worry. Once I have the money, I'll keep my mouth shut. But let's not pretend it's anything other than that. I don't think that I'm a great judge of character, but I wouldn't say Adeena is dying to get married to me. Would you?'

Mr Khan had watched Adeena's departure with the air of a loving father looking after an errant daughter. Now, as he faced me, his expression was a mask of clinical detachment. He stared at me with his dark brown eyes and said nothing at all. The friendly atmosphere that is usually generated by the popping of a champagne cork seemed to have dissipated.

'You will please go to your room and stay there,' Mr Khan said after a moment or two. 'Food will be sent to you as necessary. We will call for you when we need you again.'

I did not argue. Upstairs I sat in one of the armchairs in my bedroom and wondered about the girl I had just met. She was stunning and she was also brave: anyone who defied Mr Khan had to have a certain amount of courage – or else be foolhardy. The third thing I knew about her was that she did not like orange juice.

I didn't imagine I would see much more of her. I wondered

what was in it for her? Was she a refugee of some sort? Did she agree with this sham marriage? It didn't matter. Mr Khan would make her go through with it and then I would be free to get back to my life, but ten thousand pounds better off.

What would happen to her? I wondered. Best not to think about it. I picked up the newspaper lying on the table in front of me and turned the pages without reading them. Rain began to spatter against the window.

Then, without my being able to do anything about it, the memories started to come back; like a television set I could not switch off, playing nothing but repeats.

Four

The images had the vivid quality of a film. Time would not dull or blur them however much I wished it would.

When my half-platoon of specialists first arrived at Baghdad International Airport that spring we were met in the arrivals hall by an American non-com from Delta Force: a large man in desert camouflages holding up a name board with my name and rank on it.

'Captain Gaunt?' he asked. When I nodded he replied, 'Please follow me, sir. We have transport waiting.'

He did not smile or offer his hand. We followed him through the terminal. He walked quickly and we struggled to keep up with him, carrying our kitbags, which weighed a ton. The terminal was surprisingly busy: military personnel, mostly American; and civilians, mostly men, probably contractors, oilmen, journalists or aid workers. When we stepped outside the heat was fierce. It was spring in Baghdad. We had been told it would be getting hot and it *was*: forty degrees, at least. Our last overseas posting had been in Pristina, in Kosovo with KFOR. The springs there had been warm but they were nothing like this.

Outside, a row of Humvees was parked. I noticed that they were not the soft-skinned ones we had seen in Kosovo, but the new up-armoured version. That was comforting. They were being guarded by another soldier from Delta Force with a C7 Diemaco rifle. We'd heard that the twelve-kilometre journey into Baghdad along 'Route Irish' could be interesting. I was looking forward to the ride. I felt excited. I think we all were, although we knew this was an unpopular war at home. It wasn't like Kosovo, where we knew we were needed to stop the whole of the Balkans going up in flames, or Northern Ireland, or any of the other places I had been to in my last few years with the army. But it was action: better than sitting in Basra waiting for someone to lob a mortar at us.

I felt sorry for the Iraqis. We'd started this war to help them. Nobody I knew had ever seriously believed they had 'weapons of mass destruction'. This was about bringing peace and democracy to the people of Iraq, wasn't it? Only someone had disbanded the Iraqi army about two days after the invasion and had sent them home without pay. Then everyone was terribly surprised when they all turned up again as insurgents wearing civilian clothes; shooting, bombing and generally making the country into the most dangerous place on earth.

Anyway, we were here now, and Saddam was gone. So that was good. Sergeant Hawkes said we'd started the war to make sure we kept control over Iraqi oil, but he was a cynic. Some of us even suspected him of being too clever for his own good, but I liked him. He was interesting to talk to, and read a great deal more than the rest of us put together. I also knew that, despite his remarks, Sergeant Hawkes felt the same sense of excitement about this new mission as the rest of us.

The set-up where we were going was unusual. The Multi-National Force was headquartered in Baghdad but the city and all of central Iraq were under the control of the US military. We had been sent there in support of an operation called Task Force Black. This was a special forces job: SAS and Delta Force working together to suppress the spiralling violence on the streets of Baghdad – and practically every other town of any size in central Iraq. Our job was to provide an outer cordon: security cover for the special forces teams while they did what they were good at.

'The squadron is located in a compound in the Green Zone,' my commanding officer told me before we took the plane to Baghdad. 'But the quartermaster has run out of room for the moment. Your platoon will be quartered on a temporary basis in a villa near by. There's a Yank PMC called Green Park based there.'

'A PMC?' I asked. It was spring 2005 and some of the jargon of this war was still new to me.

'A Private Military Contractor. They are there to provide logistical services to the task force – food, accommodation and so on. You will get your orders from Squadron Command at the Task Force Headquarters in the main compound. Intel comes into the squadron via the Joint Support Group. You may remember them from Belfast. You're there in a support role, to watch the backs of the SAS.'

I did remember the Joint Support Group from the time we'd served in Northern Ireland. Its name made it sound as if it was one of those organisations set up to help distressed gentlefolk but its mission was somewhat different. In Northern Ireland it was responsible for agent-handling. I didn't know they had become involved in Baghdad, or what their new job might involve, but not all of the agents that the JSG handled in Belfast had lived happily ever after.

'Do we have anything to do with Green Park, sir?'

'Yes. Green Park are operating a Temporary Screening Facility. Any prisoners you collect should be handed over to them for questioning before being sent to the interrogation centre at Camp Nama, up by the airport.'

I'd heard of Camp Nama. It was a 'black' prison similar to the ones at Bagram or Guantanamo.

'Anything else I need to know about them?' I asked.

'They know the city so they will give you a briefing on arrival. They've got a consultant advising them called Mr Harris. He's also a consultant to Delta Force. One of their jobs is to obtain local intelligence, which they pass on to JSG. This is going to be different to any operation you've been on before, Richard.'

'I'm not sure I understand, sir.'

'Rules of engagement are different to what you are used to.'

'In what way, sir?'

In every other place I'd been our rules had been very clear: don't shoot unless someone is about to shoot you. Sometimes you had to wait until they'd actually tried to kill you before you were allowed to return fire. Sometimes you had to have written clearance in triplicate from some staff officer sitting safely in London before you could even take the safety off your gun.

'It's more flexible here, Richard. You can shoot if you perceive a threat.'

'What does that mean exactly, sir?'

'It means whatever you want it to mean, Richard. It means use your initiative.'

Our convoy was thundering along Route Irish into the city. I had been expecting the sort of landscape I'd seen on the television reports in 2003: miles of flat, sandy desert, across which the all-conquering armoured columns of the US 3rd Infantry Division had charged. But this was the Tigris valley, where the great wide, mud-coloured river flowed down to its confluence with the Euphrates at Shatt al-Arab, then on to the Persian Gulf. It was much greener than I had expected. Palm trees lined the road, and there were green fields and banks of vegetation. There was also an extraordinary profusion of litter. Piles of refuse lay by the roadside or on patches of bare land, and the smoke of dozens of small fires rose into the sky as half-hearted attempts were made to burn some of the rubbish. The air was full of dust, from traffic or from running repairs going on to damaged buildings or, occasionally, holes in the road. No doubt these had been made by IEDs.

We passed a huge white building. The upper floors were in a state of some disrepair with gaping holes in the masonry. I leaned forward and tapped the American driver on the shoulder.

'What's that place?' I asked him.

'We call it Camp Prosperity,' he replied. 'It used to be the As-Salaam palace, one of Saddam's. It's where they store his heads now.'

'His heads?'

'Yeah, big stone heads, the ones that were chopped off his statues all around the city.'

This struck me as odd.

'Why are they keeping them? Do they think they'll need to put them back on again at some point?'

The driver shook his head.

'In this place, you never know. Now if you don't mind, I need to watch the road.'

We were driving in convoy – not too close together, in case of problems – and keeping up the best speed we could in the traffic.

I shut up, and stared out of the window. It was so strange to be in this city, so often talked about, read about, seen on television: an ancient place, the cradle of civilisation. Now it looked remarkably unimpressive – like a shanty town on the outskirts, under a white-hot sky. The signs of war were everywhere: charred vehicles that had not yet been towed away, damaged buildings lining the roadside. The convoy slowed down as we approached the centre of the city and the buildings became larger and the streets a little busier; not too much traffic, apart from the military and police and a few very old cars or pick-ups that had managed to find petrol. On every street corner there were men with guns: Iraqi police and army, US army, private security. Looking up I could see half a dozen helicopters circling overhead. Above the helicopters and out of sight I knew a Nimrod or E-8 Joint Stars surveillance flight would be circling above the city.

We had to pass through several different checkpoints before we could enter the Green Zone, at Checkpoint Twelve, weaving around concrete chicanes and through anti-crash barriers that were raised and lowered to let us through. Finally we turned into a white-walled compound. As we arrived in the central courtyard I saw a man in jeans and an old khaki shirt standing at the top of the steps that led to the main entrance of the building.

'That's Mr Harris,' said my driver, pointing him out. He switched the engine off. 'He'll take care of you.'

All of us climbed out of our vehicles and clustered together, waiting for Mr Harris to come down the steps. But he just stood and watched us. Around us other men, all in civilian dress, either Arab or European, moved across the courtyard in one direction or the other. The place smelled of strong coffee, cigarettes, sweat and petrol fumes. Underlying it all was the bitter scent of blood. The roof of the building was a forest of radio antennae and satellite dishes. In another corner of the courtyard were several dusty Toyota pick-up trucks. I saw that one of them had bullet holes stitched along one side, and an Iraqi was sluicing out the tailgate with buckets of water. The sun was well up in the sky and the heat was unbearable. I mopped my brow. Finally Mr Harris came down the steps towards us.

'Captain Gaunt?' he asked.

'I'm Captain Gaunt,' I replied. 'Sir.'

'Green Park is a company, not the army. So I'm Mr Harris.'

He looked as old as Methuselah. His face was deep brown, grizzled with beard, and lined in every way it is possible for a face to be lined, as if it had been etched by sand and cracked by drought. His eyes were pale blue, the whites slightly yellow. His jawline sagged slightly, and there were pouches under his eyes. His mouth was thin, like the slit in a letterbox. It was difficult to tell what age or nationality he was.

'Get your men inside, Captain Gaunt,' he told me, jerking his thumb at the dark doorway in which he had been standing a moment ago. 'We'll give you your local briefing first, then show you your quarters.'

'Local briefing?' I asked.

Mr Harris smiled, revealing firm white teeth. It was not a comforting smile.

'We've been asked to tell you a little about what life is like in this great city.'

Once inside the building we were led to a large cool room in which several rows of chairs had been set out, with a map of Baghdad on the wall. All of us sat down. Then Mr Harris came in and sat in front of us. His shirtsleeves were rolled up, revealing forearms that looked as if they were made from some knotted tropical hardwood. His belly strained at his shirt but he did not look unfit. Patches of sweat stained his shirt under his arms but he did not look hot.

'You're here . . .' he began, then stopped and said, 'Fucked if I know why you're here. Anyone got any ideas?'

'We were told we were to provide support for a counter-insurgency operation, sir,' I said, feeling that someone should say something. Then I remembered the injunction against rank. 'I mean, Mr Harris.'

'Counter-insurgency? Forget that bullshit. We're in the real world now. Call them insurgents if you like. *We* call them criminals and terrorists. The people we are mostly fighting,' he said, 'were part of the Iraqi army, only some clever schmuck fired the lot of them, just after the invasion ended, without pay. They took to the streets, of course, so the war goes on, only the enemy isn't wearing a uniform. That's the only difference. The war never ended. And right now, we are in real danger of losing it.'

He paused, letting the silence grow, looking at us as if we were children in our first day at infant school. Perhaps that is how we appeared to him.

'You are here to fight the terrorists,' said Mr Harris. 'The Mahdi Army, al-Qaeda, Ansar al-Islam – it doesn't matter which. When they're dead they all look much the same. Your intel will come from the Joint Support Group, and from us here at Green Park. Your orders come from Task Force HQ. I am here to offer advice and support and to teach you the wicked ways of this sinful city.' It sounded dangerous. Mr Harris hadn't finished with us yet either.

'Now, you're all experienced soldiers. You were in Kosovo, right? Tell me, how do you fight terrorists?'

There was a silence while we all tried to recall our training manuals, but Mr Harris wasn't really interested in anything we had to say. He curled his hands into two massive fists and smacked them together.

'You fight them like that,' he said. 'You crush them. You fight terror with terror. You make sure these people are so frightened of you that all they want to do is hide under their beds.'

He stood up then. He was an old man: God knows how many wars he had fought in. God knows where he came from – Sergeant Hawkes told me later he thought Mr Harris was Mossad, drafted in by the Americans to give them the benefit of Israeli experience in counter-terrorism. There were some strange people in Baghdad that year. But wherever he came from and whatever he had done, Mr Harris looked as if he knew everything there was to know about terror. He looked as if he had dished it out in his time. He had probably fought in most of the dirty conflicts around the world since the last world war, and we were already more terrified of him than the insurgents who waited for us somewhere outside in the Red Zone.

'Time to go to work, boys,' he said. 'Mr al-Najafi will see you next. He will show you your quarters and give you a geography lesson.'

That was the beginning of the best and worst few months of my life. Whatever I had been expecting from my tour in Baghdad, it was not what happened. That was the last time I felt as if I was alive: really, truly alive.

Five

The next morning, I had difficulty in remembering where I was, or why I was there. Then I remembered: Mr Khan. This was my wedding day.

'I'm getting married in the morning,' I hummed to myself, 'Ding dong, the bells are going to chime,' trying to brush my teeth at the same time. The result was messy. I finished shaving and then climbed into my smart new wedding clothes, making sure I transferred my belongings into the pockets. Another hour or two and I would be clutching a large cheque, happily married and counting off the hours and days, weeks and months until I could file for divorce.

It had been a diverting interlude. My life had been so deadly boring for such a long time that the last couple of days had been an almost welcome change. If only there was someone I could have shared the joke with: walking to Oxford for a bet, being kidnapped by thugs, then married off to a beautiful girl from Afghanistan. And being well paid for it.

I caught sight of myself in the mirror: a foolish man in a wedding suit with a stupid grin on his face. Suddenly I felt sick. What the hell was I doing? How on earth could I contemplate marrying some wretched girl then simply taking the money and walking off with it in my pocket? Of course I couldn't share the joke. If I told anyone what I was up to they would look at me in disgust. No wonder I had so few friends left, apart from the card-playing vultures at the Diplomatic.

I was sick. Sick in the head even to be thinking about doing this. I ought to just get up and leave.

That would be difficult, though. After all the trouble he had gone to, Mr Khan didn't seem the kind of man who would let his guest slip through his fingers. I went to the door and tried the handle. It was locked. Even if I could get out of the room somehow, I was likely to meet Kevin. Kevin struck me as the type of person who lacked any common sense and would be quite likely to shoot me just to see what happened next.

Another thought struck me. Once Mr Khan had obtained my signature on the marriage register, was he really going to let me go just like that? Wouldn't it be cheaper and better for him if I disappeared? For the first time I began to wonder whether the situation I found myself in might not be more serious than I had at first imagined.

Before I met the girl I had assumed this was simply a rather elaborate way of obtaining a UK residency permit for another illegal immigrant: perhaps a cousin of Mr Khan's from Lahore or Peshawar, or a girl to whose family he owed a favour. But the more I thought about him, the more Mr Khan reminded me of other people I had met in the past: people whose moral values and objectives were very different from the rest of the world's. The truth was, there was no knowing what Mr Khan would do once I had completed my part of the deal. Maybe the plan they had made for me did not include a happy ending, after all.

There was a knock at the door, and I heard the key turn. David came into the room.

'It is time, Mr Gaunt,' he told me.

*

The wedding party was conveyed to the register office in two black Range Rovers. I saw the girl for the briefest moment, being shepherded by David, who had swapped his role as assistant for that of chauffeur, and the man who had kidnapped me with Kevin. His name was Amir, and he was not in the same class as Kevin. He looked much more formidable. The girl was wearing a beautifully cut dark blue jacket over a skirt of the same material. She was dressed as if for a smart day's shopping in Bond Street – unless you looked at her face, that is. Then you wondered whether she wasn't on her way to a funeral.

I travelled in the second vehicle, in the rear, while Mr Khan sat in the front and Kevin drove. Mr Khan was wearing a morning coat in the same charcoal material as my own, and there was a white rose in his lapel. He handed another rose to me and ordered, 'Put this in your buttonhole.'

We proceeded at a stately pace down a long drive with sweeping lawns and banks of rhododendrons on either side, until we came to the entrance, two stone pillars with electronically operated gates that opened slowly as we approached. We turned into a small lane and drove through pleasant rural countryside, by fields of stubble and innumerable small woods and thickets. Here and there were road signs of which I caught only the briefest glimpse. At first the names meant nothing to me, but there was something familiar about the landscape. I felt I knew it, had seen it before, perhaps from a different perspective.

The feeling passed as we turned on to wider and busier roads. I started seeing names I recognised: 'Witney' and 'Oxford'. Before long we were approaching the outskirts of

Oxford. Mr Khan turned to me as we drove towards the town centre.

'Of course, you will play your part as promised, Mr Gaunt. No wrong words to the registrar, no attempts to dash off into the crowd. Any such behaviour would be bad for you. You will not get your money. And it will be much worse for the girl, I assure you.'

'Relax, Mr Khan,' I said. 'I'm here for the money. I won't spoil the party. You'd better make sure she doesn't do something unexpected again.'

Mr Khan smiled at me. 'We have already made sure of that.'

He turned back to face the front again. I tapped him on the shoulder.

'How will you pay me? Ten thousand is quite a lot of cash to carry around.'

Mr Khan did not move his head.

'We obtained your bank account details when we visited your flat. The money will be deposited in your account twenty-four hours after the ceremony is concluded.'

I made a mental note to change my bank account as soon as possible. I wondered why I had ever believed Mr Khan would actually pay me. There was nothing I could do about it now, in any case. The feelings of doubt I had experienced earlier returned in greater strength. How on earth was I going to get out of this?

We arrived at the register office in Tidmarsh Lane. It was situated in a grey office block: rather unromantic, I thought. David and Kevin dropped us off then drove the cars away to park them, while Mr Khan, the girl, Amir and I went to sit in the waiting room until it was our turn. When Kevin and David arrived a minute or two later, Kevin was whistling

'Here Comes the Bride'. He was silenced by a look from Mr Khan. I stared at the ceiling and tried not to think too much about what I was doing. The girl from Afghanistan sat very upright, eyes downcast. She did not move or speak. Then the registrar put her head around the door.

'If Mr Richard Gaunt and Miss Adeena Haq would come through now, please, and the witnesses as well.'

Adeena stood up and said something, in Arabic, not Pashtun, as I would have expected. When I was in Iraq we were taught a few words of Arabic, so that we could hold basic conversations with locals when necessary. I had forgotten most of what little I had learned, but I was still able to understand what Adeena said.

'*Aseeb, I will not do this.*'

Aseeb? She had addressed herself to Mr Khan. Was that his name? I stood up and smiled politely at everybody. Amir stepped very close to Adeena and whispered something in her ear. She was already pale but now she flinched as if a wasp was buzzing at her head. I added Amir to the list of people I had developed a strong dislike for and mentally put him in my queue for retribution just behind Kevin. Amir took Adeena's arm and almost frogmarched her through the door into the next room. I followed, shepherded by Kevin and Mr Khan – or Aseeb, if that was what he was called. It was a Pashtun name.

The ceremony was very brief. Adeena and I stood side by side in front of the desk and listened to the registrar deliver a small speech. I did not take in a word: I was feeling more wound up by the minute. I remember Mr Khan handing me a ring to put on Adeena's finger, and Amir put a ring on my finger. Adeena wouldn't, or couldn't, bring herself to do it. Then Kevin and David signed as witnesses, and it was all over. Five minutes later we were herded back towards the Range Rovers. Soon we were driving out of Oxford.

Now that the ceremony was over, Mr Khan was in a more genial mood.

'I congratulate you, Mr Gaunt,' he said, turning in his seat to look at me, 'you have married a very beautiful girl.'

'What happens now?'

'Ah, we shall see, we shall see. All has gone well. You have done as we asked. We will fulfil our side of the bargain, you must not be in any doubt.'

But I did not see. As the minutes ticked by, and we drove farther away from Oxford, I knew I had made a serious error, once again; my life had been one long string of bad decisions over the last three years. What had started out yesterday as an amusing joke with a large cash reward now felt very different. My heart was racing. Why hadn't I run for it while we were in Oxford? What could they have done if I'd walked off? And what had prevented me from doing so? Was it the money?

As we turned off the main road and drove back along the country lanes, I wondered about Mr Khan's immediate plans for me. This was more than just a dodgy marriage ceremony to get someone an immigration visa. And whatever was going on, I was a witness to it. Would they pay a witness to their schemes, whatever they were, and then let him go with a pat on the back and a wave of the hand? I wasn't at all sure that that was Mr Khan's style. I wondered whether I would ever leave the house if I didn't wake up and do something.

As the Range Rover's wheels scrunched on the gravel and drew to a halt, I was as ready as I would ever be. Kevin got out and went around the front to open the passenger door for Mr Khan. I got out too, smiled at Mr Khan, nodded in a friendly way at Kevin and then kicked him as hard as I could just below the kneecap. As he shouted out in pain, and reached down to clutch his damaged leg, I punched him in the stomach and then drove my elbow into the bridge of his nose. He fell over, one hand clutching his shin and the other feeling for his nose, which was beginning to spout blood. The whole process gave me a moment's satisfaction; then I reflected that it had come at a price, probably around ten thousand pounds. As Kevin kneeled on the gravel I reached inside his jacket, found the gun I had noticed earlier and took it out.

'That's us settled up for the moment, Kevin,' I told him. Amir jumped out of the other Range Rover and came running towards us, while Mr Khan struggled out of the car. I could see David was holding on to Adeena's arm. She was staring at me in astonishment.

'Don't try anything,' I warned Mr Khan and Amir. I held up one hand, palm outwards. The other now held Kevin's gun.

I hurt like hell after the unaccustomed exertion and my ribs were on fire. I backed away, and Mr Khan and Amir stopped, hesitating. The electronic gates were slowly closing so I pelted down the drive and managed to slip between them before they shut. When I glanced over my shoulder as I turned into the main road, I saw that Kevin had been propped up against one of the Range Rovers, a handkerchief to his nose. I didn't think I had long.

As soon as I was out of sight I took the first footpath that led away from the main road, and within a couple of minutes was approaching the edge of a small wood. They were certain to be after me in a few moments. I had only just entered the wood when I heard a car roaring past along the road.

I did not slacken my pace but jogged as quickly as possible along the rough and muddy path that led through the narrow belt of trees. I came to a crossroads where another footpath intersected the first, and on instinct turned left and downhill, because that was where there was the most cover. Soon I found myself walking along a green and brown tunnel formed by overhanging branches. There was a constant flutter of leaves, drifting to the ground in the mild breeze. The sun had come out and its light played on me through the branches. I heard birdsong, and once or twice saw the white scut of a rabbit bounding out of my way.

After ten minutes or so I emerged from the woodland. I stopped for a moment at the edge of the trees, realising that I was still holding the gun in one hand. I was not your typical rambler out for a walk: wearing morning dress and holding an automatic pistol. I looked at the gun. It was a Sig Sauer P220, the weapon of choice for gun club target practice and professional assassins. I stuck it in the waistband of my trousers.

The path now led along the side of a stubble field, and then over a stile in a long hedgerow of blackthorn. I thought I had probably lost my pursuers, and with a lightening heart climbed over the stile. I would make my way along this network of footpaths until I came to a village, and then get a taxi, or catch a bus, to the nearest town and from there back to London. I was keen not to meet up with Mr Khan and his employees again.

As I stepped into the next stubble field I became conscious I was not alone. I found I was at one end of a long line of men, all dressed in army surplus camouflage or jeans and wax jackets. Some of them were carrying flags, others had sticks in their hands, and there were a number of dogs running about: spaniels, mostly. The man nearest me saw me and hissed, 'Bloody walkers.' Then, louder, 'Would you please stop where you are for a minute, sir – we're in the middle of a partridge drive.'

'Don't worry,' I said. 'I'm not an anti. I won't spoil anything. I'll just walk down the hill in line with you until you get to the end of the drive.'

I knew I would be safer walking with all these beaters than I would be on my own if anyone was following me. The beater nearest me gave me a venomous look, but at that moment the man in the middle of the line raised a red flag, the signal that the line could start moving off downhill. I supposed he was the keeper. I walked slowly with them, keeping in line. Then I picked up a fallen branch and used it to tap on the sides of the hedgerow as we went. I thought I was doing rather a good job as a beater, in the circumstances.

As we advanced down the long slope, partridge started to emerge in front of us: singles, then twos and threes or even larger groups, rising out of the stubble or from the hedgerows, where they had been invisible a moment before, flying away from us and gaining height and speed as they did so. At the bottom of the field, still a couple of hundred yards away, was another hedgerow running at right angles to the one I was walking along. From behind this now came the noise of shots being fired, and I realised we were approaching the line of guns. More and more partridge swarmed out of the stubble and bushes in front of us, and I saw several fall.

The keeper raised the red flag again and we all stopped, while the dogs flushed out the last few birds in front of us. The shooting from the other side of the hedge did not seem particularly accurate. Then a horn sounded, and the shooting stopped also. Now was the time to leave. I made my way through a gap in the hedgerow in front of me, scrambled across a ditch on the other side, and came face to face with Freddy Meadowes. He had a shotgun under his arm, his big moon face was beaming all over, and he was bending down to retrieve a red-legged partridge from the mouth of a liver-coloured springer spaniel.

'There, Mildred. It's dead!' He managed to take the bird from the dog's mouth, although it seemed inclined to engage in a tug of war. 'Thank you, old girl, that will do.' He straightened up with the partridge in his hand and saw me. For a moment his features expressed extreme surprise, then his beaming smile returned.

'My God,' he said. 'It's the Leader of the Pack! What the hell are you doing in my beating line? And why on earth are you dressed like that? Are you getting married, or something?'

I said the first thing that came into my head.

'It's a bet, Freddy. I'm doing it for a bet.'

Six

Freddy roared with laughter. That was his answer whenever he was confronted with any situation that was less than straightforward. The appearance of someone in a tailcoat in the middle of a partridge drive definitely fell into that category.

'Leader, I never know what you're going to get up to next! We've finished shooting for the morning, so you'd better come back to the house with us and have a drink and a spot of lunch. Unless, of course, you are keeping your bride waiting at the church?'

'No, no one's waiting for me, Freddy, and I'd love a drink if there's one going. I don't want to crash your party, though.'

'Not a bit, not a bit,' said Freddy. 'You'll know everyone, I expect. Eck Chetwode Talbot will be there. You must know him, he was in the army like you.'

Freddy turned about and I walked along beside him. I could see other guns converging on a row of Range Rovers and Land Cruisers parked by the side of a lane a few hundred yards away.

'No, I don't know him,' I said. Freddy's assumption that everyone who had ever been in the army must know everyone else was not untypical of people who had never served in it themselves.

'Bertie Razen? Caspar Weingeld? Charlie Freemantle? Willy McLeod?'

'Never heard of any of them, Freddy.'

As a matter of fact I had been here before. I now realised why the landscape had looked familiar when I glimpsed it through the tinted windows of Mr Khan's Range Rover. Freddy had asked me down to shoot a year ago, in November. It was pheasants on that occasion, not partridge, but I remembered the contours of the valley. We must be just around the corner from the country retreat I had been holed up in for most of the weekend. I wondered whether I could get Freddy to tell me anything about the house and its owner – he was bound to know something.

I had first met Freddy across the card tables at the Diplomatic. On that occasion I had looked at his big, beaming face and listened to his conversation, which consisted mostly of expressions such as 'Jolly good' and 'I say, what frightful cards you've given me' and had jumped to the conclusion that he was both rich and thick. An hour or two later, when he had gutted and filleted me through a series of bluffs and double bluffs, in an extremely canny display of poker playing, I was forced to revise my opinion. Freddy was one of those people who, whatever their apparent lack of intellectual qualities, know how to hang on to their own money and how to prise it away from other people. In fact it was on the second occasion we played together that he took so much money from me he felt obliged to ask me shooting. 'I tell you what, come and shoot a few pheasants with me down in Oxfordshire next Saturday,' was how the invitation was phrased, 'unless, of course, you have a better invitation?'

I hadn't, I thought. 'Why not?' That was how I got to know Freddy.

Freddy put his dog in the back of his Range Rover, tossed the partridge to an older man who was bracing up the shot birds and hanging them in a game cart, and motioned to me to get in the front passenger seat. As I did so, another man climbed into the back of the car. Freddy introduced us.

'This is Eck Chetwode Talbot. He and his wife Harriet have come down from Yorkshire for the shooting.'

The new arrival leant forward to shake hands with me.

'Richard Gaunt,' I replied. 'Will your wife be joining us?'

'No, she's gone to visit her mother, near Cirencester, for the day.'

'We call Richard the Leader of the Pack,' shouted Freddy as we drove away. Eck Chetwode Talbot raised his eyebrows.

I shrugged and said, 'It's an unfortunate nickname that Freddy likes to use. It's a long story.'

It wasn't far to the house and I remembered the place as soon as I saw it: a comfortable-sized, double-fronted Victorian house. As we arrived, men in tweed plus twos and shooting coats were being decanted from various vehicles. There were nine of us including me. We all straggled into the house, depositing boots and guns, or in my case mud-caked shoes, in the entrance hall. Then we assembled in a long room that was used as a library and drawing room, where a substantial collection of bottles and glasses was arranged on a side table.

'Help yourself,' shouted Freddy. 'Take no prisoners.' After a few moments someone handed me a glass of white wine that I hadn't asked for. Freddy was busy making sure his other guests had what they wanted to drink, so I found myself talking to the man called Eck.

'Forgive my asking,' said Eck. 'But do you normally dress like that when you go shooting?'

'My day started out rather differently to yours,' I replied. 'I had to assist at a wedding, but afterwards I somehow found myself mixed up with the beating line and then I bumped into Freddy.' Even as I spoke I could see how profoundly unsatisfactory this explanation was. I tried to change the subject: 'Freddy and I play cards together sometimes.'

'Everybody knows Freddy,' said Eck.

'What's that?' said Freddy, appearing at my elbow clutching a pint glass tankard full of gin and tonic and lumps of ice. 'Everyone knows Freddy? Not at all. I'm terribly shy and don't get out much.' He roared with laughter at his own joke, then said, 'Leader, I need a satisfactory explanation of your presence here. Not that I'm not delighted to see you, but do admit it, you were a very odd sight in the middle of a hedgerow.'

'I've been staying with your neighbour,' I explained. I realised that I needed to be careful about what I said. I couldn't possibly let this crowd know that I'd agreed to marry a girl from Afghanistan for money. My reputation was already dubious. Yet there was really no way to account for my behaviour over the last forty-eight hours; even if some of the events that had occurred had been outside my control.

'My neighbour? Which neighbour? What's the name of the house?' asked Freddy.

'A man who calls himself Mr Khan. Although I think he might also be known as Aseeb. Do you know him, Freddy?'

Eck gave me a very sharp glance as I spoke, but before he could say anything Freddy said, 'Khan? He's the new tenant at Harington House. An odd story: the house used to belong to a well-known local family. Things hadn't been going right for them for a long time; then one of the children inherited and burned through most of the remaining cash, so they had to sell up. It's a few years since they left now. About five years ago some City boy bought it with his bonus. Did the place up. No expense spared, our window cleaner tells me.'

Freddy lifted the tankard of gin and tonic to his lips and gargled for a moment. When he had lowered the level of the liquid by an inch or two, he went on:

'Then this one went tits up, along with a lot of others last year. Sorry, Eck, I know you used to work in the City too: tactless of me to bring the subject up. Anyway, the bank repossessed the house. I bought the land, apart from about five acres of gardens and woodland next to the house itself, but they couldn't sell the house, not at the price they were asking. I wasn't interested. I mean to say, I've got a house already, haven't I?' Freddy laughed again. 'But you can always use a few more acres for your farming. Anyway, since then Harington House has been let. Your chum Mr Khan has been a tenant for about six months, as far as I am aware. I've never met him. He's obviously well off, travels a lot; I don't think he is often there. How on earth do you know him, anyway? I wouldn't have thought he was your speed at all.'

'We just bumped into each other somewhere,' I said. I could see that Freddy would have liked a fuller explanation, but then he looked at his watch.

'Oh Lord, we'd better go through and have lunch. I promised the keeper we'd be back out again by two. Come and eat something, Leader.'

'I'd love to, but may I then ring for a taxi to get me into Oxford?'

Over lunch I was stuck between two complete strangers, but everyone was friendly, as people in shooting parties so

66

often are, and the conversation did not require much effort. Just as we rose from the table and everyone was getting ready to go outside for the rest of the afternoon's sport, the man called Eck asked me an odd question:

'Did I hear you say that Mr Khan might also be called *Aseeb*?'

'That's what I gathered. Do you know him?'

'I might have met him somewhere,' said Eck. 'It's an unusual name.'

'Not common in Oxfordshire,' I agreed.

Eck reached into his pocket and found a small diary with a pencil tucked into its spine.

'Give me your phone number, if you don't mind. I might ring you. I'm curious to know if your Aseeb is the same man I used to know.'

He was suddenly very serious and I could see he wouldn't be put off. I gave him my home number and we said goodbye. Another man was hovering beside me. He had been on the other side of the table at lunch but too far away for us to have spoken.

'Did someone mention your name was Richard Gaunt, or have I got that wrong? My name is Charlie Freemantle, by the way.'

'Yes, I'm Richard Gaunt.'

'Sorry to bother you with such a personal question, but didn't you used to walk out with a very sweet girl called Emma Macmillan?'

I felt a sharp stab of remembered pain when I heard the name.

'Yes, but that's all over now. Do you know her?'

'I've met her. She's a very attractive girl. I'm sorry you're not with her any longer. I suppose that means anyone can have a crack at asking her out now, doesn't it?'

'I suppose it does,' I said.

'Come on, everybody, hurry up,' roared Freddy. 'This isn't a cocktail party – we're meant to be shooting things!'

I waved goodbye to Freddy and shouted my thanks across the room.

'Come again, Leader, but do try to dress in something more appropriate to the countryside next time.'

As they left, I spotted a phone on the hall table, sitting on top of a telephone directory. Within a few minutes I had arranged for a taxi to pick me up and take me into Oxford. There I bought a pair of jeans, a tweed jacket and some new shoes, and put all the clothes I had been wearing into a carrier bag and stuffed them into the first litter bin I could find. I kept the gun. Then I walked to the station and took the next train to Paddington.

On the train I sat and stared out of the window. It had been an odd couple of days, to say the least. On the whole, I could not look back on my behaviour with any satisfaction. Even the temporary thrill of punching Kevin a couple of times had dissipated. It seemed to me I had, without much reflection at all, sold my soul for ten thousand pounds: a Faustian bargain of the most useless kind, as I was unlikely ever to be paid. The thoughts kept rattling around my head. So I did what I always did when what remained of my conscience gave me trouble: I tried not to think. Outside rain streamed across the window.

Nature abhors a vacuum and into my empty mind came thoughts of home and family. It had been raining the last time I had been home. I remembered that very well: the sheets of rain descending from low streamers of dark grey cloud as I drove down the winding road, trying to avoid the occasional sheep that strayed in front of my car, through the remote green Cumbrian valley towards my parents' house. I had left the army: my last two leaves had been spent with Emma and I hadn't been home for nearly two years. I felt strange about seeing my parents and my little sister again, but I longed to be with them too. Home would make me feel better.

Hardrigg Manor sat in a steep-sided valley at the western edge of the Pennines. Dark fir woods clung to the slopes and grey stone walls divided the hillside into small compartments filled with the white dots of grazing sheep. The grey walls were covered with lichen, and the winter grass was an exhausted brown. Above where the walls ended was a wilderness of fell and rushes, where fell ponies and sometimes red deer could be seen.

The house itself was a jumble of Elizabethan, Jacobean and Victorian Gothic: an extraordinary confection of turrets and gabled roofs and false crenellations. Leaded and mullioned windows looked out across the valley. My mother had made a water garden, using slates to create little cascades and rills, so that if you were walking near by, the music of the water was always with you.

It had been a wonderful place to grow up. I had scrambled among those hills as a child, had lain on the floor in the book-filled space that my parents had used as a drawing room, reading every book they would let me get my hands on. It had been a very happy childhood and now, coming back home after all this time, I anticipated the warmth, the feeling of security and comfort that would course through me as soon as I walked through the front door. I felt I could almost smell the woodsmoke from the fires even though I was still half a mile from the house.

My parents and Katie were waiting for me in the hall. At first our meeting was wordless. We hugged one another, and then my father stammered out a few phrases in which 'old chap' and 'good to see you' were the only distinct words I could hear. My mother had tears in her eyes. My sister Katie, my little sister, now in her twenties, smiled her crooked smile at me. For many years that smile had carried a message: 'They may love you more, but I'm the one who looks after them.' Now I saw only that she was pleased to have me back home. I wished that Emma had been there as well, the girl I had been engaged to since my mid-twenties and whom I had known since I was fifteen. It had long been understood that Emma was the girl I would one day marry. But that meeting was for another day; tonight was just for family.

Greetings over, I was allowed some time to myself, and went up to the bedroom that used to be mine. It was warm and welcoming. The curtains had been drawn against the darkening evening, clean towels had been set out for me on the bed, the lamp had been switched on, and at one corner the sheets had been pulled back. The thought of climbing straight into that bed and sleeping for a week was almost overwhelming.

Instead, I had a bath, and then changed into 'home' clothes: jeans, a pullover, loafers. When I went downstairs the three of them were waiting for me, their faces happy and smiling. A bottle of champagne had been opened, too. I didn't really mind whether I drank the stuff or not, but I knew it would make them happy if I did, so we all raised our glasses and my father said, 'Here's to your safe return, dear boy. We're so glad to see you.'

Over dinner my mother, fortified by a large gin and tonic on top of the wine, recovered the power of speech.

'Was it very hot in Afghanistan, dear?' she asked.

'Very hot by day, and very cold by night.'

'Oh,' she said. 'What a wonderful climate. So much easier to get a good night's sleep if it's cold, don't you think? Did you get the silk underwear I sent you?'

'I'm sorry, Mummy,' I told her. 'I don't think I did.'

My father cut in. 'I know you must have been busy and probably didn't have time – but did you manage to follow the cricket while you were out there?'

'I'm afraid not,' I replied. An image came into my mind of myself trying to pick up the cricket scores on Radio Five Live against the background noise of small-arms fire and incoming RPGs as we drove towards Musa Qala.

'I'm surprised,' said my father. 'You used to be so fond of the game. As it happens you didn't miss much. The whole series was a disgrace from start to finish.'

I supposed my parents wanted to keep the conversation light; I supposed they wanted to help me forget what I had been through. But I didn't want to forget.

The three of them – my beloved family – couldn't have been nicer to me, or more careful of my comforts, or more concerned. They made sure that I was not too tired, not too hungry, not too full, not too hot, not too cold. They gave me the best cuts of the leg of lamb we ate for dinner; my father kept topping up my glass of wine, telling me that this was Château so-and-so, and the best vintage, nineteen something or other. I smiled, and nodded my thanks, and ate the lamb, and sipped the wine.

To me, the lamb tasted like cloth. The wine tasted of mud. The temperature in the room seemed at one moment to be oppressively hot and stifling, so that I could scarcely bear it; at another, I was freezing and wished I could be nearer the fire that blazed at one end of the room. We ate by candlelight, and in the gloom I thought my father's face had become red and pompous; my mother's dull and stupid; my sister's narrow and scheming. I couldn't breathe properly. I couldn't think of anything to say when someone spoke to me. The conversation, lively enough at first, began to falter.

'Won't you tell us a little bit about what you have been doing, Dicky?' asked my mother. 'We haven't seen you for so long and we haven't the least idea of what your life has been like. It's been so hard for us, not knowing where you were or how your days have been.'

No, you haven't the least idea of what my life's been like, I thought. Aloud I said, 'This lamb is delicious.'

'He can't talk about it. Disclosure policy,' said my father. 'I was in the army. I know what it's like, coming home after a long tour.'

No you don't, I thought. You served for three years in Germany and the most exciting thing you did was drive your Golf into a tree near Bielefeld. You were invalided out and you never heard a shot fired in anger.

'You're right,' I said. 'I can't talk about it.'

My silence had nothing to do with the disclosure policy. We had all signed it when we left the army. We weren't meant to talk about what we had done but most of us didn't want to, anyway. I certainly couldn't talk about the last few months. I couldn't talk because someone had imprisoned me behind a wall of glass. I could see people around me, I could see their mouths opening and shutting, but the words never reached my brain. And I couldn't answer questions. I could hardly bring myself to say 'Yes' or 'No' or 'Two lumps of sugar, please' or 'Thank you.'

Nobody who hadn't been there could understand what it had been like: the adrenalin rush, the fear, the occasional random, sudden moments of horror; the excitement. I was alive then. Now I felt as if I were in a trance, or as if I were half-dead.

When I came back to Britain after finishing my brief tour in Helmand I decided to apply for Premature Voluntary Release. The next move for me would have been to spend two years behind a desk. But I had never been interested in promotion or passing exams. I felt that I wasn't capable of sitting behind a desk. I longed to be back in the action; and I dreaded going back to it at the same time. The truth was that I'd done enough; I'd seen enough; I wasn't sure I could take much more. So I put in my papers.

Before I left I was sent to see the Regimental Medical Officer at headquarters. He had a file on his desk and he interviewed me for five minutes without showing much interest. Then he said:

'People who have experienced the sort of things I see in your file sometimes suffer from post-traumatic stress disorder. Do you know what that is?'

'I've heard of it, obviously,' I said.

'We do have some limited facilities for treatment of particularly severe cases. It's up to you to seek help if you feel you need it.'

'OK.'

'You can't claim on your insurance, you know. It's not recognised as an insurable illness.'

I didn't know, but I nodded my understanding. The

medical officer scribbled something on a piece of paper and then looked up at me.

'Plenty of sleep, that's the ticket. Have a good rest. They say art therapy can help. Painting pictures, that sort of thing. Sounds like a lot of nonsense to me. You're a fit young man. You may experience flashbacks and perhaps have some difficulties adjusting to civilian life, but no doubt you will manage very well.'

The interview was soon over. He had many other people to see that day – and every other day. Some of them were a lot more damaged than I was.

So that was it. I was out; and nobody would look after me except myself.

As I sat at dinner with my family that evening I began to wonder whether there *was* something wrong with me after all. I hardly spoke again before I went upstairs to bed and at breakfast I didn't speak either, except to say good morning. After a while the silence I imposed on myself fell like a wave of cold air on the rest of the household. They thought I didn't care for their company, that I was bored, that I was not grateful for everything they were doing to make me feel welcome, that I found their lives meaningless, that I wasn't interested in anything but myself. Affection was replaced by puzzlement; puzzlement by dismay; dismay by irritation; irritation by anger. And there was nothing I could do about it. I could see their hurt, but I couldn't ask for help. There was my pride; and besides, how could they help? How could anyone help, if they hadn't been where I had been and done what I had done? Most of the people who had shared those experiences with me were dead, or far away from England.

Even while this estrangement was creeping in, one part of me still remembered fondly the kindness and support I had been offered as I grew up. I was the golden boy: nothing was too good for me. My mother and Katie adored me. I grew up in a simple, straightforward world where I expected everything to work out for the best, and everyone expected the best for me. That wasn't how things were now.

My visit lasted three days. At the end of that time I couldn't stand being there any longer. The house had become totally silent. No one spoke to anyone else, at least not when I was there, and I felt as if I had brought a curse upon the place. So I left and went back to London. I hadn't been home since.

I looked out of the carriage window and saw we were just pulling out of Reading. Two noisy youths arrived, carrying a six-pack of lager. They opened a couple of tins, spattering me slightly with foam, and seemed to have every intention of necking down not just the two cans in front of them, but the rest as well. I got up and managed to find another seat.

I was in an odd frame of mind when I returned to my flat in Camden. Perhaps getting married and separated from one's new wife on the same day would do that to you. And I wondered whether Mr Khan and his friends might have followed me here. They'd had enough time. I approached the street where my flat was with caution, but I saw nothing to alarm me.

I unlocked the door, and saw that all my post had been picked up, opened, and left in a pile on the kitchen table. It must have been Amir who had done that, when he visited the flat a couple of days earlier. I somehow felt violated, even though most of the post was just unpaid bills and bank statements.

There was a letter from my landlord about unpaid rent. I

put it aside to read later. There was a card from my regimental association acknowledging my acceptance of the invitation to Lancaster House to be presented to the president of Afghanistan on his forthcoming state visit. A note from my commanding officer was enclosed. It said, 'The invitation is for you and Mrs Gaunt – I presume you have married by now, although I didn't see the announcement.' On the card it said: *'Please bring this card with you and show it to Security.'*

There was a letter in my sister's handwriting, and the usual junk mail. I threw the letter and the rest of the unwanted post into the bin. I had given up reading Katie's letters: they always contained the same mixture of reproach and lecturing.

I noticed that the bin was full, which set me thinking about the state the flat was in. I wandered into the bedroom and saw the unmade bed, sheets unchanged for a couple of weeks; clothes all over the floor, almost everywhere, in fact, except the wardrobe. The bathroom was a mess, the bath stained with scale. The so-called 'spare bedroom', which was nothing more than a box room, was the same dismal jumble of dusty suitcases and the little pile of photographs that had followed me round from one place to another. Among them was a photograph from school, all the boys in my house sitting in rows behind a depressed-looking master.

There I was in the back row, a tall, fair-haired eighteen-year-old wearing a sunny smile. My hair was short, my tie was properly knotted. I looked clean, tidy and organised. That was how my parents had thought of me: head of house, in the eleven, no great academic, but a thoroughly decent ordinary schoolboy. Another picture in a similar vein showed me on the day of my passing-out parade at Sandhurst: I looked like an advertisement for a recruitment campaign –

cheerful, optimistic, ready for anything. I could do no wrong back then. My parents worshipped me and poor Katie was quite in my shadow. On top of the pile of photographs were the leather cases containing my campaign medals. These had been opened: another trace of Amir's visit.

Nothing else had been disturbed although the place was so untidy it was hard to tell. The sitting room was covered in old newspapers and unwashed mugs, some with coffee still in them going mouldy. A couple of empty bottles of Chilean Sauvignon had rolled across the carpet. It was a depressing scene.

Suddenly, I couldn't stand the sight of the flat any longer. I felt a wave of disgust at the life I lived, the person I had now become. Although it was past six o'clock there were still a couple of supermarkets open. I left, slamming the door behind me, and went shopping. I bought a mop, washing-up liquid, dusters and polish. I bought food for the store cupboard; and butter and milk for the fridge, which was empty except for a few murky jars whose 'best before' dates were at least a year old. I bought bin liners and air freshener and a bottle of what looked like hydrochloric acid, which it was claimed would remove stains from anything. I bought so much I had to get a taxi back home.

Once inside, I began cleaning the flat. I opened all the windows that would open, to let in some air. I scrubbed out the bath. I poured cleaning fluid down the loo until it began to erupt in a violent-looking chemical reaction. I found the vacuum cleaner in a cupboard, and cleaned every square inch of the carpets. I mopped the kitchen floor and used the bottle of faux hydrochloric acid on every stained surface. It worked frighteningly well. Then I changed the sheets on my bed, remade it, hung up all my clothes and had a shower. I washed my hair and I scrubbed myself. I scrubbed until my skin was quite sore, standing so long under the hot water that it started to run cold.

When I had finished drying myself and had dressed in clean clothes, I took six bin liners full of rubbish along the street to a builder's skip I had spotted outside someone's house. Then I went back to the flat and flung myself on the sofa and looked about me. It was a completely different place to the one I had returned to a few hours ago. Not cheerful, but definitely clean and tidy. I wondered whether it would make me feel better about myself. I didn't really feel any cleaner, as if the events of the last few days had stained me in some way that soap and water could not remove.

I sat there for a few more minutes, recovering from my exertions. Then a thought struck me. I went to the window and checked the street. No black Range Rover; no sign of anything untoward. All the same I kept the gun stuck in my waistband. After a while I decided that they would either come or they wouldn't. The thing was to have a drink and relax.

Drink. That was the one thing I had neglected to buy. I looked at my watch. There was a newsagents-cum-deli run by a cheerful Bangladeshi family a few hundred yards away. I might just be able to buy something there. I went out again. Mohan was just closing up, but I managed to get him to sell me a bottle of white wine straight from the fridge. I thought I would allow myself a couple of glasses, and then go to sleep between clean sheets. In the morning, I would go out and look for a job.

The entrance to my flat is up some steps and through a side door. The door opens into a lane that runs into a larger road. I occupy a part of the house that is separate from the main building, a sort of annexe with a generous-sized sitting room. The other flats are entered via a front door that leads on to the main road and I had almost no contact with the other occupants of the building. So when I saw someone standing beside my door, I wondered for a dreadful moment whether I had got it wrong and Mr Khan and his mates *had* caught up with me. But it wasn't a man. As I approached, my visitor moved slightly out of the shadows and the light from the streetlamp fell on her face. I stood quite still. I knew that face: not well, but I knew it.

It was the face of the girl from Afghanistan: Adeena. It was my new wife, standing there, waiting to be let in to my flat.

Seven

'Hello,' I said. 'What are you doing here?' It was not the traditional way to greet one's new wife on her wedding day.

Adeena stared at me, as if she did not speak any English. I stared back. Then I realised I couldn't just leave her standing there. I motioned to her to follow me inside, with a wave of my hand, as if I were inviting her to enter a palace and not a poky little flat, then I locked the door behind us. I switched on the lights and we stood looking at each other in my small kitchen.

'Come into the sitting room,' I said, 'it's more comfortable there.' I remembered I was still holding a bottle of white wine in one hand. 'Would you like a glass of wine? Can I take your coat?'

She shrugged off her coat and gave it to me. It was a brown tweed and far too big for her: it looked like a man's coat. Underneath she was wearing the same dark blue suit she had been wearing for our marriage ceremony.

'I do not drink alcohol,' she said, in perfectly clear, if slightly accented, English. 'May I have a glass of water?'

I ran the tap and filled a glass, then opened the bottle of wine and poured myself a large measure. I felt I needed it. We went into the sitting room and I slumped on the sofa while she sat demurely on the edge of the only other chair. I sipped my wine and looked at her. She kept her eyes fixed on the floor. No immediate subject of conversation occurred to me. Our engagement had been too brief to establish any common ground between us. All I knew about her was that she did not seem to like orange juice. And she spoke Arabic. I repeated my question.

'What are you doing here? How did you find me?'

'I took a taxi.'

'Yes, but how did you know my address?'

She looked at me as if I was an idiot.

'Your address is on our marriage certificate.'

'Oh yes, of course.'

There was a silence. I sipped some more wine and wondered whether it would make a very bad impression on my new wife if I refilled my glass. She might as well know the worst. She sipped a little water delicately, as if she were crossing a desert and needed to conserve supplies.

'You like our London water?'

'Yes, thank you, it is very good water.'

There was another silence. I found myself thinking that a wife who does not talk too much is a pearl beyond price. I returned to my original question:

'Why are you here?'

'Where else should I go?'

I stared at her with a blank look and she stared back. After a moment she added:

'I did not want to stay with those men. They are very bad people. When you left, it gave me a chance to get away from them.'

I raised my eyebrows, but she said no more, so I tried again:

'How did you get here?'

'I drove a car from the house to London, and then a taxi to this street.'

'What I meant to ask was, how did you get away from Mr Khan? I didn't think he would just let you go.'

'When you struck that man they call Kevin they were very surprised,' she said. 'I was also surprised. Until then I thought you were a friend of those people.'

'Yes, I felt quite pleased when I hit him too,' I told her. 'But how did you get away?'

She held up her hand to stop me talking. 'I will explain.' She put her hand down and folded it with the other one in her lap. Her gestures were graceful and she was elegant in the way a model might be, except that in her case the elegance was entirely natural. She looked quite out of place in my shabby flat.

'When you struck this man they helped him up. Then they all left in the car – Aseeb, Amir and Kevin – except for the servant David. I thought they would quickly find you and perhaps they would kill you.'

She paused to sip some more water, then put the glass down carefully on the floor.

'The servant took me inside the house and put the car keys on a table in the entrance. His mobile rang. I think it was Aseeb who was calling him. The servant walked to the other end of the room because he could not hear properly, so I took his coat from the chair and his car keys from the table and ran out to the car. There is a box in the car that opens the gates. I have seen them use this. You press a button. I pressed it and drove out of the gates. The servant came out running and shouting but I was too fast for him.'

'That was brave of you,' I said. She made a dismissive motion with her hand. She didn't want me to interrupt.

'I drove the car until I found signs to Oxford, then to London. It took me a long time to get to London. I have not driven in England before and I got lost many times. At last I found a street where there were taxis, so I stopped the car and left it there. I left the keys in the car so that they can drive it back when they find it. I am not a thief. I had some pounds I found in the servant's coat. They were enough to pay for a taxi. Now I have no money.'

She seemed breathless at the end of this speech, as if she had used up a lot of energy remembering all those English words. How come she spoke English so well, if she was from a remote valley in the Hindu Kush?

'You left the Range Rover in a busy London street with the keys in the ignition? Well, that's the last Mr Khan will see of his car, I'm afraid.' It had been a bad day at the ranch for Mr Khan. But I still didn't understand what was going on.

'Tell me again why you left Mr Khan,' I said. 'And why do you call him Aseeb?'

'Why?' asked Adeena. 'You ask me why?' Her voice rose in anger. 'You ask me why I leave a man who has held me prisoner and made me marry a man I do not know?'

'Hey, I didn't ask to be married to you either,' I said. 'We were both prisoners. Kevin knocked me down.'

'I thought you were like them,' said Adeena. 'Then when you hit that man I saw that I was wrong. It was very good that you hit him so hard. I was pleased when I saw you do it. I wished you had struck Aseeb also.'

'Well, maybe next time,' I said. 'Anyway, you keep calling him Aseeb. Is that his first name?'

'At home in Kabul his name is Aseeb. Many people know of this man. He is a very bad man, but with powerful friends.'

'Then how do you know him?' I asked.

83

'I was working for an aid agency in Kabul,' said Adeena. 'You know that in Afghanistan it is very new for women to be allowed to work. Only the aid agencies and a very few government departments will employ us. I studied English language in school and then I found a job in Kabul, after 2001 when the Taliban left. I was working as a translator for two years. Then a few weeks ago the Taliban shot two people from our aid agency in the street.'

As she spoke I remembered reading about similar incidents. This part of what she was telling me sounded true at any rate. I reproached myself inwardly. Why shouldn't her story be true?

'They shot one good German man,' Adeena continued, 'and his bodyguard, right outside the office, in front of their car. I did not see, but I heard the shots and ran to the entrance. My friends were lying in the road. The men who had shot them just walked away. It is a busy street but no one tried to stop them. Everyone knew it was the Taliban. The police did nothing when they came. One policeman said to me: "They will shoot you too, because you are committing a crime against God, working for these Christians."'

Adeena yawned, covering her mouth with the back of her hand as she did so.

'So how did Aseeb come into your life? You still haven't explained that.'

'Because I am very tired,' said Adeena. 'It is hard for me to remember and speak English at the same time. Aseeb came to me one day soon after. The people I worked for were talking about closing the office and going back to Europe. Aseeb came to my home. He told my brother to go outside and my brother went quickly. He gave me a look. He wanted me to be careful with this man. When we were alone, Aseeb told me that the Taliban knew who I was and where I lived, and would kill me in the next days because they wanted to show the Europeans that they could protect no one, *no one*, who worked for them. This was important politics for them. Aseeb told me this. "It is not you yourself they want to kill, but they need to kill you as an example." "What can I do?" I asked. "Where can I go?" He told me he could help me. He took me away in his BMW before my brother came back. He said he would get me to England and give me an English passport as a favour to me, and in memory of my father, whom he once knew. He took me by plane to London.'

Adeena looked at me, as if asking me to understand. I nodded encouragingly. I was having difficulty, picturing Aseeb in the role of Good Samaritan.

'How did he get you a visa?'

'He told me to say I was his niece coming to learn English at a language school. It is easy to come if you say you are a student. But when I got to England he took me to that house and told me I would have to marry an Englishman, as a favour to him, in order to get an immigration permit and then an English passport. He said he would ask me to do certain favours for him in return.'

'What favours?' I asked. It seemed like a very important question, but I did not get an answer.

'I am tired now,' said Adeena. She stood up. 'I wish to go to sleep. Can I stay here tonight?'

I stared at her. She looked so vulnerable when she said those words.

'Yes, you can stay,' I replied. 'In the morning we will talk some more about what to do.' I too felt overwhelmed by sleep as I spoke. It had been a long day. 'That is my bedroom, through that door there. The sheets are clean. And that,' I said, 'is my bathroom. I'm sorry everything is so cramped. You can sleep in my room and I will sleep here on the sofa. Tomorrow we will decide what must be done.'

Adeena seemed relieved by these arrangements.

'Thank you,' she said. Then she asked, 'What is the time now?'

'Nearly midnight.'

'Please wake me before dawn. I must pray at sunrise. I will go to sleep now.' She went into the bathroom and then, a few minutes later, I heard the bedroom door close. I stripped down to my shirt and boxer shorts and pulled a rug and a few pillows over me and tried to sleep. At first I couldn't. What on earth was this woman doing in my house? She would be nothing but trouble to me, I felt certain.

She was good-looking, though, I thought sleepily. For a while I considered going into my bedroom and getting into my bed and curling up beside her. It would be very cosy in there, warmer than on this bloody sofa, with its springs sticking into me and draughts swirling in through the badly fitted windows. Then I thought that, if I did that, I might never get rid of the girl. I might be stuck with her. I couldn't quite understand how little control I seemed to have over my own life. There was something wrong here, but I was too tired to work it out. I fell asleep.

At four in the morning I awoke as suddenly as if someone had shaken me by the shoulder. This had happened to me before, but not since I left the army. Some sixth sense would warn me that something was about to happen and my instinct was nearly always right. Now I sat up on the sofa, my brain working furiously.

Why was the girl here? There were two possibilities. Either

the whole thing was a set-up: in which case Khan and his two thugs would be here any minute. She was here to make sure I stayed in one place long enough for them to be able to deal with me. Or. Or it wasn't a set-up and she had left Khan because he had kidnapped her and had plans for her that she didn't like. In which case Khan and his thugs would come to get her back. My flat might not be the most obvious place to look, given Adeena's earlier distaste for my company, but they would get round to it soon enough, I was sure.

The only miracle was that I hadn't woken up to find a gun at my head.

If all three of them came – Mr Khan, Amir and Kevin – things might get very nasty very quickly. I still had Kevin's gun and I was sure they would bear this in mind and would come armed accordingly. The idea of taking part in a gun battle in Camden did not appeal to me.

I was wide awake now. I dressed, pulled aside the curtains, and looked out. There was still no sign of the enemy. That didn't mean there wouldn't be. Warning signals were going off somewhere deep inside my brain. I had to move. I had to get away from here. Was I being paranoid again? I didn't think so.

What about the girl? I couldn't just leave her here. Or could I? For a moment I thought that maybe I could, that she wasn't my problem. Why should I take responsibility for her, just because I had married her? But I knew, even as I had these thoughts, that I wasn't simply going to abandon her. I had sunk fairly low in my own estimation, but not that low: not yet. Going home to my parents' house didn't seem like a good idea. Could I ring Bernie and ask whether he could loan me a hideaway? Not tempting: and besides, he never did favours for anyone, and certainly not for me. Nor would he keep his mouth shut. Then an idea occurred to me.

I knocked on the door of my bedroom. A sleepy voice answered after a moment, at first in slurred words I could not make out, but which were not English. Then, 'Who is it? What do you want? Is it the hour for prayer?'

'No. It might be. I don't know. It's quarter to five. Adeena, you must get dressed. We must go. Aseeb will find us here. I know he will.'

'I will come.'

A few minutes later Adeena came out of the bedroom. She was dressed in her blue wedding suit, but still looked half asleep.

'I must pray,' she announced. 'I will do it in your other room. There is light beginning in the east of the sky.'

'There is no time to pray,' I said. 'We must go quickly.'

'There is always time to pray,' said Adeena. 'Today of all days I must ask God for guidance and help. I do not pray every day, as I should. But this morning I must.'

I felt her warmth as she brushed past me. Then she shut the door of the sitting room. There was a phone in the kitchen. I went to it, and looked at the little black book where I kept phone numbers. I looked up the one that I wanted and then dialled. It was early here, but not quite as early where the phone was ringing. After a moment another sleepy voice, this time a man's, answered in bad French.

'Ed,' I said. 'It's me, Richard Gaunt.'

'Do you know what the fuck the time is?'

There was a pause, but before I could say anything, Ed Hartlepool's voice came again, this time sounding more awake.

'Richard? I was expecting you to call. Richard, I'm so

sorry.' I had no idea what he was talking about, but it seemed like a good time to get on the front foot in what might be a difficult phone conversation. The very fact Ed Hartlepool was calling me by my given name rather than the irritating nickname they all used meant that for some reason I had the upper hand.

'So you should be,' I said.

'I simply overslept. We went on playing cards at the Diplomatic after you left to walk to Oxford – some fool suggested one last hand and I didn't get into my bed until five o'clock. I slept right through my alarm clock and woke up about midday, just in time to cancel my lunch date with my uncle. Then I remembered about you, walking all the way to Oxford, but your mobile didn't seem to be working.'

It wouldn't have done. It was at the bottom of the Thames, or inside a fish. I couldn't believe what I was hearing. I had – or I would have – walked all the way to Oxford to complete my part of the bet, and this idle bastard hadn't even got out of bed in time to drive there in his Mercedes. In other circumstances I might have taken the next plane to the south of France, found Ed's villa, and strangled him. But these were not other circumstances. I needed his help.

'I walked all that way, Ed, for nothing. What are you going to do about the bet?'

There was a silence.

'Could you bear to cancel it?' he asked, in what I think he hoped was a contrite voice. 'Not the card debt, I mean. I'll honour that whenever I see you next. But the double or quits bet: the extra three thousand pounds. Could you see your way to letting me off the hook?'

I let him dangle for a bit. Then I said, 'If you will do me a favour in return, I'll think about it. It won't cost you anything, either.'

'Name it,' said Ed. 'Anything, just tell me what it is.'

'I need a bed for a few nights, somewhere out of London. A couple of beds, in fact. I was thinking of Hartlepool Hall. Is it completely shut up when you are away?'

This time Ed laughed.

'Hartlepool Hall? Are you sure it's going to be big enough for you? Who are you taking with you? Who is she?'

'Never mind all that,' I said. 'I'm not looking for somewhere to go and bonk someone. I'm trying to help a friend who's in a bit of a jam and needs to be out of the way for a while.'

'How long's a while?' asked Ed.

'Say a week?'

Ed thought for a moment. Then he said. 'Fair enough. I'll call Horace. Do you remember him?'

Horace was the Hartlepool family butler.

'Yes, I do.'

'I'll call him. He lives in a flat at the back of the house, and Mrs Dickinson, the housekeeper, lives in a cottage near by. They assist with the occasional functions that we have to have there – weddings and such – to help pay the bills. I may not go there much myself, but the bills keep coming in. I'll ask them to make up a couple of rooms for you and get some food in. Don't expect spectacular cooking, but you won't starve.'

'It's a deal,' I said. 'Do this for me and we can consider your debt cancelled. One other thing . . . it's very important.'

'What?'

'Don't tell anyone. I mean no one.'

*

As I turned from the phone Adeena came out of the sitting room. She must have finished communing with God.

'We can go now,' she said.

I called a taxi to take us to King's Cross, then I hid the gun. I didn't want to be carrying it around with me. I packed a change of clothes. The taxi arrived and we left.

Ed's house was an enormous pile in County Durham, about half an hour's drive from Darlington Station. On the train there, I tried once or twice to get Adeena to talk, but she shook her head. On her face was the expression she had worn when I first met her: a look of desperation so profound I wondered what on earth was the matter with her.

When we arrived in Darlington we went to the shops, where Adeena bought some clothes and other necessities. Then we climbed into a taxi and I told the driver to take us to Hartlepool Hall. He didn't need directions – everyone in that part of the world knew of the house. Adeena asked me no questions about where we were going, and I didn't bother to explain. You couldn't explain a set-up like Hartlepool Hall. You had to see it. As the taxi drove down the narrow country lanes, I thought about the very first time I had been there.

Eight

The first time I went to Hartlepool Hall was to a dance when I was in my early twenties. I forget the occasion for which the dance was given – it was a mixture of young and old people, and I think Ed's father and mother gave the dance rather than Ed himself. It was a grand enough affair. There were over three hundred guests that night, as far as I recall. Hartlepool Hall is an enormous house but even so it had been necessary to erect a couple of adjoining marquees on the lawns outside. In one, drinks and dinner were served. In another a dance floor had been erected, along with a platform on which a group of men in white tuxedos played orchestral versions of songs such as 'Yesterday' and 'I Did It My Way'. By common consent the band yielded to disco music towards midnight, and all the younger members of the party swarmed on to the dance floor.

I already knew who Emma Macmillan was, because our parents were friends. We had been in each other's houses and I knew that I liked her, but had never got beyond a feeling that I liked her on the few occasions when we had met. Most of the people of my age at that party were from Yorkshire or Durham or Northumberland and I didn't know that many of them. In those days the Pennines were a social as well as a physical divide and I was on the wrong side of them that evening, as far as I was concerned. Then I recognised Emma, sitting at a table talking with two other girls, so I asked her to dance. We bopped away energetically to a couple of songs and then left the marquee, which was very hot, and went into the house to cool off. Quite a few people were wandering about in the enormous marble entrance hall, or staring at the pictures. There was a drinks table attended by a waiter in one corner, and I managed to obtain a couple of champagne cocktails. As we sipped our drinks I asked, 'Emma, why do I have to come all the way to Yorkshire to meet you when you only live an hour and a half up the road?'

'You must know the answer to that question better than me,' she replied.

I smiled. 'Fair enough. Do you think you could face another dance with me when we've finished these drinks?'

We returned to the dance floor a few minutes later and, as luck would have it, it was a slow number. Some time during this dance, I pulled Emma very close to me and we kissed. When we did this, I felt a tingle like an electric shock go right through me to the bottom of my feet. Emma seemed to have experienced something similar, for I felt her body quiver against mine. It was very hard to let go of her when the kiss ended. Nothing further of consequence was said or done that night, but when we said goodbye – she left with her parents at about one o'clock – both of us knew that something momentous had happened.

That dance was at the end of August, and in September my leave ended and I went back to my regiment. But it was the beginning of my long affair with Emma. After a year we became lovers, during one of my leaves. Two years later we were engaged, but our agreement was that I would take the junior staff course I had put off for so long and apply for promotion when I was thirty. Then I would become a major and we would get married. We were both faithful to each other. As far as I knew Emma never even looked at another man. And with each leave it was like the beginning of the affair all over again, except that Emma lost her plump, puppy look and her features became more finely drawn. She was a grown-up woman with her own job and her own life. She would have been a catch for anyone but, miraculously, she kept herself for me.

But the innocent schoolboy in the photograph – the person who had gone to Sandhurst all those years ago and was going to be a colonel one day – had disappeared. I had gone into the army feeling cheerful, optimistic, certain that I could help make the world a better place, confident in the expectation of a happy future when I came out. It hadn't worked out like that.

It took me a while to realise what had changed. At first I thought it was everyone else who was behaving oddly. After a while I realised something had gone wrong inside *me*. Very wrong. Emma was the only person who understood what had happened, and the only person who tried to do anything about it.

The taxi slowed down and I saw that we were approaching the twin stone pillars and the lodge that marked the entrance to Hartlepool Hall. Adeena was sitting bolt upright. The taxi entered the long drive that led in a great curve first underneath an avenue of limes, the leaves now turning golden, then an avenue of wellingtonia, then blue cedars. Adeena spoke for the first time in what seemed like hours: 'Where are we going?'

'This house belongs to a friend of mine. He is away in France so the house is empty.'

At that moment Hartlepool Hall came into view. You can

visit the website, or look it up in Johansens or Hudson's, but nothing quite mirrors the effect the house itself has on you when seen for the first time. The grand front was interrupted by a portico with a great colonnade. Uncountable windows gleamed in the late-morning sunshine, and the house was crowned with a stone balustrade above which appeared leaded roofs and a central dome of white marble, contrasting with the grey stone all about it. Behind the house were stables, estate offices and a sign that indicated the way to the gift shop and tearoom (closed until Easter).

The taxi pulled up in front of the house and I paid the driver, then unloaded my overnight bag and Adeena's carrier bags from the boot. Horace appeared silently at my side and took the bags from my hand. I turned, startled.

'Lord Hartlepool called to say to expect you, sir. Everything is ready for you.'

Horace was ageless. Silver-haired and slightly stooped, he nevertheless betrayed no evidence of the fatigue that many decades of buttling for the Hartlepools must have brought upon him. By now he would have been well into his seventies, but his face was unlined and rosy-cheeked and his eyes were clear. He turned and bowed to Adeena, who stared at him.

I said, 'This is . . . you'd better call the lady Mrs Gaunt, Horace.'

'Congratulations, sir,' said Horace, without a flicker. 'Lord Hartlepool did not mention that the person accompanying you would be your wife. I had been instructed to make up two bedrooms, Mr Gaunt, sir. I hope that is correct.'

'I'm a bad sleeper,' I replied. 'That is correct.'

Adeena and I followed Horace up the wide stone steps and into the hallway. This was a vast space, with a black and white marbled floor, and walls covered with pictures depicting scenes from naval battles, rural idylls or stories from Greek mythology. At one end of the hall was an enormous white marble group portraying a she-wolf suckling the twins Romulus and Remus, a testimony to the deep purse and imperial longings of an earlier Lord Hartlepool, who had purchased it on his grand tour. At the other end was an enormous fireplace, unlit. Beams of light shone down from the circular dome above the hall.

Adeena gazed around her in amazement. Horace stopped and put the bags down.

'I have lit a fire in the Green Drawing Room, Mr Gaunt. If you and Mrs Gaunt would like to go there I will have these bags taken up to your rooms. May I bring you some refreshment?'

I declined anything for the moment and steered Adeena towards the drawing room. A log fire burned merrily away and, after the hall, the room had a more human quality. The walls were hung with green silk, and yet more enormous oil paintings hung from the picture rail. On a side table stood a drinks tray. I looked thirstily at it, and wished I had accepted Horace's offer of a drink.

Adeena looked around her for a moment longer, then turned to me and said:

'Your friend: is he a government minister?'

'No.'

'Or a general?'

'No, he is just the man who owns the house.'

Adeena went to the door of the room and stood looking again at the cavernous splendour of the hall.

'Why is your friend not here?'

'He lives in France,' I explained.

'If he is in France, who lives here? How many families?'

'Nobody lives in the house just now. My friend may come back here again one day.'

Adeena shook her head in disbelief.

'*One* man lives in this house? One man only?'

'Well, he isn't here at the moment. They keep the place going, though. I expect it gets used now and again.'

'There is enough wealth here to buy a whole province in Afghanistan,' Adeena said, 'Why do the British bother to come to our country when they have such houses as this?'

Horace returned before I could think of an answer.

'Your rooms are ready, sir, and I have taken the liberty of unpacking your bags. Lunch will be served in the dining room in half an hour, sir, if that is convenient?'

'Fix me a gin and tonic, please, Horace,' I said. 'And the lady – Mrs Gaunt – would like . . . what would you like to drink, Adeena?'

'A glass of milk.'

When Horace had served us our drinks I took Adeena out through the French windows at the other end of the room. We stood on a stone terrace, looking down across banks of dark green rhododendrons towards the lake. A family of mallard, disturbed by our arrival, skittered across the water half in flight, then subsided back on to the surface a few yards farther on and paddled away demurely. Clumps of water lilies floated on the water. From the other bank a heron flapped lazily into the trees.

'It is very beautiful here,' said Adeena suddenly, her tone different to before. 'I have never seen a place like this. So green, and so quiet.'

We walked to the end of the terrace, where there was a view of the formal gardens beyond the house.

Adeena drank her milk and gazed thoughtfully at the scene. Then she said, 'I would like to stay in this place for a while. I feel safe here.'

'I'm afraid we can only stay for a few days,' I replied.

'Why is that so? If your friend does not like his English house and stays in France, why should we not stay here longer?'

It was a good question.

A little later Horace appeared at the doors that led from the drawing room on to the terrace and announced that lunch was served. After lunch Adeena and I went for a walk in the formal gardens. It was a glorious autumn afternoon. The sun still felt warm: a last memory of summer. There were displays of dark green topiary, plain avenues of yew, bushes that had been sculpted into birds, dogs or other shapes too indistinct to define. As I walked, Adeena followed quietly just behind me, not speaking. I was trying to work out what I was doing here, and what I was going to do next. Since Kevin had knocked me over in his car four days ago, I felt as if I had never got my balance back. Although I had been off balance for a lot more than four days.

I couldn't understand why Adeena was here with me. Why hadn't she gone to her embassy and asked for help? Why had she come to me? And what on earth was I going to do about her? That was the real question. I was beginning to feel responsible for her, just because I had married her, even though we both knew that was a sham.

I looked at her as she walked along the gravel path and suddenly she smiled for the first time since I had met her. Since we had arrived at Hartlepool Hall she had become a different person: the haunted look had left her face. Now she

wore the expression of someone who found herself unexpectedly on holiday.

'You are wondering what to do about me,' she said,
breaking the silence. 'You were tricked into marrying me
and now you want to find a way to get rid of me. Is that not
so?'

She had not wanted to marry me, to say the least. When I
met her for the first time it seemed as if she would rather cut
her own throat. But now she appeared to have accepted,
for better or for worse, that she was stuck with me for the
moment.

For better or for worse: I wondered whether they used that
phrase in Afghan marriage ceremonies. Because of my own
habit of agreeing to almost anything anyone suggested to me,
I had ended up getting married to a girl about whom I knew
nothing and with whom I had even less in common. She was
without doubt easy to look at, but she would never be easy
to talk to: we had no friends in common, no memories that
we shared. I had mostly seen her country from inside an
armoured vehicle because the people who lived there sometimes shot at you or tried to blow you up.

I was beginning to realise what I had to do. Instead of
running around the country with her, I had to get her back to
London and then she could either go to her embassy or back
to Aseeb. It wasn't my problem. I turned to face her. If we
were going to have a difficult conversation, the sooner the
better.

'Adeena,' I said. 'We need to talk.'

She came up to me and put her arm through mine. The
physical contact was unexpected and pleasant.

'This is a place like paradise. I have never seen such a

house, or such gardens. Thank you for bringing me here. It is so peaceful. There has never been any war here, has there?'

'Not in a long time.' I saw a stone bench set against a yew hedge a few yards along the path. 'Let's sit down for a moment.'

We sat side by side. The view across the gardens carried our gaze westwards, across to the encircling woods. Beyond was a hint of hills: the dales, running up to high moorland far away. My parents' home was thirty or forty miles from here. The sun was lower in the sky now, and I had to shield my eyes from it. Adeena's eyes were closed and she had tilted her face to catch the warmth of the sun. She looked tired and sad again. I felt sorry for her, but I knew what I had to say.

'Coming here was a mistake. Another mistake.'

'Why was it a mistake?' she asked. 'Did you mean to go somewhere else?'

'No, I didn't mean that. It seemed like a good idea. I was worried Aseeb would find you if we stayed at my flat. Maybe I was wrong. Maybe he wouldn't have bothered . . . just cut his losses.'

After a moment Adeena replied: 'I know Aseeb. He will kill us both if he finds us. He does not like people who do not do what he wants. He is full of anger. You do not know him.'

This seemed a bit melodramatic to me.

'Well, maybe. But I shouldn't have married you, you shouldn't have followed me to London, and I shouldn't have come here with you.'

There was another silence. Then Adeena asked: 'Why *did* you marry me? Was it as a favour to Aseeb?'

I swallowed. I couldn't speak for a moment, I felt so ashamed of what I had to say.

'He offered me money,' I told her. 'It was thousands of

pounds. I don't have a job at the moment and the money would have been very helpful to me.'

Adeena was silent. Then she said:

'It is normal for money to be given when a husband takes a bride.'

'It was an immigration problem, wasn't it?' I asked her. 'You needed an English husband to get a residency permit. Do you know what Aseeb's plans were for you after that?'

'I cannot say,' Adeena told me. She looked away and again I had the feeling she was contemplating something unpleasant. 'But Aseeb would have kept me, and the things he would have made me do . . . would have been very bad. And if I did not do what he wanted he would find my brother in Kabul and harm him. Or he would send me back and give me up to the Taliban. That is why I had to escape. And when I escaped, to whom should I go? I know only one other person in the whole of this country.'

'But even if I am your legal husband . . .' I began. Adeena put a finger to her lips.

'No more now. I understand what you will tell me. But I do not want to hear it. I am tired. I have not slept properly since I left Kabul. Take me back to the house and ask the servant to show me to my room.'

I awoke after sunset. I opened the curtains and wandered next door to have a bath. By the time I had finished wallowing – it was one of those deep, old-fashioned baths in which you could lie flat out without your toes touching the taps – it was nearly time to go downstairs for dinner. There was no sign of Adeena. I wondered whether I should knock on her door, but decided to leave her to wake up in her own time.

Downstairs I found that Horace had lit a fire in another

room lined with books from floor to ceiling. On the drinks tray behind the sofa was a selection of bottles and glasses including a jug of milk with clingfilm over the top. I helped myself to a whisky and water and sat by the fire. Then there was a rustle and Adeena appeared at the door. She looked like a different girl; someone who was used to coming downstairs dressed for dinner in a house like this. She was wearing a long black evening dress with silver edging. It had not been one of her purchases that morning.

'Where did you get that dress?' I asked, getting to my feet.

'The kind servant put it on the bed for me. He said it belonged to – I cannot pronounce her name – the woman who lived here before your friend. His mother. Do you like it?'

The dress could have been made for her. She looked wonderful in it.

'You look fantastic.'

Adeena was pleased with the phrase.

'Fantastic! That is how I feel – like I am living in a fantasy.'

Later, over dinner, I tried to return to the afternoon's conversation, but Adeena would not let me. She surprised me by using my name for the very first time.

'Richard, I know what it is you wanted to say to me this afternoon. You are right. We should not have been married. You should not have taken the money, and I should have not let Aseeb threaten me.'

'But you were scared. You have every excuse for what happened and I have none.'

'Please,' said Adeena. 'I do not want to talk any more about it. Just for the next few hours, I would like to pretend. I would like to live in this fantasy house, in this fantasy dress, and pretend it is all mine. There is no Aseeb, no Taliban, and we have always lived here. Let us agree that it is all real, and not just a dream. Will you not do so?'

She seemed so earnest. I smiled and said, 'Of course.'

After dinner we went back to the library and Horace brought us coffee. We sat for an hour or so, not talking very much, but this time the silences were not awkward. When it was time to go upstairs, I followed Adeena to the landing outside her room, opened the door of her bedroom for her and said, 'Goodnight. I'll see you in the morning.'

She did not reply but stood there in her black evening dress, her blonde hair falling to her shoulders, giving me a look that could have meant anything. I thought it meant that I could go through that bedroom door with her if I wished. I knew that I would like to do that – I would very much like to do that – but also that getting any more involved with this girl would be absolutely crazy.

'Goodnight,' I said again.

'Goodnight,' she replied, then shut the door softly behind her.

Nine

The next morning, after breakfast, Adeena asked me whether she could phone her brother in Kabul, to make sure that he was safe. I referred the matter to Horace.

'Of course, sir. There is a telephone in the library. Lord Hartlepool suggested you might like to ride while you were here. If that would suit, I can call the groom and arrange for some horses to be saddled up and brought around to the stable yard.'

The idea pleased Adeena. As she hurried off to make her telephone call, a thought struck me.

I said to Horace, 'Is there another line I can use?'

'Of course, sir. There's one in the estate office, if you will come with me. All the phones have ten lines. Just press any button that isn't lit.'

I found the phone and made my call. It was to my bank. It had just been an impulse, because I felt certain I knew what the answer would be. I was wrong. Someone had transferred the sum of ten thousand pounds into my account.

Why had Aseeb done that? I had felt sure that the moment I kicked Kevin, I had sacrificed my pay-off. In fact, I had also felt a little better about myself, knowing that I had not taken the money after all. But Aseeb had paid anyway. It wasn't a good feeling. Whoever this man was, it would now look as if I was on his payroll. I returned to the breakfast room, trying to think through the implications of this, but before I could reach any conclusions Adeena came back.

'Did you speak to your brother?'

'Yes, after a while I found him. He is well, thank God.'

'You didn't say where you were, I hope?'

'I don't *know* where I am, Richard. Only that it is in England, somewhere very nice.'

We went down to the stable yard and met the groom, who was leading out two horses. Adeena mounted her horse as if she had been doing it all her life. The groom told us where we could find a bridle path that would take us in a wide loop past the home farm and through the fields, then into the woods on the far side of the lake. He said we would be back to the house in time for lunch.

It was another soft autumn day. We jogged slowly along past stone farm buildings, then along through fields of barley stubble, and round into the woods. As we rode among the trees a golden light filtered through the branches and I felt a great sense of well-being. After living a semi-nocturnal life in London for so long, the unaccustomed fresh air and exercise were doing me good. But it was more than that. I was enjoying being with Adeena in a way that, a day ago, I would not have imagined possible. I was riding behind her and found myself admiring the straight-backed, elegant way she sat upon the horse.

I paid for this loss of concentration a moment later. As I nudged my horse to jump over a fallen tree trunk, it sensed my inattention and decided to jump it as if it were taking the last fence at the Grand National. I fell off, slowly, and landed upside down with a gentle bump in a huge cushion of fallen leaves. Gentle or not, the fall reminded me of the cracked rib and bruises that Kevin had inflicted on me. My horse gave me a look, then wandered down the track. Adeena stopped, and dismounted, leading her horse back to me.

'Are you all right?' she asked. She was smiling down at me.

'I'll live.'

'I thought all English gentlemen could ride? Is that not so?'

'I was in the infantry, not the cavalry,' I said, sitting up and rubbing my back. Adeena laughed. She bent down to give me a hand.

'You look so funny, lying there on the ground.'

I was almost overwhelmed by an impulse to pull her down beside me. Then I remembered that was exactly what I had decided I was not going to do. I climbed to my feet and brushed the dead leaves from my clothes.

We found my horse cropping grass in a clearing. It did not object to being remounted and we rode back through the woods towards the house. As we approached I saw an old Land Rover parked by the front steps. I hoped it had nothing to do with us.

After riding the horses around to the stable yard and handing them over to the groom we walked back through the house into the hall. There was a stranger standing there, a man of about my own height, quite red-faced and with bright blue eyes. There was something familiar about him. As we entered, he came forward and said, 'Good morning.'

'Hello.'

'You don't remember me. I'm Eck Chetwode Talbot. We met at Freddy Meadowes' in Oxfordshire a day or two ago.'

'Oh yes, of course. I'm Richard Gaunt. And this is . . . Adeena.'

'I am Mrs Gaunt,' said Adeena in a formal voice.

'Delighted to meet you,' replied Eck. 'I'm sorry to drop in on you like this. You know I tried telephoning you after we met, but there was no answer. Then when we got home last night I rang Horace to find out if Ed was expected home this autumn. I should explain I'm an old friend and a neighbour. Horace mentioned that you were staying. I thought I'd look in and say hello.'

'Of course,' I said. 'Nice to meet you again.'

I wondered what he could possibly want. I should have recognised him but his appearance here at Hartlepool Hall was so unexpected.

'I must go upstairs and change,' said Adeena.

'We've been out riding,' I explained to Eck. 'I fell off.'

As Adeena walked away and started up the stairs Eck asked, 'Adeena . . . where is she from?'

'Afghanistan.'

He seemed surprised.

'Really – she looks quite European: a very striking girl. Congratulations. Have you been married long?'

'Not long,' I replied. I waited for him to get to the point and explain why he was here. Instead he asked another question.

'Were you in the army in Afghanistan? Is that how you met?'

'No,' I said. 'I mean, I was in the Middle East, but mostly in Iraq. I did one tour in Helmand.'

'What did you do in Iraq?' asked Eck.

'I was with the Special Forces Support Group. We were providing support to Task Force Black.'

'Oh yes,' said Eck. He gave me a look, as if seeing me for the first time. 'I've heard about that operation. They killed a lot of insurgents, didn't they?'

'We took a few people off the street. You were in the army yourself?'

'I came out some years ago. I was in Afghanistan briefly – that's why I was surprised when you told me your wife was Afghan. She doesn't look much like the ones I met.'

I knew I ought to have offered him a drink, or invited him to stay for lunch. That would have been the civilised, good-mannered thing to do. But I didn't. This person was clearly going to ask me about Aseeb. That was why he was here. Now I remembered our conversation at Freddy's house and the way he had looked at me when I mentioned the name: as if a large snake had just entered the room. Then he would ask me again how I had met Adeena: a lot of questions I didn't want to answer.

'Last time we met you said you'd been staying with a man called Aseeb.'

'Yes, that's right.'

'How do you know him?'

'I don't know him. We sort of bumped into one another.'

Eck tried another tack.

'Maybe it's not the same person,' he said. Then he described Aseeb down to the last detail of his almond-scented hair lotion.

'It sounds like the spitting image of the man I met,' I admitted. 'But he called himself Mr Khan.'

'But you used the name Aseeb when we last met.'

'I heard someone call him that, yes.'

'Well,' said Eck, 'if it *is* the same man, I can tell you that I met him just over a year ago and he is extremely dangerous. I found out – it doesn't matter how exactly – that he was laundering cash for the Taliban.'

I remembered Freddy saying that Eck used to work in the City. Maybe that was how he had come across Aseeb.

'Really?' I said, trying not to sound too concerned.

'Yes, really. The security services would be very interested if they knew he was back in the country. He could be involved in worse things than money laundering.'

I already knew that Aseeb was bad news. This was confirmation of the worst sort.

'You need to tell someone about him,' said Eck. 'You need to tell someone right now.'

'Tell who?' I asked.

'I used to know someone in the army called Nick Davies. He works for the security services now. He had a particular interest in Aseeb at the time I came across him. You should ring him and tell him what you know. Aseeb is a very dangerous man. They nearly got him last time he was in the country. If he has come back here, he's taking a big risk, so there must be a reason why he's here, and it's probably not a good one.'

I was in a difficult position. If I involved the police or the security services, I would have to go through the whole embarrassing story of my 'marriage' to Adeena. And what would happen to her? I was very vague about immigration law, which seemed to change every week. I felt sure they would decide my marriage to Adeena was a sham, and try to deport her. Only a day ago I had been wondering how best to separate myself from her as quickly as possible. Turning her in to the immigration service, or the security services, would certainly do the trick. And yet now I found the idea difficult to contemplate. I wished I had never met Eck. I wished he had not come here and bothered me with his questions and his unwelcome information.

'Give me your friend's name and number,' I said. 'I'll get in touch with him.'

'You should do it soon.'

Eck took his diary out of his pocket, wrote something on a page at the back, then tore it out and gave it to me. I read the name 'Nick Davies', and a mobile phone number. I put the paper in my pocket. As I did so I saw Adeena coming back down the stairs. She had changed. I turned and smiled at her then turned back to Eck. He was holding up a mobile phone, gazing at it.

'Just missed a call from my wife Harriet,' he said cheerfully. 'Anyway, so nice to have met you again; and you too, Mrs Gaunt.'

Adeena gave the faintest nod of her head in acknowledgement, and Eck left. We heard the sound of the Land Rover coughing into life, then the crunch of the wheels on the gravel. Only when the sound had faded did Adeena speak again.

'I did not like that man. Who is he?'

'Someone I met for about five minutes last weekend. He was staying with another friend of mine.'

'Why was he here?'

I hesitated.

'He wanted to find out when Ed Hartlepool – the owner of this house – was going to return.'

'Well, I hope we do not meet him again.'

Adeena's mood had changed once more and her face had hardened.

'Let's have some lunch,' I said. She shook her head. The carefree happiness of the morning had vanished to be replaced by a suspicious gloom.

Ten

Eck's reaction to the name 'Task Force Black' was not the first time I had seen such a response. To most people, it then meant nothing, but to a few, those who had experienced or knew something of the world of special operations in the Middle East, the name meant a lot.

In autumn 2004, the Coalition forces were losing the war in Iraq, the war that everyone had said was over. Ground had been taken, but was not being held. Coalition forces were pinned down in a few semi-secure spots: the palace at Basra, the International Zone in Baghdad, various fortified bases across the country where mortar shells and rockets landed almost daily. The cost of maintaining the 'peace' was horrendous: half a billion dollars in cash was being shipped into Iraq via Baghdad Airport every month to pay contractors and the burgeoning private armies, and to pay off politicians and tribal elders. The result was supposed to be a safe, peaceful country that was moving towards a bright and democratic future. It wasn't working.

Each week civilian deaths mounted alongside a steady stream of Coalition casualties, and by the time I arrived in Baghdad in January 2005, they were running at a thousand a month. By the time I left later that year, the Coalition and its Iraqi allies were bringing so much peace and security to the people of Iraq that the monthly civilian death toll had trebled. People were being killed at a faster rate than Saddam had ever achieved. Nearly as many civilians were dying every month as were killed in the Troubles in Northern Ireland over twenty years. That was before the 'surge', when central Iraq was swamped by American troops for a while.

'Task Force Black' was about gathering intelligence and disrupting the insurgents. Our job was to provide support, but the line between support and direct action was often blurred. The job of the task force was to go after the insurgents where they lived, find and shut down the bomb factories, take the gunmen off the streets.

The targets changed from week to week. Sometimes we had to go into the narrow alleys of Sadr City after Shia followers of Muqtadr al-Sadr. Sometimes we cordoned off the Thieves Market in Tahrir Square while the special forces went looking for fedayeen gunmen, or the ex-army officers who now called themselves Ansar al-Sunna and the insurgents and AQ foreign fighters embedded with them.

At night we returned to the Green Park compound. The Green Park people didn't mix with us or talk to us except when they had to. They were mostly Iraqis, but there were other nationalities too: a lot of Americans; a few Israelis; South Africans. We were just there for bed and breakfast. All the same, we couldn't help finding out some things about our new neighbours.

Green Park was not just another Private Military Company. There were contractors whose job it was to act as 'bullet-stoppers' for visiting VIPs; others who provided security for the oilfields and pipelines, so that at least a trickle of oil made it from Iraq's vast oilfields as far as Basra and the oil terminals. Others made sure the generals and colonels in the Green Zone received their filter coffee and their choice of premium beers whenever they briefed journalists in the Babylon Hotel.

Green Park did none of these things. We knew they were there to screen prisoners before sending them up the line for further interrogation. We never knew what their mission was in its entirety, but it appeared to be the ultimate outsourcing operation. It seemed as if it was there to do the work that governments couldn't admit to approving or even knowing about. No doubt their work was just a line in someone's defence estimate, under the heading 'Intelligence Gathering' or 'Security Services', but sometimes the Green Park teams went out in their old Toyotas and took people off the streets. Then they processed them. That meant: finding out what they knew.

For the first few weeks our own missions could still broadly be described as cordon support: daylight patrols, keeping the streets safe or manning checkpoints around the edges of the Green Zone. But once we had become more familiar with the city, things began to change.

There was a pinboard in one of the rooms at the Mission Support Station. On it were the photographs of men the special forces wanted to get hold of: bomb makers, people who organised the gunmen or who planned the roadside ambushes. Sometimes these photographs were razor sharp, taken with high-resolution cameras from one of the helicopters that thudded overhead day and night. Sometimes they were blurred, like an image snatched by a mobile phone. Sometimes there were no photographs, just names typed on a piece of paper. Lines connected these images to words, intended to suggest relationships: tribal, religious or business. These were the task force 'targets'.

Our job, when we were not providing support for other

task force teams, was to help collect some of these people. It was a strange and very scary time for all of us. Sometimes we drove into al-Amariyah or even worse parts of the Red Zone. At other times we worked the checkpoints to see what might be caught in the net.

I will never forget that day at the checkpoint in Yafa Street. Although it was nearly summer it was for once a relatively cloudy morning. The sky was grey and heavy. A song crackled from a loudspeaker hung from a nearby streetlamp. It continued playing all through the incident, and its haunting melody stayed with me for a long time. One of the first things I did afterwards was to go and ask a startled shopkeeper, unharmed by the blast, who the singer was. I even wrote down the name he gave me, as if I planned to listen to the song again.

We had been letting the Iraqi police and the US Marines do the talking, coming forward to take a look if the soldiers at the barrier stopped someone who might be of interest. A watermelon seller was trying to do some business with the people in the queue of cars and trucks. I was talking to an American soldier about fifty yards back, one eye on the checkpoint, when I saw a slender boy of about sixteen come around the corner of the street. When he saw the checkpoint, a big smile came over his face, visible even from that distance. That was good thinking: smile at the nice soldiers, smile at the nice people with guns. As he approached the line of vehicles, I noticed his odd shape underneath his dishdasha. He was spindly at the top and what I could see of his legs looked spindly too, yet around the middle he was as plump as a partridge. I started to run forward, shouting, 'Down! Everybody get down!'

Whether the boy activated the vest bomb because he heard

my shout, or more likely because he reckoned he had got as close as he ever would, I do not know, but he blew himself up. Bombers like cloudy days. The low pressure encourages the force of the blast to go sideways rather than straight up into the air, causing maximum damage on the ground. The force of the blast shattered the cluster of vehicles around the checkpoint and shredded the human beings standing around them. I was sent flying backwards, landing heavily but otherwise uninjured apart from a temporary deafness. The vehicles had erupted in flame as their fuel tanks detonated. Something round and gory and horrible rolled towards me, covered in red pulp. It came to a stop by my feet and I made myself look at it. It was the remains of a watermelon.

Sixteen people died instantly in that single attack, and there were many more casualties. There were ten such vest bomb attacks around the city that day. The next night we joined up with the special forces teams and went after the men who had organised the attacks. We were given three targets. We found none of them, but we brought back some people for 'processing' by Green Park to see whether we could improve our information. That was when I learned what else went on in our compound.

Working like that, if only for a few days, does something to you. After weeks and months the changes work their way deep inside you. To start with, and to end with, you have to deal with the fear. The fear is always there. So you have to suppress it. You must never show it. That wasn't the way things worked in our regiment. We were taught that we weren't afraid of anyone; other people were afraid of us.

But all the same, some of us were afraid. Some of us knew that you were likely to live longer if you allowed the fear to come, because it kept you sharp and vigilant. And with the fear came a feeling of being alive that was so intense it was like a drug. Don't believe anyone who has worked on this sort of operation and says they don't know that feeling. If they don't then they probably never went to the places we went, walking in the shadows down narrow alleyways in the shanty suburbs of Baghdad, never knowing when we might be shot at by a sniper, or discovered by an angry crowd anxious to tear us limb from limb and hang our mutilated remains from a lamp-post.

As the weeks passed something else became clear. The odds of getting away with it grew worse over time, not better. You knew the arithmetic was against you: the more you went out there, the greater the chance that something would go wrong.

It wasn't only the tension that changed you. It was the things you had to do. The task force was there to 'take people off the streets'. That might mean one thing in London and another in the backstreets of Baghdad. Most of our intelligence came from Joint Support Group, but it also came from a variety of other sources, including the 'processing' that went on in the Green Park villa. That part of the villa was sealed off from the bunk-rooms where we were housed. That part of the villa had steel doors which were rarely opened. When they were, we glimpsed dark and humid corridors that were badly lit, with rooms leading off on either side. We never saw inside those rooms. The windows were always shuttered.

People who had to be 'taken off the streets' were identified in a number of ways. Sometimes they were caught by aerial photography monitored by the analysts at Camp Balad. Sometimes the intel came from mobile phone calls which were pinpointed by the electronic intelligence teams working in the Green Zone, linking through from GCHQ in Cheltenham or the National Security Agency listening posts in the USA. In the last year the *Iraqna* mobile phone network had been activated, operated by the Egyptians, using US communications satellites.

In a country where the average income was only six hundred dollars a year, everyone still wanted a mobile phone. Our enemies used them all the time. Sometimes – until the Coalition authorities got wise to the fact and started using jamming devices – they managed to use mobile phones to activate roadside bombs and blow up American or British soldiers. Often they used them for one-time calls, from principal to bomb maker; from bomb maker to suicide bomber. Then the phone would be discarded or sold. So we might be out looking for the man who made the call and end up arresting some unfortunate who had picked up the same phone, with pay-as-you-go units still on it, from a market stall.

From time to time the Green Park 'processors' would obtain the name of a target from one of the people they interviewed in the shuttered rooms of the compound. That might mean that the person being questioned knew something of value. Or maybe he had given us the name of someone with whom he had a score to settle, or whose job or wife he coveted; or maybe the person being interviewed by Green Park just wanted the 'processing' to stop and was prepared to say anything to make it do so.

Sometimes the right people were caught or killed, and sometimes it was the wrong people. It's just that we never knew which was which. The special forces teams went into houses, and found a family at supper. Then two soldiers would hold the children and the wife at gunpoint, offering them chocolates and chewing gum, while someone else led the man of the house outside and 'took him off the streets'. Sometimes a bomb maker would be caught in his factory, fiddling with home-made electrical circuits. But the high-value targets, the people who organised the suicide and car bombs, were usually sitting in a village in Syria or Iran.

This was the kind of life we led. For a while I didn't quite know how to cope with it, but I found a way. I stopped caring. I anaesthetised myself, the part of me that worried about walking into a booby-trapped building, or being bottled up in a cul-de-sac with an angry crowd, or shot in the back by a sniper. Instead I was up for everything. It didn't matter what I was asked to do. There was only one answer to give whenever anyone briefed us on a mission. The answer I found was in a question: 'Why not?' because 'Why not?' stopped you from asking yourself 'Why?' 'Why not?' was the right answer to give people who might be wondering whether you were about to crack up, or whether you still had any nerve left in you. 'Why not?' wasn't really a question at all: it was a way of life.

In between missions we lay on our cots and smoked, even those of us who had never touched a cigarette before. Sometimes we talked a little, in low voices. We never talked to the Green Park people unless we had to. We never discussed what went on in the sealed rooms. We had a feeling it would be very unhealthy to express any criticism of what was going on here.

That didn't stop Sergeant Hawkes talking. Nothing would. He read too much, he thought too much, and he definitely talked too much. I didn't mind. Sometimes he said the things I was thinking, only he expressed them better than I ever could.

'Do you think we're doing any good here, boss?' he asked me quietly, one night.

'Good? In what way, good?' I asked. I wasn't sure I understood.

'I mean that we go and take out a few of the insurgents. Or we hand them over to the Iraqis, who lock them up. Or the people next door take them off our hands. But that man last night was no more an insurgent than you or I, sir. You saw him. But sure as hell his children will grow up hating us. They'll never forget what we did, charging into their house with guns and taking their father away.'

'I suppose not,' I said, dragging on my cigarette. I was trying not to think about last night.

'He's upstairs being interrogated,' said Sergeant Hawkes. 'Do you suppose he has anything to tell them?'

'I don't know. I hope so, for his sake.'

'I mean, how can you win a war when you keep killing the people you're meant to be liberating?'

'I don't know,' I said again. 'Shut up for now, Sergeant Hawkes, there's a good chap.'

'Yes, boss.'

The rock music started at that moment. It was very loud. Tonight they were playing 'Hotel California', an old favourite of Mr Harris's, judging by the number of times we had to listen to it. He was in the locked rooms of the villa, the part we could never enter, and didn't want to. That was where the interrogation teams worked, 'processing'. The music was turned up. When that happened we all turned away from each other and lay on our sides or closed our eyes so that we did not have to look each other in the face.

Above the plaintive voices of the Eagles, we could occasionally hear a noise like the screeching of owls.

Eleven

After Eck had left, Adeena remained silent all afternoon. At dinner she was sullen, replying only in monosyllables to my attempts at conversation. She barely ate, and afterwards, when we went through to the library, I lost my temper with her. She was standing by the windows leading out into the garden, staring at the dark, her back to me.

'What's the matter?' I asked her. 'You're not still thinking about Eck, are you? I didn't bring him here.'

Adeena looked at me as if I were a child.

'Of course I am thinking about that man. He will tell someone I am here and then we will have to leave.'

Suddenly her eyes filled.

'I don't want to go. It is so peaceful here. I feel safe.'

She looked at me with such anguish that my bad temper disappeared. Without any thought of the consequences I walked across the room and put my arms around her. She clung to me.

'You don't understand what it's like to be me,' she said.

'No, I don't.'

'Wherever I go I will never find peace. I will not be safe.'

'That's nonsense,' I told her. She started to tremble. The passion that swept through me was overwhelming. I let go of her and stood back.

'We mustn't,' I said, more to myself than to her.

'You are my husband,' she said. 'It is your legal right. You can come with me upstairs to my room.'

'I was paid to marry you. I can't take advantage of you now.'

'Take advantage of me? An Afghan man would say that is what wives are for,' replied Adeena. 'Do you not find me attractive?'

'I find you very attractive,' I said, gritting my teeth.

'Perhaps you have other wives? A girlfriend?'

'None at the moment.'

'I don't want to be alone,' said Adeena. 'If I am alone I will be afraid.'

'Afraid of what?'

'Of what is going to happen to me.'

Later we went upstairs to her bedroom and I waited outside until she had got into bed. Then I went into the room and lay down beside her still fully clothed until she went to sleep. As she dozed a hand came out from beneath the blankets and I took it. She mumbled some words: not English, not Arabic. I couldn't make them out. For a long while I just lay there, wondering at the comfort that lying next to her gave me. She slept peacefully, as if whatever memories haunted her, whatever dark thoughts occupied her mind, were for the time being expelled. It was a long time since I had felt closeness like this: not since I had left Emma more than two years ago. It was the middle of the night before I could bear to leave her, letting go of her hand as gently as I could and easing myself off the bed. As I left the room I heard her murmur:

'*Papa, où est-tu?*'

I headed back to my own room and went to bed.

*

When I awoke it was daylight. I looked at my watch and saw that it was after eight o'clock. I got up and after I had showered and dressed I went to the window and pulled back the curtains. Outside the golden weather of the previous day had been replaced by glowering skies. As I stood there, I saw a silver-coloured people carrier with tinted windows come down the drive and pull up in front of the house. For a while nothing happened. It spooked me, the way it just sat there. No one got out.

Then at last a passenger door slid open and a man stepped out. He was tall, thin and dark-haired. His face was shaded with stubble. He was wearing a pale raincoat, and clutching a mobile phone. He looked up at the house and instinctively I moved back from the window. Another man got out of the vehicle. He was wearing a leather jacket and jeans and trainers. He started talking to someone else inside the car, then straightened up and looked at the first man. They both examined their watches.

Perhaps these men were here to read the meter, or to measure the place for double-glazing, but I didn't think so. The way they stood, waiting for some signal that would spur them into action, reminded me so vividly of the way I had once behaved, at the beginning of an operation: those moments of false calm before the adrenalin started to flow and everything speeded up. Maybe that memory was what pushed me into doing what I did next. I stopped thinking altogether and something else took hold.

I hurried along to Adeena's room. I could hear her splashing about in the bath, so I opened the bathroom door. She was lying in a mountain of foam, soaping herself. She gave me a melting smile.

'Adeena, we've got to go.'

'Go? Go where? Why must we go?'

'Some men have come to the front of the house.'

Adeena's whole demeanour changed in an instant.

'Get out of the bath and get dressed.'

I went back outside into the corridor and waited. She was very quick. She came out of the bedroom wearing a grey pullover and jeans, her hair still damp.

'What men have come? Is it Aseeb?' she asked.

'I don't know. I don't think so. Are you ready to go?'

I was becoming more and more jumpy. The right thing to do would have been to go downstairs and sort it all out. Open the door and confront these men with that well-known phrase: 'What seems to be the trouble, Officer?'

But maybe these men weren't policemen. They didn't look like policemen, so perhaps they were from the security services. Eck had decided I wasn't going to do anything about calling them so he had called them himself. In which case all I had to do was hand Adeena over to them so that she could answer their questions. And I could go and make myself a cup of coffee.

Except I wasn't going to do that.

I wasn't going to do that because I thought I knew what would happen next if I did. We would be put under restraint and driven back to London. We would be taken to wherever these men conducted their business – maybe the building known as 'Legoland' at Vauxhall, maybe some darker hole. There we would be separated. We would be interrogated. They'd ask me about Aseeb. I didn't know whether they would believe my story: I could hear myself telling them how I had met Aseeb and Adeena and I could hardly believe it myself. I could imagine them asking me about the ten thousand pounds in my bank account. And I had no idea what sort of questions they would ask Adeena. I couldn't see them thanking us for our co-operation and allowing us to walk back into the sunlight while they waved goodbye. I thought there was a good chance I would never see Adeena again: that she would be deported, or taken to some place beyond the reach of the human rights lawyers.

Adeena was looking at my face. What she saw there, I don't know, but she didn't like it.

'It is that man who came here yesterday,' she said. 'He has told the police to come here. He has told lies about me.'

'Maybe,' I replied. 'But there's no time to discuss it. We have to leave now.'

I took her hand and we hurried down the stairs, then headed along corridors and through silent halls towards the back of the house. Far away I heard the insistent ringing of a doorbell. We walked swiftly through the stable yard, past endless buildings that had once housed bakeries or brewhouses, and past the walled gardens until we found the road that led behind Hartlepool Hall and out towards the farm buildings.

'Where are we going?' asked Adeena.

'I don't know,' I said. 'Away from here.'

Every move I made was the wrong one, but for the right reasons. Another Rubicon had been crossed. Now I felt even more responsible for Adeena. I should have given her up back at the house, and I hadn't. Now I had to keep her out of trouble, for as long as I could.

Did I feel anything for her? I hardly knew her, although I knew her a lot better than the first time I had seen her, standing frowning in the drawing room of Aseeb's house. I thought she was very beautiful. I definitely wanted to sleep with her. But I couldn't work out how our lives had become so entangled. Only someone like me could have got into a mess like this.

We walked briskly past the farm buildings. There was no one about. Adeena said nothing, but kept her head down. A faint drizzle began to fall from the grey sky. Now we were walking between two stone walls along a track. On either side of us were fields, ploughed and sown, with the faintest dusting of green from the new crop showing on the brown soil. The track took us now through a long dark plantation of firs. We were both beginning to feel quite wet. Adeena suddenly stopped walking.

'Where are we going?' she asked again. 'I cannot walk for ever.'

'Neither can I,' I said. 'Look, there's a road ahead. We ought to be able to find a village and get a bus or a taxi.'

'And what then? Where shall we go?'

'I don't know yet. Let's get away from those people first, and then worry about what happens next. Come on, let's keep moving.'

As we came to the edge of the road, a single-track affair that looked as if it led from nowhere in particular to somewhere quite similar, Adeena stopped again. She turned to face me.

'Why are you helping me?' she asked.

I didn't know how to reply so I said with a flippancy I did not feel: 'Because I'm your husband.'

She made an almost indescribable gesture with her hands, as if dispelling clouds of vapour, to show what she thought of my answer.

'You know you do not have to look after me. This has been an accident: an accident has happened to me, and another sort of accident has happened to you. We have met like two people whose cars have crashed in a road. I come from such a different place to you. How can I ask you to look after me? I cannot.'

She was nearly weeping as she said this, the first time I had seen her really start to lose control. Suddenly I saw the world as I imagined she must see it: not much more than a week ago she had been living her own life, in a faraway country. She may have been happy or unhappy there, but it was her world. Then, in an instant, everything had changed. The men she worked with had been shot and she was spirited away – kidnapped might be a better word – and taken to a house in Oxfordshire. Her feet had hardly touched the ground when she was told she had to marry the first tramp that Kevin and Amir picked up from the roadside. That tramp, as it turned out, was me.

'But if I don't look after you,' I said without thinking, 'who else is there?'

She ran into my arms. We stood there for a moment in an embrace. I could feel the fierceness of her grip. She was holding me so tight that my ribs hurt. I stood still until she stopped sobbing into my shoulder. Then she straightened up and let go of me, wiping her face with the sleeve of her jersey.

We started walking along the road. After half a mile it joined a larger road at a T-junction. Here was a sign indicating that we were fifteen miles from Darlington. I looked to either side, hesitating. Main roads meant people, people in cars, which is what we wanted. But I did not want to meet a silver-coloured people carrier with tinted windows. At that moment a bus came around a bend in the road, displaying the word 'Ripon'. Ripon was in the opposite direction to Darlington. Those men would definitely think about watching the station at Darlington. They might have the resources to do that: what they couldn't do was check every town in the Yorkshire Dales.

We started waving at the bus and by a miracle it stopped.

'What we're going to do,' I told Adeena, as we climbed on board, 'is get over to the west side of the country and then take the train down to London. They won't be looking for us on the West Coast line.'

Adeena nodded as if she believed I knew what I was talking about. The fact is I had no idea exactly who was looking for us or where they would look. But it was important to sound as if I had a plan.

'And then?' she asked.

'And then – then we'll see.'

From Richmond we took another bus deeper into the Dales, and then another and another. We passed through villages whose names I remembered from my childhood: Muker, Thwaite and then through Hawes and Garsdale Head. Once a police car overtook us with its lights flashing and Adeena shrank against my side. It probably had nothing to do with us. Probably.

It was a cloudy, windy day with sudden patches of sunlight sailing over the fell, transforming it into a green and gentle place; then the sun would go in and the landscape would become dark and threatening. There were so many questions I wanted to ask Adeena but on the bus it didn't seem safe to talk, even though we could hardly have been heard over the noise of the engine. Adeena's head lolled once or twice and then she fell asleep with her head on my shoulder.

It was many bus journeys and a taxi later that we arrived at Oxenholme. That was the station we always used when we travelled to London from home. By that time I was out of cash but I found an ATM and took out a few hundred pounds. It was Aseeb's money but I was using it in a good cause. We bought tickets and headed south.

Twelve

The train to London was half empty. We sat opposite each other at a table and at last it was possible to talk.

'We can't stay at my flat tonight, it's too dangerous. But we can probably risk going there for a few minutes. I need some clean clothes and I need to get my passport. Then we'll find a hotel. Tomorrow we'll go to your embassy.'

'And then what?'

'Then we will ask them to help you.'

'What can they do?' asked Adeena. 'Send me back to Kabul where the Taliban will find me?'

'Perhaps they can help you apply for refugee status. I don't know. But right now I think we've got the security services looking for us. And we have Aseeb to worry about as well. I'm not that clever. I can't think of any more places where we can hide.'

'You want to get rid of me,' said Adeena. 'I understand. You are right. I am putting you in danger. You don't have to look after me when we get to London. I will go to the embassy myself in the morning, if you will tell me how to get there.'

'I don't want to get rid of you,' I replied. 'I want to *help* you. But I don't know how else to do it. If you have a better idea, tell me what it is.'

'We have been together now for four days,' remarked

Adeena after a while. 'To me, it seems like a much longer time. If we could stay in one place, and not be hunted by Aseeb or those other men, those secret police friends of that man who came and disturbed us, do you think we could have been happy? I do. But now we will not have four days more . . .'

We looked at each other. In those four days I had felt as if I had begun a completely new life. I thought: yes, four more days together is the least amount of time that I would like to spend with you. But it wasn't going to happen. As for a relationship of any sort with Adeena – I wasn't good at relationships. Why would I be any better at this one?

'I am sorry we left that house so quickly,' said Adeena. 'I felt safe there, like a different person. I haven't felt that way since I was a child.'

A memory came into my head of Adeena lying in her bed at Hartlepool Hall.

'You talked in French in your sleep,' I told her. 'Why did you speak in French?'

Adeena put her hand to her mouth as if she wanted to stop it betraying her a second time.

'I spoke French?'

'You said – *Papa, où est-tu?*'

'Did I say anything else?'

'Nothing I could understand.'

'I spoke in French because I am part French,' she said after a moment. 'I was brought up in Paris. Once my father was a French citizen.'

I was astonished; yet it made sense. I had been wondering how a woman who was supposed to be from a remote mountain province of Afghanistan could speak English so well, and look and behave like a European girl. She *was* a European girl.

'But Aseeb said you were from some place with a strange name where Afghan women had fair hair.'

'Aseeb told a lie. That is not unusual for him. If he has a choice between the truth and a lie he will always tell a lie.'

'So you are French,' I repeated, still getting used to the idea.

'I said part French. My mother was a Palestinian. My father worked in Beirut. That is where he met my mother. They came back to France together. I was born there and we lived in Paris for a long time.'

'Why did you not tell me this before? You said you were from Afghanistan.'

'I did not. Aseeb told you that. I told you I worked in Kabul. That was all.'

'Then how did you get to Afghanistan from Paris?' I asked. 'How did you get into so much trouble if you are a French citizen?'

Adeena was silent for a moment, looking at me. Then she said slowly, as if speaking to a small boy:

'You don't listen. I said I was part French. I said my father was a French citizen. After he came back from Beirut he became a journalist. He was a man of the left. My mother was very anti-Western. How could she not be, after life in the camps?'

I thought about what she had and hadn't said to me. It was true she had never directly told me she was from Afghanistan, but she had allowed me to believe it. Now she was telling me another story. At least this one made more sense: so far.

'My father was offered a job by an Arab news agency.'

'Al Jazeera?' I asked. I'd heard of that one.

'No. Not Al Jazeera. My mother had contacts with a pro-Palestinian organisation. It was through them my father got his job. We all moved to Qatar when I was seventeen. I learned to speak Arabic. My father was away a lot. He travelled in Afghanistan; in Pakistan; in Iran; in Syria. He told the other side of the story.'

'The other side of which story?'

'The other side of the stories you are told in the West about what is happening in Iran, and Pakistan and Afghanistan. My father used to say that history is written by the victors. He wanted to report on how the losers felt.'

'Sounds like a dangerous thing to do,' I said, without thinking.

'It was dangerous. He knew that. But he wanted to do it. He had a reputation as an honest man. His writing was often printed in the Western press, especially in France.'

'So how did you end up in Afghanistan?'

'My father took us with him. He had an assignment to report on what was happening in the tribal areas in north-west Pakistan. He thought we would be safer with him than back in Qatar. He thought people might try to get at his family to stop him filing his stories.'

'Which people?'

'He didn't say. People like those men who came to find us this morning . . .'

She stopped talking.

'Is that it?' I asked.

'I don't want to talk about it. It changes nothing. I am a citizen of nowhere. The French don't want me. My father has always been in trouble with the authorities in France, ever since 1968. The Qataris won't let me back. The only people who looked after me were in Afghanistan and now I can't go back there either.'

'Is Adeena even your real name?' I asked.

'Yes. It is what they called me in Afghanistan. They could not pronounce my proper name. In France I was called Nadine: Nadine Lemprière. I was brought up as a little French girl. I had friends I played with at school, friends whose houses I visited. I was a normal, bourgeois child.'

Adeena spoke of her past with an odd mixture of regret and contempt for the little middle-class girl she had once been.

'What should I call you?' I asked her. 'Adeena, or Nadine? Which name do you prefer?'

She shrugged.

'It doesn't matter. 'Now I have told you enough about my family,' she said. 'You must tell me more about yourself.'

So I told her a little about how I had been brought up by my parents to believe I should go into the army.

'Why the army?' asked Adeena. 'In Afghanistan it is very dangerous to go into the army. The people don't trust the soldiers. It is not a good thing to do.'

'We think it is honourable to serve our country,' I stated, sounding pompous even to myself.

'You were in Afghanistan with the army? Aseeb said so.'

'Yes,' I replied. 'And in Iraq. I was in the army for about ten years.'

Adeena frowned.

'Why do British and American soldiers come to such a poor country? I understand about Iraq. You want their oil. But in Afghanistan there is nothing. Some walnuts. Some goats.'

That was easy. We had been told the answer in briefing after briefing.

'We went into Afghanistan because al-Qaeda blew up the World Trade Center in New York. The Taliban would not surrender al-Qaeda to the Americans. That's why we went there.'

'No Afghan people blew up anything in New York . . .'

'I don't know about that.' I shrugged. 'They said we have to stop the Taliban growing opium. And we have to get rid of al-Qaeda. And we have to build roads and hospitals and make the country safe for democracy.'

'The Taliban never used to grow opium,' said Adeena. 'They used to punish people who grew it, or made it into drugs. Now they grow it, it is true, but only to get money for the fight against the British and the Americans.'

'I don't know why you are defending them,' I said. 'You told me the Taliban were trying to kill you.'

'Yes. But still I do not understand why all these foreign soldiers are in Afghanistan. They are there to protect politicians who don't help the people, who take bribes, or who live from drug money. The aid money doesn't get to the people who need it. I worked in an aid agency in Kabul. I know who gets the money that the British and Americans send. Not the poor people. If you go to Shirpur, where the rich people live, you will see what happens to the aid money. You will see the big houses and the armed guards and the big American cars. The bridges that are built collapse because once the bribe money is paid there is almost nothing left to do the work. The schools and clinics are not built, or they are built so badly they fall down straight away. After the bribe money is paid there is nothing left for teachers, or books, or medicines. The politicians don't stop this. Their hands are dirty.

Everyone knows this. That is why the Taliban can keep finding new recruits.'

It was the longest speech I had heard Adeena make since I had met her. She did not raise her voice. Nobody else in the carriage took any notice, but by the time she had finished talking her voice was shaking.

I couldn't argue. Maybe Adeena was right. The truth was, I wasn't really sure why we had been sent to Iraq or why we had been sent to Afghanistan. At different times we had been told it was about bringing democracy to the Middle East, or it had something to do with the 'war on terror'. But when we were there it often seemed as if we weren't wanted. It seemed as if a lot of the people we had been sent to save wanted us either dead or gone.

Some of the soldiers I had served with thought a tour in Afghanistan was the ultimate adventure. It was a 'hot' war and they got the chance to shoot off thousands of rounds of ammunition. Other less fortunate men may have had a different view: especially if they had been shot or blown up in a roadside ambush. We didn't really go around thinking much about bringing democracy to the people, we concentrated on staying alive.

'So what do the Taliban want?'

'The Taliban want life as it was fifty or a hundred years ago. They dream of a time when all the land was fertile and there were no ruined villages and no foreign invaders. Perhaps there never was such a time. The Taliban want their villages rebuilt and their orchards replanted. They want the fields resown and the pastures cleared of landmines. They want the people to renounce the ways of the West. That is what they want.'

After that she didn't speak again, but sat looking out of the window at the darkening sky.

'God knows what we are doing there,' I said after a while. 'I'm sure I don't know what to believe any longer.'

She was silent. Then she asked: 'Then why were you there if you don't know what you believe in?'

'Do you know what you believe in?' I asked her.

'I know exactly what I believe in, Richard,' she replied in a soft voice. 'And that is more than you can say. That is more than any of you can say.'

For a long moment we looked at each other and then I looked away. I couldn't face her gaze. I didn't want to know any more. I didn't want to think about what she had said.

We arrived at Euston in the early evening and made for the Underground. I hurried Adeena along through the crowds, clutching her arm above the elbow to keep her with me.

'Why are we hurrying?' she asked.

'In case someone is looking for us at the station.' I was thinking about how I had used an ATM earlier in the day. Could the security services have picked up on that transaction already? How efficient were they? I didn't know, but I wasn't going to take any risks. We took the tube to Camden Town and then walked through the streets to my flat. When we came to the head of the road, opposite Mohan's grocery shop, I hesitated.

'Adeena, go into that shop and buy something. Here's some money.'

'Buy what?'

'Anything. I just want you out of sight for the next five minutes while I look around the flat and make sure that nobody is waiting for us. Can you do that?'

She took the money, nodding, and hurried across the road. I walked on, looking for . . . I was not quite sure what. Large unmarked vans or silver people carriers with aerials sticking up from the roof; men peering into shop windows and not moving on; people fiddling around at manholes, pretending to be workmen or telephone engineers. As far as I could remember most of the cars parked along the road were familiar. But this was Camden, not Baghdad. I hadn't a hope of spotting a watcher if there was one in this safe, familiar environment.

There was no point in waiting. I went back up the road and found Adeena coming out of the shop with a family-sized pack of porridge oats.

'What am I meant to do with that?' I asked.

'I don't know. I had to buy something. This is English food, is it not?'

We walked back to my flat, and I opened the door with my key. I stood for a moment on the threshold. Was there an unfamiliar smell? A stale smell, of someone's body odour? I sniffed for a moment and then shook my head. I was imagining it. I looked into each room to check no one was lurking there, but it is difficult to lurk in a flat the size of a shoebox.

'Are we going to stay here tonight?' asked Adeena.

'No. It's too dangerous. Let me get some things and then we'll go and check into a hotel for the night. In the morning we'll decide what to do next.'

I found a bag and packed a few clothes, then grabbed my passport and my chequebook. I thought about taking the gun from its hiding place in the sofa but hesitated. If I was stopped and searched with that on me, life really would become very difficult. I hid it in a new place, in my sock drawer. That would fool them.

We were not in the flat for more than ten minutes. I had it covered. Keep moving, and they can't catch you. I was determined to be too smart for whoever might be interested in us: the man called Nick Davies that Eck had told me about. Or Aseeb, wanting Adeena back.

From the moment we left my flat my pulse started racing. I was paranoid: that was all there was to it. Two years of living on the edge in the Middle East had turned me paranoid. I was looking over my shoulder again. I was imagining people following us. There was a man walking along the pavement opposite, keeping abreast of us. As I glanced at him he went into a takeaway. It was probably nothing. I tried to calm down. We walked back to Camden High Street. From time to time I glanced behind me. The man I had noticed earlier was nowhere to be seen. God, I was jumpy.

As we passed a large supermarket Adeena said:

'I need to get some things.'

'What things?'

'Woman's things. Please can you give me some money? I have none.'

I gave her a couple of twenty-pound notes.

'You go in there,' I said, pointing her in the direction of the entrance. 'Keep walking until you find what you want. I'll wait for you here by the newsagent's stand.'

'Then afterwards we can eat,' she announced. 'I am hungry.'

While Adeena was in the supermarket, I tried to think where we could stay that wouldn't involve too much more walking; and where we could eat. I wondered what sort of food Adeena liked. We could try a little Indian restaurant I knew not far from here.

After a few minutes there was no sign of Adeena. I waited a few minutes more, then decided to try to find her.

She wasn't in Fresh Fruit and Vegetables. I imagined that she was probably in that shopping trance people sometimes go into, staring at the shelves. If she'd just come here from Kabul she wouldn't be used to shops like this. She wasn't in Wines and Spirits. She wasn't in Dairy Products, or Frozen Foods. Then where was she? She wasn't at the Bakery, or the Fish Counter. I continued to walk along the last aisle. Then, not finding her, I started to search the shop more thoroughly.

I felt a little 'ting' of anxiety going off in my head. I walked along the front of the shop, looking at all the checkout queues, but couldn't spot her. She wasn't in any of the aisles. I hurried from one end of the shop to the other, attracting curious glances from one or two shoppers. Still no Adeena.

I ran outside, my heart thumping within my chest, as if it would burst. She wasn't in front of the shop. She wasn't in the street anywhere that I could see. I went a few yards in one direction, and then a few yards in the other. Every now and then I blinked, as if a film showing another world had fallen across my eyes, and if I wiped it away, there would be Camden High Street as it really was, with Adeena standing there smiling at me. Perspiration was running down my forehead. I stopped for a moment, trying to make myself think.

There was no Adeena. There was no sign of her anywhere. She had vanished. It was as if she had never been.

Thirteen

I don't know how long I stood there, opening and shutting my mouth like a stranded fish. I took a step, and then another step, quite unable to think of what I should do next. My mind was utterly blank. Then a question formed in it, like a single message scrawled on a huge sheet of paper:

'*Did she run, or was she taken?*'

I needed to do something. I could not stand here for the rest of my life. In any other emergency I had ever been in, training and reflexes took over. I never hesitated; I went straight into action. But not on this occasion. I tried to get a grip of myself and started to walk rapidly along Camden High Street in search of Adeena. As if I would find her, among ten million people. As if she wasn't miles away by now, being carried off in a car, or walking rapidly away down side streets, doubling and turning to confuse any pursuer. After a few more moments I gave up and walked slowly back to my flat. There was no point in going anywhere else now.

When I arrived at the entrance to the flat the door was still locked. All the same, when I opened it and stepped inside I called out: 'Adeena? Nadine?'

There was no answer.

I went into the sitting room, sat down in a chair near the window and tried to think. She wouldn't have left me;

someone had taken her. It must have been Aseeb. In a few minutes, when my heart had stopped racing, I would get up, go to Oxford and find that house again. Aseeb was no different to some of the people I'd dealt with in Baghdad. I could deal with him too. It wasn't a great plan, but in my present state of mind I could not think of a better one.

Then a new thought struck me. She was gone: did it matter? Wasn't that the idea? I should thank whoever had so neatly removed Adeena from my life. Yes, it was a bit brutal. But I had had no idea what to do about her. She was a problem. Of course, she was also my wife – legally or illegally – but easy come, easy go. Problem solved. Job done. Tomorrow I would use Aseeb's money to pay off the arrears on my rent, and start looking for work.

I got up and went into the kitchen and put the kettle on. An image of Adeena talking to me on the train suddenly came into my mind, her body leaning forward, her face vivid and animated. It was as if I could reach out and touch her.

While I stood there waiting for the kettle to boil I realised that in the last few days Adeena had got inside my head in a way that nobody had done since Emma. There was no question about it: I had to find her, and bring her back.

As I was getting ready to go I heard faint sounds outside: a step on the stairs; a sound that could have been a whisper; a creak. Before I could react there was a bang as the front door of the flat flew open. Several men were suddenly in the kitchen with me: large men, moving very fast. Someone kicked my feet from under me and I was on the floor, catching my forehead on the edge of the kitchen table as I fell. A man dropped on top of me, pinning me to the ground. More doors banged, and someone shouted:

'No one else here.' Another voice replied: 'Well then, go back to the van and wait while I have a word with Matey here.'

From my vantage point on the floor I could see little. Then two pairs of feet came into view: one wearing trainers, the other, battered suede shoes.

'Let him up,' said the voice that had spoken a moment ago. I was released and I heard someone leave the room. I took a moment or so to get my breath back and then got slowly to my feet. I found my handkerchief and wiped away the trickle of blood that was running into my eyes from the cut on my forehead. I was not at all surprised to see the man in the pale raincoat I'd spotted outside Hartlepool Hall, standing in front of me. He didn't look happy. His thin, unshaven face was scowling as he held up a warrant card.

'Richard Gaunt?' he asked.

I nodded.

'Security services,' he said. 'My name is Nick Davies. Where's the girl?'

There was another man in a leather jacket, jeans and trainers beside him. I recognised him as well. He was the second man who had got out of the silver people carrier. Nick Davies pushed past me and went into the sitting room. I followed, while the other man lounged against the door jamb, watching us both.

'Where the hell did you go this morning?' asked Nick Davies, without any further preamble. 'You were at Hartlepool Hall last night, weren't you? Why did you run? What are you afraid of?'

'Hang on a second,' I said. 'Before we go any farther with this, I don't know anything about you. Who are you, and why the hell did you break down my door and assault me?'

'We didn't break down the door,' said Nick Davies. 'We slipped the catch. And I'm sorry if our entry was a little noisy. My colleagues from CO15 didn't quite know what to expect when we got here. You've seen the warrant card. You know why we want to talk to you and the girl.'

'I haven't a clue,' I replied. My head was aching from where it had struck the kitchen table and I wasn't feeling very helpful.

'Eck Chetwode Talbot rang us and told us you had met up with a man called Aseeb. He also emailed us a photograph of a girl. We understand she has some connection with Aseeb, and that she's a foreigner. We want to interview her. We also very much want to find Aseeb.'

'I'm not responsible for what Eck does, or says. I barely know him.'

'Don't waste time,' said Nick Davies. 'Where's the girl? And Aseeb?'

I hesitated. I didn't know what to say. Nick Davies reached into his coat pocket and pulled out a small photograph in a clear plastic envelope. He handed it to me.

'Do you know who this is?'

It was a picture of Adeena at Hartlepool Hall, looking straight into the camera, an expression of displeasure on her face. For a moment I didn't understand: then I remembered Eck holding up his mobile phone and fiddling with it. The sneaky bastard had been taking a picture of Adeena.

'Her name is Adeena,' I said. Then I added: 'She's my wife.'

'She's your wife, now, is she?' Nick Davies leaned back on the sofa and yawned, then said to the other man, who was still leaning against the kitchen door frame:

'Basil, make us all some coffee, would you? I'm dead.

We've been up and down the length and breadth of this country chasing after you, Mr Gaunt, and a cup of coffee would be much appreciated. Your wife's name again?'

'Adeena.' I spelled it out for him. 'She's from Afghanistan.'

'You say you're married. For how long?'

'We were married at Oxford Register Office four days ago,' I told him.

'And where is your wife now? Out shopping in the dark?'

'I don't know where she is.'

Nick Davies looked at me as Basil came back in and handed us both mugs of coffee.

'You don't know where she is,' he repeated. 'Married life going a bit stale already, is it, Mr Gaunt? Not too bothered about her whereabouts? And how do you know Aseeb?'

The sudden switch in the questions threw me off balance.

'I met a man who called himself Mr Khan in a house in Oxfordshire,' I said.

'Is this him?'

Nick Davies pulled another photograph from his pocket, and showed it to me. It was of a man in a dark suit, getting out of a car. He was half turned towards the camera and it did not look as if he knew he was being photographed. I could see just enough of the face: the high forehead, the dark hair brushed straight back, the dark eyes and aquiline nose. I nodded.

'That's him.'

'Then your Mr Khan is our Aseeb. Where exactly in Oxfordshire was this house? What were you doing there?'

I told Nick Davies the name of the house and where I thought it was. He turned to his colleague.

'Phone it in, Bas. Ask them to get someone down to the location to take a look. Not a copper in a panda, though.

Send a team with a search and entry warrant, as soon as they can get one.'

He turned back to me.

'So how exactly did you come to be Aseeb's guest at this house? How did you meet?'

'One of his employees knocked me down with a Range Rover, and then took me there in the boot of the car.'

Nick Davies stared at me. Then he laughed.

'Well, that's different. Are you capable of telling me the whole story, or do I have to drag it out of you bit by bit?'

I saw there wasn't any point in concealing anything from him. I needed this man's help, now I knew for certain he was not the one who had taken Adeena. So I told him the full story: the kidnap; the 'arranged marriage'; my escape. As I told it I felt a renewed sense of self-loathing. How could I have behaved like that? Nick Davies did not bother to hide the look of contempt that spread over his face as I talked.

'So you married this girl for money, did you, Mr Gaunt? No wonder you're not that bothered where she is. You've cashed the cheque, I suppose, had a bit of fun with her, so now she can just look after herself. Is that the idea?'

I shook my head. I wanted to object to this view of my behaviour, but I couldn't find the right words.

'So you really don't know when she'll be back? I can't decide, Mr Gaunt, whether you are just another one of the people Aseeb has duped, or whether you are working for him. You tell me that he paid you ten thousand pounds. That puts you on his payroll, doesn't it? A court might consider your evidence to be contaminated by that payment.'

He paused and looked at me.

'We work in counter-terrorism. The girl appears to be an associate of someone we think organises and finances terrorism so we need to talk to her as a matter of urgency. She will know something about Aseeb and what he is doing back in this country. She may not know she knows it, but she will know *something*.' He looked at his watch. 'We've been sat here for a quarter of an hour already. Is she coming back here?'

'Adeena has disappeared,' I told him.

'How do you mean, she's disappeared?'

'I mean that one minute she was with me, in a super-market, the next she was gone.'

I had to go over that part of the story again, in detail. When I had finished Nick Davies asked, 'Why didn't you call the police?'

'Call the police? By the time I'd finished explaining every-thing to them they'd think I was mad. I'd probably have been arrested.'

'So what *were* you going to do?'

'I was just about to go back to Oxfordshire and look for her,' I told him.

'You were going to go and get her back? Who do you think you are? James Bond?'

Nick Davies stood up. He took a card from his pocket.

'Leave that kind of thing to us. That's our job. We don't want civilians interfering. We'll check out the house in Oxfordshire as soon as we can get a warrant. In the mean-time, don't go anywhere. We'll keep an eye on your flat in case your friend Aseeb decides to come here, but you stay put. This is our business now, not yours. Here's my phone number,' he said, handing me the card. 'If I don't answer, someone else will. What's your mobile number?'

'I don't have one,' I told him.

'Then go out and buy one as soon as the shops open

tomorrow. If the girl gets in touch, you need to speak to me straight away. Don't go anywhere, don't do anything; just call me. We'll be looking for Aseeb, now that we know he's in the country, and if we find him or the girl, we'll let you know.'

A moment or so later the two of them left. I didn't feel I had made a very good impression on them but I didn't much care. At least they would be looking for Aseeb. They had the resources to do it. My own plan had been a little thin on the detail. Leave it to the professionals, I thought.

Just then the phone rang. I snatched up the receiver, wondering whether it was Adeena.

'Don't you have any manners?' a voice asked. After a moment's confusion, I realised who was speaking. It was Ed Hartlepool.

'I'm sorry? Is that you, Ed?'

'Yes, it bloody well is me.'

'What's all this about manners?'

'Don't you know how to behave?' he asked, sounding annoyed. 'You borrow my house, you borrow my horses, you even borrow my butler. Fine. We agreed you could stay at Hartlepool Hall for a few days. But then you up and leave – you and your girlfriend – without so much as saying thank you or goodbye. Horace was really upset. He rang me to say that Mrs Dickinson had gone into Darlington and bought some kippers for your breakfast, and you just disappeared without saying goodbye: without a word, in fact.'

'Some people we didn't want to see turned up. We had to leave in a hurry.'

'Some people?' repeated Ed. He sounded more and more angry. 'They told Horace they were from the security services. He nearly had a heart attack. What kind of people are you mixing with these days, Richard? Who was the girl?'

'I'm awfully sorry, Ed. They were just some old army acquaintances I wanted to avoid.'

'That sounds likely. What opinion do you think the staff will have of me if I let people like you stay in the house?'

'I'm awfully sorry,' I repeated. I was beginning to get annoyed with Ed. He hadn't finished ranting.

'You didn't even leave a tip for Horace. He didn't say so, but when I asked if you'd left anything in your rooms he said, "Only their clothes, sir." I could tell from his tone of voice that you hadn't left anything for him. I call that thoroughly bad manners. Or are you going to tell me you were unhappy with the way he looked after you?'

'He looked after us beautifully,' I said. 'I'm sorry to have left Horace in the lurch like that. I'm sorry about the kippers too. I'll put a cheque in the post. What's the going rate these days?'

Ed sounded slightly, but only slightly, mollified.

'A hundred quid at least.'

'I'll send him a cheque today.'

'What do you want done with your clothes?' he asked. 'I hope you don't expect Horace to post them to you?'

'Burn them,' I told Ed, and hung up.

I sat by the phone, trying not to think about what might be happening to Adeena. I had a very bad feeling about Aseeb. If he was some kind of terrorist and if Adeena was in his way now, or a risk to him, then he might do anything to her.

Whenever I tried to empty my mind of unpleasant thoughts, it often happened that even more unpleasant ones came along and filled it. The medical officer had told me I might have flashbacks. 'You'll get over them,' he had said.

We tried hard not thinking about what happened in the interrogation rooms, but it was no use. One of the men said he thought they were waterboarding people. He had seen Mr Harris going up the stairs one night with a roll of plastic film in his hand. It was used to wrap people from head to toe and then strap them to a board. The interrogators would then pour water over the subject so that he felt as if he were drowning. He *was* drowning, but the process allowed the interrogator to cause the sensation of imminent death to recur over and over again.

Sergeant Hawkes once had the courage to ask Mr Harris about it when he attended a briefing session.

'You would like to join us?' asked Mr Harris. He gave a comfortless smile. 'We can train you in the work if you are interested. We only use information-gathering techniques approved by the US authorities, you know. You aren't getting soft on these terrorists, I hope, Sergeant Hawkes?'

'Just asking, sir.' Sergeant Hawkes went on calling Mr Harris 'sir' and Mr Harris had given up correcting him.

If his answer was meant to be reassuring, it wasn't. And anyway, I didn't believe it. I had heard other noises through the music that still haunted me. Not just the screaming. Twice now I had heard the unmistakable whine of an electric drill. That didn't sound like something approved by the US authorities. I hadn't mentioned it to anyone, although I knew that if I had heard the sound, then some of the others probably had as well. But if we admitted we knew what was happening upstairs we would have had to say something, or else remain silent and be complicit. So we said nothing to each other. It didn't happen, and we didn't hear it happen. Yet the sounds that were audible at night haunted my dreams so that sometimes I awoke covered in perspiration, sweating at the shame of my knowledge and my silence.

Then we started to take casualties ourselves.

The first had been a month previous: Corporal Gerrard had been shot in the back by a sniper while on foot patrol in Rashid Street. He died on the spot. The second was Trooper Samuelson. He went mad: that was the only way to describe what happened. Over the last couple of weeks, he'd become withdrawn and very jumpy. I'd noticed this and put in a request to Task Group Headquarters that the man should be allowed some leave or at least be restricted to duties in the villa for a while. Instead I was told that we were under-manned; request denied.

I nearly went and told headquarters to get a grip, but of course I didn't. Then Samuelson had some sort of fit when we were leaving the compound one morning. He jumped out of the back of the jeep just as we were about to set off on a patrol, and ran back into the building. Sergeant Hawkes was after him like a cat. I followed a moment later. I found Sergeant Hawkes pinning Samuelson against a wall. A pistol lay on the floor.

'He tried to put it in his mouth,' said Sergeant Hawkes, breathing hard.

After a while a medic came and gave Samuelson a shot of something. A little later he was taken away to Ibn Sina Hospital. Or so they said. We never saw or heard from him again. But someone must have decided that the rot had set in. A few days after this incident, I was called to headquarters and told that our tour in Baghdad was over.

The next day, as we loaded our gear into the transport that Green Park was providing to take us back to Baghdad

International Airport, Mr Harris came into the yard and strolled over to us.

'I hear you've done good work, boys,' he said. 'If ever you feel like coming to work full time in the private sector, just let me know. Six hundred bucks a day. Beats working for the regular army, don't you think, Captain Gaunt?'

'Thank you, Mr Harris,' I told him. 'I think I've had enough of Baghdad for now.'

'Well, we'll get you back as far as Basra safe and sound, and then you can all sit in the airport until they send you home. Just one thing, boys?'

We all looked at him.

'What goes on at Green Park stays here,' said Mr Harris. He wasn't smiling now. 'You don't ever talk about it. Not to anyone. Not to your colonel, not to your comrades, not to your wife, not to your sister. We don't like people talking about us. Isn't that right, Sergeant Hawkes?'

'Of course, sir,' said Sergeant Hawkes politely.

On the trip to the airport Sergeant Hawkes was very nervous every time the Humvees slowed down in the traffic. The highway was busy that day.

'I wouldn't put it past that bastard Harris to blow up one of his own cars as long as we were in it,' he said. 'He won't want us to talk to anyone about what goes on in that villa.'

'He knows we can't talk about it,' I said. 'He knows we wouldn't want the grief of spending the next two years of our lives mixed up in some sort of inquiry. Anyway, they're Americans. It's up to the US Army to keep their contractors under control. It's not our problem, Sergeant Hawkes.'

'If you say so, sir,' said the sergeant, in his most wooden voice.

We reached the airport without incident. From Baghdad

we flew to Basra, expecting to be put on the next flight back to Brize Norton. That was not what happened. Our commanding officer was waiting for us. He had news.

'We're all very pleased with the work you did. I'm sorry about your losses.'

'Any news of Samuelson?' I asked.

'Samuelson? Oh yes, Samuelson. He's been shipped back to a specialist hospital in the UK. He's not very well, I'm afraid.'

'Perhaps we can go and visit him when we get home,' I suggested.

'Perhaps you can. But that won't be for some time yet. You're off to Helmand tomorrow, via Camp Bastion. We've been rather caught out by operational requirements and we're under strength there until the next rota comes in from home, so I've had to scratch together what I can from here. There's a C-17 leaving tomorrow at six in the morning, and you're on it.'

Fourteen

Talking about kippers with Ed Hartlepool had reminded me that it had been a very long time since food had passed my lips. It was all very well sitting around in my flat, but it wouldn't do anyone any good if I starved to death. It wouldn't do me any good, at any rate.

I put on my jacket, left the flat and started looking for somewhere to eat. After five minutes I came to the little Indian restaurant that I sometimes favoured. But that was where I had intended to take Adeena for supper and I didn't feel like going in there now. I walked on. Next came a short row of restaurants: a Chinese; then a Thai; then a Greek café offering all-day breakfast. Instead of making me feel hungry the smell of food that wafted out from these places made me feel sick. I hurried on.

Presently, as had happened before, my footsteps led me down a familiar road. It was as if I had no will of my own, but was programmed to return to this place. After twenty minutes I found myself outside the empty glass windows of Emma's restaurant. 'Emma's' was what we had called it, after many arguments. After all, it had been her idea, her planning, and mostly her money that had made it all happen. The name of the place had been painted out on the fascia board, and 'To Let' signs were plastered across the windows, with an estate agent's board fixed above the door. I pressed my face against the glass. Inside was just an empty room with concrete floors and a few bits of rubbish. Two years ago these windows had blazed with light on our opening night. Now it was hard to see inside.

After I came home from Afghanistan, I had stayed for only three days at home, then I moved in with Emma. Emma would make everything all right. She had been expecting me to come to her after I had stayed with my parents for a few weeks. Then we were going to look for a bigger flat to live in together.

The speed of my arrival took her by surprise. I was at her door just as she was leaving. She was beside herself with excitement at seeing me again. She rang her work, which was cooking boardroom lunches for various banks in the City, and told them she was sick. I could tell she felt bad about letting them down, but she wanted to show me she would drop everything for my sake. We went to bed five minutes later. Then we spent the rest of the day talking and catching up. In the evening we went out to dinner and celebrated my return, then came back to Emma's flat in Parliament Hill. In the middle of the night I got out of bed feeling restless and suddenly I was violently sick. I just managed to get to the bathroom in time. I did not wake Emma. The next morning we breakfasted together before she went off to work.

'So what are your plans now you're in London?' she asked.

'I don't know.' I looked at her. She was smiling, but a faint worry crease had appeared between her brows. 'Spend time with you, mainly.'

'But I work all day, Dick. Or do you want me to give up my job? Then we'll have no money at all coming in.'

'I don't know,' I said again. I stood up and went and stared out of the window of her flat. You could see Hampstead Heath from there, and the green space called to me. I wanted to go and walk in the sunshine with her. I wanted to go to bed with her. I didn't know what I wanted. She came and put her arms around me.

'What are we going to do with you?' she asked.

'I'll be all right,' I told her. 'I just need a bit of time to get used to life outside the army.'

'And now I have to go to work,' she said. 'Or I'll get the sack.'

For the next couple of days I hung around Emma's flat and read the newspapers. I bought a notepad in order to write down ideas for how I would conduct my life now that I had left the army. Its pages remained a complete blank. The fact was I had never given the slightest thought to what I would do with my life. At school I had rarely looked farther ahead than the end of the week. Then my father had told me I was going to go into the army, which was fine by me. It was what he had done when he was my age, and what his own father had done. I knew I didn't want to go to university. And once I was in the army, my life was mainly organised by other people. Now I was out, I had to think for myself for the first time in my life. It gave me a headache.

It was Emma who cut through my doubt and confusion. She came home one evening with an air of excitement.

'What is it?' I asked.

'Tell you later. I'm going to have a bath.'

I went and sat on the edge of the bath while she lay in it.

'Did you have a good day?' I asked.

'Mmm. Very. And you?'

'Don't know where the time has gone,' I said. 'One minute it was breakfast, the next minute you were back here again.'

'Didn't you go out for a walk or anything? Did you do the shopping I asked you to do?'

'Oh God, sorry. I forgot. I'll take you out to dinner instead.'

It was true. I had sat in a chair all day and my mind had gone blank. I suppose I must have been thinking about something. I don't believe I slept. I just stared at the wall, nagged by a feeling that I ought to go outside and take some exercise, or that there was something Emma had asked me to do. Now I remembered what it was: buy stuff for supper.

We went out to a little restaurant about four streets away. It had the merit of being cheap, and when you ate the food you could forgive its shortcomings because you knew you weren't being overcharged. I was fussy about food. I was even quite interested in it, interested enough sometimes to ask Emma what she had prepared for her boardroom lunch. But when Emma told me what was on her mind, it still took me by surprise.

'I've been talking to one of the other girls at work,' she announced, as we chewed our way through overcooked steak. 'There's a restaurant not far from here called Chez Angela. I don't think you've ever been. I have, once or twice. It wasn't very good.'

'Wasn't? Has it closed?'

'That's just it. Angela Bright is the girl who owns it, and the girl I know, Mary, has been doing temporary work for her in the evenings. Angela offered her the business. She says her heart's not in it any more. I think her husband left her, or something.'

I didn't see what was coming.

'My friend Mary says she could never take it on and she doesn't have the money. Angela doesn't want much, just someone to take over the lease and pay a nominal amount for the catering equipment and whatever else she's leaving behind. So I told her to tell Angela that I might be interested.'

'*You* might be interested, Em? What about your job?'

'Well, what I was hoping, Dick, was that *we* might be interested.'

I looked at her for a moment. Her eyes were bright with enthusiasm and she was smiling, her lips parted, as if she couldn't wait to hear what I would say.

My first instinct was to say, 'Not in a million years.' It would never work. I knew nothing about running a restaurant. But as I looked at Emma's face and realised how very hard she was trying to think of something that would make me wake up and take an interest in life, I hadn't the heart to discourage her. Looking back at that moment, I wish it had been otherwise.

We left the restaurant we had been eating in and walked through the streets to Chez Angela. As we walked Emma explained that she had some money her parents had given her which might be enough to buy the business and put it back on its feet. She wasn't sure whether Chez Angela was still making money, but it had done at one time. The staff were good, according to her friend Mary, and Mary herself would come and help out if she was needed. Emma also thought the bank would give us a loan for working capital. She had it all worked out.

'What would I do?' I asked her. 'I'm not going to put on a white jacket and become a waiter.'

'You have to put on a suit and tie every night, look nice, greet the customers, and make sure everyone's happy. You can help take orders and serve drinks when we're busy. Which we will be.'

'OK, I've got the picture – I'm a waiter in a suit. What will *you* do?'

'Plan the menus, order the food, help with the cooking, recruit the staff and tell them what to do, count the stock, do the accounts and fill in the VAT returns.'

'Sounds fair,' I said. 'I can help with the paperwork. I don't mind that.'

Emma stopped in the middle of the street and looked at me.

'Do you think we really might do it, Dick?'

'Hang on, I haven't even seen the place yet.'

We walked on. I could feel Emma almost vibrating with enthusiasm, as she hung on my arm. When we got to Chez Angela, it wasn't very exciting. Inside it was dull and badly lit, with that slightly run-down feeling that places sometimes get when they are no longer loved. The menus looked a bit dog-eared. The tablecloths had been washed too often and the glasses and cutlery didn't sparkle the way they should have done. We ordered a couple of glasses of wine and sat in the bar area, watching the ebb and flow of business. It was more ebb than flow.

But after a few minutes I began to see what Emma had in mind. With new cutlery and glasses, and new white linen, and better lighting, and more cheerful staff, and a bit of bustle, it could be an inviting place. The location was good, a street with two or three smart dress shops in it and a hairdresser's; we might get the 'ladies who lunch' crowd during the daytime and we could do even better in the evening. Suddenly it didn't seem like such a mad idea after all.

And what else was I going to do? I didn't think I was

capable of mapping out a new career for myself. In any case, what was I good at? What I was good at would never appear on any résumé, and would likely horrify any prospective employer. Besides, I had heard that restaurants kept you busy and that it was a very demanding job. That, I thought, was what I wanted: to be kept too busy to think.

We didn't buy the place straight away. Emma was more careful than that. It was her own capital she would be spending, a good part of the inheritance given to her by her parents plus her own savings, and I knew the idea made her nervous. If she lost the money, she wasn't likely to get her hands on any more.

A few nights after our first visit, we had dinner at Chez Angela. We introduced ourselves to the owner, a tall, care-worn woman who seemed to be close to the end of her tether. She welcomed our interest, and was disinclined to haggle when we named a very low price. A day or two later she sent us her accounts, and Emma employed her own accountant to help her put together a business plan.

I didn't do much apart from looking through catering equipment catalogues with Emma, and helping her write lists of things she wanted to do. I didn't bother myself too much with the details. It was her idea, and I was happy to come along for the ride. After a couple of weeks we had a plan, and the offer of a bank loan for our working capital. We called Angela Bright, and the deal was done. The restaurant was ours.

So now the idea had become reality and for a while I was as caught up in it as Emma was. She gave in her notice at work and for a week there was a whirlwind of planning: meetings with shopfitters, with catering equipment suppliers, with decorators, with electricians. Emma interviewed staff and sometimes I sat in, but after a while she discouraged it.

'You make them too nervous, darling. It's the way you sometimes look at people. Go and do some menu planning instead.'

But the menus I planned weren't very good. They cost about twice as much to cook as we could possibly have charged for them, so Emma, who was more practical, took over that side of things as well.

In the end I became an odd-job man. But I was enjoying myself too: that is to say, the listless feeling that threatened to overwhelm me most days receded a little, and the days went past quickly enough. And of course, Emma couldn't have been happier.

'It's perfect for both of us,' she said to me one night just before we exchanged contracts with Angela Bright. 'I love cooking, and you're keen on food and wine too. The restaurant will be a hit. I've arranged for lots of press releases to go out before the opening night.'

'I don't know why you think I'm going to be any good at looking after customers,' I said.

'Please try. You can be so nice when you want to be. Remember, the customers are paying our wages. At least, I hope they will be.'

'I'll do my best to be nice to everyone. But don't say I didn't warn you.'

'It will be wonderful to work together, won't it?' Emma looked at me, almost pleading. 'It's not as if we've seen that much of each other over the last few years. You won't get bored of being with me all the time?'

'I won't get bored,' I promised her. The truth was, I didn't really know.

The plan was that for the first year Emma and I wouldn't take any money out of the business. We could just about afford to do that, because we both had modest incomes from other sources and I had just qualified for my army pension plus a cash grant. But it would mean no holidays and no new flat. I didn't mind. If Emma was happy, she could look after me, and then in time I felt sure I would be happy too. It's just that I'd forgotten exactly what that word 'happy' meant.

Meanwhile the new restaurant took shape. Emma planned an entirely different table layout, which meant we could seat a few more people, yet had extra space between the tables so that you didn't risk putting your elbow in your neighbour's soup while you ate. New linen, glasses and cutlery were ordered and new menus were designed and printed. The wine list and the drink stock were changed and expanded so that the bar became a place where people might want to drop in for a drink rather than just a waiting area for diners. Emma was clever with the lighting, too. The whole place sparkled and there was a bright, cheerful feel to it.

Then came the opening-night party.

We served drinks and plates of tapas. Sample menus and wine lists were scattered around. The champagne flowed. I certainly wasn't drunk – I don't really drink that much – but I'd probably had more than I usually do. Everything was going swimmingly and I was working the crowd: 'Hello, I'm Richard. What do you think of it all? Marvellous. Thank you for saying so. Hope we'll see you here in the future.'

I thought I was doing quite well. Occasionally I caught glimpses of Emma through the crowd – it was amazing how many people we had crammed into a not very large space – and she gave me a brilliant smile. Once we found ourselves next to each other. She was talking to the restaurant critic from the *Evening Standard* so I thought I'd better leave her to it, but she reached behind her back, found my hand and squeezed it. I could see she was enjoying herself and I felt proud of her. I turned away and bumped into a girl standing behind me. I didn't recognise her. I must have caused her to spill some wine, because she gave her glass to the man standing next to her and started wiping her hand with a tissue.

'I'm sorry. Did I do that?'

'It doesn't matter,' she said briefly. She took her glass back from her companion. She was a tall red-haired girl, with blue eyes.

'I'm Richard Gaunt.'

'Oh yes. Emma's boyfriend.'

She didn't sound especially friendly. I didn't blame her. I smiled encouragingly.

'You're the soldier, aren't you?'

'I'm a restaurateur now,' I replied, still smiling.

'I remember Emma telling me. Iraq and Afghanistan. Did you ever think about what you were doing there, or did you just believe what the politicians told you?' She turned and addressed her companion, a chubby man wearing a dark blue suit with receding black hair. 'How anyone could believe shooting and bombing all those innocent people was going to bring back democracy is beyond me.'

The chubby man removed his horn-rimmed spectacles and wiped them. He was smiling at me in a nervous, ingratiating way.

'Griselda's terribly anti-war, aren't you, Grizzle?'

I smiled back at him and said, 'It wasn't quite like that.'

'Well, what was it like, then?' asked Griselda. I thought for a moment before answering her. I was about to come out

163

with the usual platitudes: 'The people of Afghanistan are grateful we are there' or 'We liberated them from the Taliban' but the words that came out were not what I expected.

'I don't know why we were there,' I told her. 'But I know we paid for it. I once picked up a friend and found he had no legs. There was just the trunk of his body left. He'd lost an eye, too. That was an IED. Roadside bombs. And all you fucking people do when we come back is lecture us about human rights, and upsetting the Muslim world. We're just soldiers. We do as we're told. And then, when we get home, we have to put up with people like you.'

'For Christ's sake,' said the balding man. Griselda had gone deathly pale.

I said, 'Since you brought the subject up, that's how it was.'

I turned away. The two of them made off through the crowd and I went and stood on my own for a moment, waiting for my pulse to drop back down to normal. What had happened to me? Why had I behaved like that? I shook my head. The crowd was thinning now, and people were leaving. I hoped that was because it was late, and that it didn't have anything to do with my behaviour. With luck, Emma would never hear about it. But I was out of luck. She was standing near the door, saying goodbye and thanking people for coming. I saw the tall redhead and her friend stop and say a word or two to her.

A little later we were on our own, apart from the staff, who were clearing up the empty glasses and dirty plates. Emma came across the room to where I was standing, watching everyone else at work.

'That went very well, on the whole.'

'Yes, you did brilliantly, darling.'

She was frowning a little. She hesitated and then asked, 'What did you say to Griselda? She seemed distressed about something.'

I wondered what to tell her. 'She made some anti-war remark. She doesn't like soldiers. It upset me, I'm afraid.'

'Well, you upset her too. The poor girl was in tears when she left. I know Griselda can be a bit punchy at times, but honestly, darling, what on earth did you say?'

'I can't remember. I'm sorry if I upset her. But she shouldn't have been so bloody rude to me.' My voice rose in volume as I spoke.

Emma put her hand on my arm.

'All right, darling. Calm down. I'm not criticising you. Only these are our customers, OK? The people we need to keep happy. Can we do that, do you think?'

I didn't like the way Emma was looking at me.

'Whatever you say, darling.'

Two years later, I stood once more in front of 'Emma's'. You could still just about make out the trace of the name in the orange glow of the streetlights. When the restaurant had been put into administration, the receivers had rashly invested in a can of white paint to remove poor Emma's name, thinking they could relet the place quickly. It hadn't done them any good. The restaurant had changed hands too often in the last few years and people who checked on its past decided it was jinxed. Now it was just the ghost of its former self, a cold empty building that had once echoed with noise and life.

I turned and walked back towards home. I wasn't hungry any more. I felt sick: sick with memories. When I got to my flat I unlocked the door as quietly as I could and crept in.

I suppose I hoped Adeena might have returned. I'd been lost in my own memories for a while but now the anxiety came surging back.

I sat in the empty flat and tried not to think about Adeena. Instead, recalling that night at Emma's restaurant and my row with her friend Griselda triggered another memory.

We were on the road to Musa Qala, in Helmand Province in Afghanistan. We had left the base at Sangin in the morning with orders to reinforce an operation that was clearing Taliban out of the orchards and irrigated fields of the plain. When we arrived at the base from Camp Bastion, we were shown the vehicles we would be travelling in. To my horror I saw they were Snatch 2 vehicles, a desert version of the Land Rover with token armour cladding that gave its occupants about the same amount of protection from IEDs or rockets as if they were sitting inside a tin can.

I complained to the major in charge of the vehicle park, but he wasn't helpful.

'It's that or walk,' he told me. 'We don't have anything else at the moment.'

Sergeant Hawkes was gloomy when I told him what we would be travelling in.

'Do you think they actually don't want us to survive, boss? Perhaps we know too much.'

The same thought had occurred to me, but I dismissed it. I couldn't see anyone being that well organised. It was chaos here, not conspiracy; just as it had been chaos in Iraq.

An hour later we drove off towards Musa Qala. It was a pleasant day in late spring, but we were driving along dusty roads in a noisy Land Rover with a diesel engine that sounded as if it had been driven flat out for most of the

166

Second World War, then dropped off a cliff. Travelling in this fashion, it was already too hot for comfort.

We passed through fields of green wheat. Farther back from the road were groves of trees covered in white blossom. Small children waved at us from the roadside and here and there we could see the figures of farmers working in the fields.

We were about half an hour from our destination when, a long way ahead of us, something pulled out into the road.

'Where have all the people gone?' Sergeant Hawkes said.

'What?'

'I said where have all the people gone?'

A moment ago there had been people everywhere, dotted around the fields, or standing by the roadside watching our convoy drive past. Now the fields were empty. Ahead of us I could see a cart, pulled by a donkey and being guided by a single man. As we watched, it came to a halt by the side of the road. The brake lights of the vehicle in front came on as the driver slowed in order to manoeuvre around the cart without hitting it. The whole convoy slowed down in response.

'Don't slow down, for fuck's sake!' shouted Sergeant Hawkes. 'Keep the speed up—'

At that moment there was a whoosh and a rocket slammed into the side of the vehicle in front. The explosion wrecked our windscreen and the vehicle in front vanished. I heard the driver scream as our Land Rover left the road and tipped slowly down an embankment into a shallow irrigation ditch. I was out of the door almost before the vehicle came to a stop. Behind me I heard small-arms fire, then the sound of a heavy-calibre machine gun. I thought the fire was coming from a grove of trees to the right of the road.

I wiped blood from my face – my own or someone else's –

and grabbed an automatic rifle from the vehicle. The driver was dead. Sergeant Hawkes was sitting in the back, moaning, his hands covering his eyes. Blood trickled between his fingers.

'I can't see, sir,' he said. 'Sir? Are you there?'

'I'm here,' I said. 'Get your head down. Hang on a moment.'

I looked back down the column of vehicles. All of the other Land Rovers had stopped. There was nowhere to go: the road was too narrow to turn around in and there was an embankment on either side. The ambush site had been well chosen.

Up and down the line soldiers had spilled out of the Land Rovers and were returning fire. I could see black-gowned figures moving towards us through the knee-high crops. I ran down the line and shouted at the driver of the radio vehicle to call in air support. He was already on it. I had just turned back when there was another whoosh and a rocket slammed into the road beside my own Land Rover. There was another explosion. The vehicle was on fire now, and badly damaged, but I managed to open the door. There was a lot of blood, and human tissue everywhere. It was like some insane operating theatre. Sergeant Hawkes was still moving and making bubbling sounds so I grabbed his shoulders and pulled him out. It was surprisingly easy and he weighed much less than I expected. It was because he no longer had any legs.

The firefight lasted half an hour or so, and we took more casualties before the air support arrived. Then the grove of trees the Taliban had been hiding in was incinerated, and the firing stopped. The last I saw of Sergeant Hawkes was his tiny figure under a blanket on a stretcher, being loaded into a helicopter that would take him to the military hospital at Camp Bastion.

I visited him once when I was living with Emma, after the restaurant had opened and the scene with Emma's friend Griselda had brought him back to mind. I decided that for once I should stop thinking about myself and would go and see him. Tracking him down was another matter, but in the end I found him.

I knew that he had nearly died at Camp Bastion, but the battlefield surgeons had saved him and he had been shipped to the hospital at Selly Oak. From there he had been sent to a regional rehabilitation centre in Yorkshire. That was where Sergeant Hawkes had spent the last twelve months of his life.

I went by train to York, and then by rented car. The 'Regional Rehabilitation Centre' was a series of single-storey brick buildings, of that peculiar school of architecture that is associated with former prisons, lunatic asylums or isolation hospitals. I parked on a potholed area of tarmac and followed the signs through to reception. Through the double doors I found a lino-clad waiting area with a few canvas-backed chairs placed along the walls. The receptionist's cubicle was empty. Somewhere a phone rang. It rang for a long time, then stopped.

At last someone appeared – a young girl of about seventeen, I guessed, wearing a white tunic. She was holding a magazine.

'Hello,' I said. 'I've come to see Sergeant Hawkes.'

'You what, love?'

We stared at each other.

After a moment she said, 'I'm new here. Is he a patient?'

'Yes.'

'Only there isn't anyone about today. Everyone's off on a training day. Can you come back tomorrow?'

'No, I can't,' I said. 'Which way are the wards?'

At that moment a porter appeared pushing a trolley with a tea urn. I turned to him and obtained directions, leaving the receptionist staring at me with her mouth open. After a moment she lost interest and went back to her magazine.

My footsteps echoed as I walked along the corridors. The place felt empty and it smelled empty. In one room I saw a man in pyjamas sitting on his bed smoking a cigarette. There was nothing obviously wrong with him: he had all his limbs at any rate. All the other rooms off this corridor appeared to be empty.

'Sergeant Hawkes?' I asked. The man jerked with his thumb, indicating that I should keep going. At length I came to a ward marked 'Prosthetics Rehabilitation Unit'. I pushed open the doors. The room beyond was large, cold and green: green lino on the floors, green paint on the walls. At one end was a large television screen. At the other end was a single bed. Next to it stood a wheelchair. Sergeant Hawkes sat there with a blanket over his knees, or at least over where his knees had once been.

'Hello?' he called as I opened the doors. His voice was thinner than I remembered, more shaky.

'Sergeant Hawkes?'

'Captain Gaunt? Sir?' Then: 'It's very kind of you to come all this way, boss. I hope it wasn't just to see me.'

I walked towards him, then reached out and took his hand. For a moment I clasped it in both my hands and then let go. It felt clammy and cold.

'How are you?' I asked, sitting down on the bed.

'I am as you see, boss. Much improved. I'm being fitted

with prosthetic legs next week. There's a bit of a waiting list for them. This unit is at the back of beyond, you must have noticed, sir. They're waiting for the funding to be released, so that they can equip the place properly.'

'That's a bloody long time to wait.'

'They had to wait until the wounds had healed properly. It took a long time. There were complications: secondary infections and suchlike. But I'm better now.'

'You look well,' I lied. His face was thin and hollow-cheeked and there were dark circles under his eyes. One eye was entirely red underneath a drooping eyelid. The other looked normal, but there was a patchwork of scars around both of them.

'How's your sight?' I asked.

'I lost it in one eye when that windscreen blew in. I've got about fifty per cent vision in the other one, though, so that's something to be thankful for. Not quite eyeless in Gaza, sir, but definitely legless.'

I didn't understand the allusion. Sergeant Hawkes was always quoting bits of poetry or literature that went straight over my head.

'Well, that's good,' I said. 'Are you the only one in this ward?'

'I am at the moment,' said Sergeant Hawkes. 'When they get the money there will be more patients here. My only regret is that it's a bit far for my family to come. My parents live in Kent.'

'And are they looking after you well?' I asked. Sergeant Hawkes didn't answer for a moment. The loneliness must be awful, I thought. Even when the staff weren't on a 'training day' I imagined the place must be as quiet as a tomb.

'Oh yes,' he said finally. 'The people here are marvellous.

They're all away on a jolly: team-building, they call it. But Ben the porter keeps an eye on me when there's nobody else around. He's an ex-soldier too.'

We sat and chatted for a while. Sergeant Hawkes became more animated as we talked and his face flushed an unhealthy red. He had great plans for the future. As soon as his new limbs were fitted and he learned how to use them, he was going to apply for a desk job in the regiment.

'Even if it's just stuffing forms into envelopes,' he said, 'it'll be something to do. I don't want to leave the army, if they'll have me back.'

He asked what I was doing and I told him about the restaurant.

'A restaurant, boss? That doesn't sound like you.'

'It keeps me out of mischief,' I explained.

For a while we talked about the regiment and about other people we had known. He nodded, but didn't seem very interested.

Then he said, 'Do you think it was all worth it, sir?'

'What do you mean?'

'The war. The war in Iraq; the war in Afghanistan. I hear we've pulled out of Basra now and there's talk about NATO getting out of Afghanistan. What was the point of us going there in the first place?'

'I don't know,' I said. 'Our job was to go wherever they told us to go.'

'I watch television all day, every day,' said Sergeant Hawkes. 'I watch the news channels a lot, when they remember to leave the remote somewhere I can reach it. It seems to me that not much has changed in the countries we've been fighting in. People are getting killed every day. Some say half the politicians in Afghanistan are on the take. You wonder what the point of it all is.'

'Best not to think about it too much,' I suggested.

'Well, you always used to say I read too much, thought too much, and talked too much. And you were right.' Sergeant Hawkes laughed. 'But there you are: that's me, always complaining about something.'

We talked for a while longer, but the silences grew between remarks. At last I looked at my watch.

'Well, I have a train to catch,' I said.

'It was so kind of you to come all this way just to see me,' said Sergeant Hawkes.

'I should have come before,' I said. 'Keep in touch. Let me know if they move you. I'll visit again, wherever you are.'

Sergeant Hawkes took my hand as if to shake it, then patted it with the other hand. I knew I wouldn't come again. I couldn't bear seeing what had happened to him.

On the train back I thought about Sergeant Hawkes and what he had given up for his country. He had given up what most of us called a life: to live out his days partially sighted and heavily disabled doing some administrative job in the back office of a garrison camp was the best he could look forward to. I had two or three newspapers in front of me to kill the time: they were full of stories about a new football coach at Chelsea; a row between the government and a banker; a celebrity who was dying of cancer. There was also a small article, less than an inch of single column, about a car bomb killing sixty people in a market in Baghdad.

There was nothing else in the papers that day about the wars that had taken away so much of Sergeant Hawkes's life. Nobody knew where these places were, or what they looked like, apart from a few glimpses of rock and sand on television. Nobody knew what the lives of the people had been like before we invaded, or what their lives were like now. Nobody knew why we were there: either they didn't believe the official explanations or, more often, they simply didn't understand them. Recently the public had begun to take more notice of soldiers coming home on leave: there were a few well-reported funeral parades; a few welcome-home parties in the local pubs. But what did it really mean? Most people felt it had nothing to do with them, after all. It was a war on terror which had produced yet more terror, and everyone had already forgotten how it started, what lies had been told, or what truths had emerged.

I turned the pages and found no more allusions to the terrible conflicts that were raging so many thousands of miles away, so I read the cricket results instead.

Fifteen

The next morning I went out and bought a mobile phone. I rang the number Nick Davies had given me. There was no answer, so I left a message on his voicemail. Back at the flat I tried to keep calm while I waited to hear whether he and his team had managed to get a warrant to enter the house in Oxfordshire. I kept wondering what might be happening to Adeena. I couldn't bear the thought of them questioning her, or perhaps worse, asking her questions about me that she couldn't answer. I felt like screaming with frustration at my own inactivity. But still I waited: some instinct told me to stay where I was, and wait a little longer.

It didn't take long before my patience was exhausted, and by the middle of the morning I'd had enough. God knows what might be happening to her. I put on my jacket and went to the front door and pulled it open. Nick Davies, who had been standing outside, practically fell on his face.

'Christ, you gave me a surprise,' he said, when he had recovered his balance. 'Do you always answer the door like that?'

'I didn't hear you ring,' I said.

He didn't look any less tired or better dressed than the last time I saw him. Instead of his raincoat he was wearing a navy blue blazer and a rather grubby white shirt, open at the neck.

'Can I come in?' he asked. 'We need to talk.'

I made way for him and then closed the door. 'Coffee?'

'Please.'

I made two mugs and we went and sat at the kitchen table. For a while he did not speak, but sipped at the coffee as if it was the only thing that might bring him back to life. Then he said, 'We didn't get a warrant, you know.'

'Why not?' I couldn't believe what I'd just heard and I had difficulty in keeping my voice down. A day had passed and nothing had been done to find Adeena and bring her back.

'Nowadays every request for a warrant of that sort has to go through our tame solicitor's office. They check through the Human Rights Act, and the Criminal Justice Immigration Act, and the Terrorism Act, and the Immigration, Asylum and Nationality Act and who knows what else. On this occasion they decided that we had insufficient proof that your Mr Khan was our Mr Aseeb. Go away and get more evidence, they told us. They didn't tell us where to get it from.'

'I see,' I said. But I didn't see. 'So you've done absolutely nothing.'

'Oh yes, we had someone drive by the house. It's occupied. That's probably where your friend Mr Khan is right now. And the girl – I'm sorry, your wife . . .'

I said nothing. There was a long silence while Nick waited for me to speak.

'I read your file, you know. Your service records.'

'Really?'

'You were with Task Force Black.'

'We were in support.'

'You used to kill terrorists. So why are they now part of your social life?'

I didn't feel his remark deserved an answer.

'Tell me about the Aseeb set-up. Who else was there?'

I told him about Kevin and Amir.

'Your friend Kevin doesn't sound like a problem,' Nick said after a moment's thought.

'Not until he gets behind the wheel of a car.'

'But this other guy Amir, we don't know about him. That's a worry.'

He sat and worried for a moment. Then he asked: 'What else can you tell me about the girl? She sure as hell doesn't look like an Afghan.'

I hesitated and then said, 'Well, she might be part French.'

'Part French? What's the story there?'

So I told him about Nadine Lemprière, her father the journalist and her Palestinian mother.

'She has two names now, has she? Do all your friends have two names?'

'I got the impression that her parents are dead. She adopted an Afghan name when she worked there.'

'That's what we call a legend,' said Nick. 'Normal people don't need two names.'

'What are you suggesting?'

'I'm not suggesting anything. We need to know more. I can't send anyone into that house until our departmental solicitor takes his thumb out of his arse and gets us a warrant. Why don't you go?'

We stared at each other. I couldn't believe what I had just heard him say.

'But yesterday . . . you told me not to.'

'I've seen your file since then. You *might* cope better than the average man in the street. And we have got to do something. If you can find out what's going on, then that might be better than nothing.'

'I want to find Adeena,' I said to him. 'We've wasted nearly a day while you lot were trying to get your act together. I'll find her if she's there, and I'll bring her back.'

'And if she comes back with you, then we'll know she didn't want to be with Aseeb in the first place.' Nick paused and then added: 'We need to know she's not part of Aseeb's project.'

'What project?' I asked.

'Whatever he brought the girl into the country for. Whatever he paid you ten grand for. There's something going on here, Richard. This is a man with a plan and we need to stop him. The trouble is, the girl might be part of it. You know that, don't you? Our allies in Afghanistan might want to ask her a few questions too.'

Nick watched my face as he said this. He was talking about rendition. It didn't happen, and no government would ever admit that it happened. But I knew he meant sending Adeena to Bagram airfield in the south-east of Afghanistan: the other Guantanamo, the one that didn't appear on the television news.

'She's not part of anything,' I told him. 'She's just got caught up in something. The same way I did.'

'Of course,' added Nick, 'Aseeb may not want to let Adeena go. He may have decided to move her, or sell her on. You may have to persuade him to see things from your point of view.' He stood up. 'If you find her, call me straight away. We need to talk to her. Thank you for the coffee.'

'Hey, thanks for all the help—' I said, but he had already left.

I sat for a while longer, and then I went and dug out the Sig Sauer I had hidden in my sock drawer. It had a full clip of eight .45-calibre rounds, the sort of thing you could stop an elephant with. I knew Nick was using me. He was like a man throwing a stone into a pool, to see what stirred. I didn't care. I was going to go anyway.

I was beyond worrying now about being found with a gun in my possession. And having it altered the odds slightly in my favour, although I was quite sure that by now Kevin would have another gun. Perhaps they were all armed. I would soon find out.

I took a train to Oxford. Near the station I found a budget hire company, rented a car and obtained a map. Then I made my way to Harington House. I had no plan in mind except to get there and rescue Adeena. It did not take long, but by the time I arrived at the house it was four in the afternoon and dusk was approaching. I drove past the black iron gates, which were shut, and pulled the car into a small overgrown track that led off the road about a hundred yards beyond the house. Then I walked back until I came to the wall that ran around the grounds. The gates might be locked, but the wall didn't seem too challenging.

I climbed over a fence into a ploughed field and walked along the headland beside the wall until I found a tree with a low-hanging branch. I used this as leverage to pull myself on to the top of the wall and sat there for a moment, listening. There were no sound of baying guard dogs, or of alarms going off. I didn't think that Aseeb was that worried about his security – he probably felt a lot safer in Oxfordshire than he did in Afghanistan. I dropped down into a pile of dead leaves and then made my way into the garden.

The house was as I remembered it, although the last time I had been there I had not really paid its external features much attention. It was a large, pleasant-looking building: a substantial stone-built country house designed with the comfort of its occupants in mind, rather than any aspiration to great elegance. A single black Range Rover was parked outside. Either they hadn't recovered the other one, or it was out somewhere. I was fairly sure all the doors of the building would be locked, which meant breaking in through a window, or else ringing the front doorbell.

Only an idiot would ring the bell of a house that might be full of armed terrorists, so I walked along the gravel to the front door, found the bell and pushed it. I heard it sound inside. Nothing else happened for a while, except that my pulse moved from its normal seventy up through the one hundred mark. I rang again. This time the door was answered almost the moment my finger left the bell-push. It was Kevin himself, wearing a dark blue suit and his trademark wraparound dark glasses. He stared at me.

'Butler's day off?' I asked. Kevin breathed out through his nose, drawing my attention to the fact that the area around the bridge of his nose was discoloured.

'What the hell are *you* doing here?' he asked.

'Is the master of the house at home? Might I have a word?'

'You'd better come in, old man,' said Kevin, recovering his self-possession. 'If you would be so kind as to wait in the hall, I will go and see if Mr Khan is available.'

He walked off briskly. I waited. The house was quiet. No sign of anything amiss: no Kalashnikovs lying on the sideboard; no mullahs in black turbans with long beards wandering about. Presently David himself appeared, carrying a silver tray.

'How nice to see you again, Mr Gaunt,' he said. 'Would you care to follow me into the library? Mr Khan will be a few moments. He thought you might like a cup of coffee while you waited.'

'Absolutely.'

I followed him into the library and sat down at the table where only a few days ago I had signed the forms they gave me in order to process my marriage to Adeena. It seemed like a lifetime ago. What I wanted to do was run through the house, banging doors open, and look for her. But I knew it was better to wait. I had a few questions I needed to ask Aseeb. So I sat and sipped my coffee. It was very good.

Presently the door opened, and Aseeb came in, followed by Kevin and Amir. The last two leaned against the door and stared at me. Aseeb came and sat down opposite me and poured himself a cup of coffee. Then he smiled suddenly: a big smile showing off his white teeth.

'How very nice to see you again, Mr Gaunt,' he said. 'You left so suddenly the last time you were here, we never had a chance to say goodbye.'

'I'm sorry about that,' I said.

'So was I. So was Kevin. Poor Kevin. He was quite sore for a day or two. I had to give him paracetamol. Why did you thrash the unhappy boy so severely?'

I ignored the question. I could still feel the spot where Kevin's car had hit me less than a week before.

'Mr Khan,' I said, 'I've come to collect Adeena. I think she's here, isn't she?'

'My dear fellow. Now why on earth would you want to see poor Adeena?'

'She's my wife, isn't she?'

Aseeb looked at me in mock astonishment. Then he threw back his head and roared with laughter. Amir gave a little giggle, a sound at odds with his large and forbidding exterior. Kevin did not join in the joke.

'Oh, Mr Gaunt, Mr Gaunt,' said Aseeb. 'How you do surprise me. We had a contract. I thought it was very clear. I paid you some money for your services. In return we agreed that you would grace Adeena with your family name and confer on her the immense benefits of a future as a British citizen. It was a simple proposal. You take the money. You attend the register office. You sign the documents. Then you go away. Adeena is no longer part of your life, Mr Gaunt.'

'But she's my wife,' I pointed out again.

'That is a technicality, Mr Gaunt,' said Aseeb. 'If you remember, you were a passer-by – a man collected from the street in order to assist in a commercial transaction. I am a commercial gentleman, Mr Gaunt, and Adeena is here to assist me in some of my business ventures. You must forget all about her.'

'Then why did she leave you and come to me?' I asked him.

'She is young, and young people are often foolish and do not know what they really want.'

I tried again.

'But I like Adeena,' I told him. 'Maybe I want her to stay with me. Have you thought of that? Shouldn't she be free to choose what to do with her life?'

'Ah,' said Aseeb, with a fond look on his face, as if he were listening to one of his grandchildren. 'If women were free to choose what they wanted to do, where would we all be? I have to decide what is best for Adeena. I must tell you very frankly, my dear Mr Gaunt, you are not part of her life any more.'

We seemed to have reached an impasse.

'I must be honest. I'm not very happy with what you are telling me.'

'I am so very sorry. But you do know that business is business.' Aseeb shook his head regretfully. 'Besides, she tells me you have been followed everywhere you go by policemen. Is this true?'

'Someone has been following us around,' I told him. 'Not because of Adeena herself, but because of her connection to you. They think you are a man called Aseeb. That's what Adeena calls you as well.'

When I said this Aseeb looked pensive for a moment.

'Then what is the point of Adeena returning to be with you? She is much better off with me. Forgive me for saying so, Mr Gaunt, but she will be safer here.'

He gave me a sharp look, and it seemed as if my answer might matter very much. His brown eyes fixed on me as he waited to hear my reply.

'Maybe,' I told him. 'But I'm the one who's going to look after her, not you.'

Aseeb sighed, but for some strange reason I felt my answer had pleased him.

'Ah, Mr Gaunt. You are a very persistent gentleman. Adeena spoke of this. Indeed, we thought you would visit us again. It has been a pleasure to speak with you once more. You are most unlike the other English gentlemen I have done business with. But now, I must get on with my day. I have a lot to do before I go back home. So nice to see you again, Mr Gaunt. Goodbye.'

I stood up.

'I'd still prefer to take Adeena home with me,' I said. I turned my back on all of them and I took the gun from my coat pocket. When I turned around. Aseeb was still sitting at the table. His mouth opened when he saw the gun in my hand. Kevin was pulling a pistol out of the waistband of his trousers. I watched Amir and Aseeb closely but they did not appear to be armed, so I took aim and shot Kevin in the leg, just below his left knee. He collapsed on to the ground screaming.

'You can take some paracetamol for that,' I told Kevin. I pointed my gun at Amir and gestured to him to go and stand beside Aseeb at the table. I bent down and picked up Kevin's gun and took out the clip. I put it in my pocket and threw the empty gun into a corner of the room. Then I aimed my own pistol at Aseeb's forehead.

'I really am quite serious about this,' I said. 'Tell Amir to bring Adeena here. If he tries anything funny or produces another gun, I will shoot you, Mr Aseeb Khan, or whatever your name is. I might shoot you anyway. I haven't made up my mind yet.'

Aseeb said something in Pashto to Amir.

'He will bring Adeena to us,' he said. 'Then we will see what she *chooses* to do.'

Amir left the room in a hurry. Kevin was rolling around on the floor, clutching his leg and whimpering. I don't know what it was about Kevin. I needn't have shot him. I needn't have hit him, the week before. Maybe it was the wraparound sunglasses, or his awful personality. He was just one of those people it's easy to be unkind to.

'Shut up, Kevin,' I told him. 'Or I'll shoot you again where it really hurts.'

The whimpering subsided a little. I turned my attention to Aseeb.

'I have a question for you, Mr Khan. If I take Adeena

away, will you leave her alone? And me? Because if not, I think I had better kill you.'

Aseeb watched me with his dark brown eyes. He didn't seem to be afraid, just wary.

'I am a businessman, Mr Gaunt. If you are going to take Adeena away, then pay me back my ten thousand pounds and we will regard the matter as closed. I will ignore the fact that you have injured my employees, wasted my time and abused my hospitality. I will not come after you. I have better things to do with my time.'

I didn't believe a word he said. I held the gun pointed at the exact centre of his forehead and wondered why I shouldn't pull the trigger.

'You know, I believe you *would* kill me,' Aseeb said. 'When Kevin brought you here in your evening clothes, I thought you were a typical English playboy. But I misjudged you. You do not object to shooting people.'

'It used to be my job,' I told him.

'Your job? Where I come from, people shoot other people for lots of reasons: because they have killed a relative, or stolen a woman, or invaded our country. But I have never heard someone call it a *job* before.'

I could hear the sound of footsteps. I drew in my breath and my finger tightened on the trigger. I could see Aseeb watching my face. For a moment I think we both believed I was going to shoot. It would make everything much simpler if I just shot him in the head. But those days were over. This was not Baghdad or the Helmand Valley, but Oxfordshire. And I wasn't in uniform any more; I was just an unemployed ex-restaurateur. Probably better not kill anyone today, I decided.

I breathed out. Amir came into the room, propelling

Adeena in front of him with the flat of his hand. She was wearing a black burka that covered her from head to foot, although she wasn't wearing the veil. It was like looking at a completely different person. Her face was very pale. When she saw me she moved as if to come towards me, but I held up one hand to stop her.

'Amir, go and sit beside your boss,' I told him. Kevin was lying with his back against the wall, still clutching his leg, his eyes screwed up with pain and hatred. There was a lot of blood staining his trouser leg.

'We are going to leave now,' I said. 'I suggest that you look after Kevin before he bleeds to death. Do not try to follow us. My flat is being watched. Come anywhere near me, and the security services will have you. You should go back to wherever it is you came from. That's my advice, for what it's worth.'

Aseeb and Amir said nothing. I pointed the gun at Aseeb again, then at Amir.

'If I do see you again, this will be the last thing you see.'

Finally Aseeb said, 'Adeena, do you *choose* to go with this man? Because if you do that you are taking a step you cannot draw back from.'

'I do choose to go with him,' said Adeena in a low voice. She did not look at Aseeb as she spoke.

'It is your life,' he said. 'You must dispose of it in the best way you can.'

I turned and, taking Adeena by the arm, walked out of the room. I glanced back one last time. Amir was looking grim but Aseeb was inscrutable. I shut the door on them. On the hall floor was a large canvas holdall.

'That is my bag. Can we take it?' Adeena said.

I picked it up. It was heavy.

'I am sorry. All my things are there, everything I was allowed to bring from Kabul.'

We hurried to the front door. David, the assistant, was nowhere to be seen. I hoped his job description didn't include the use of firearms. With luck he was keeping his head down.

'Is there any way of opening the gates from here?' I asked Adeena. Then I saw something like a TV remote lying on the hall table. I picked it up and pressed it and a green light came on. We rushed down the drive and went out through the gates, running towards the lane where I had parked the car. We hadn't exchanged a word since we left the house. I unlocked the car and flung Adeena's bag on to the back seat.

'Get in,' I said. She climbed in on the passenger side and I was gunning the engine before she had even closed her door.

We drove very fast down the lane away from the house and I kept the speed up as much as I dared until we came to the main Oxford road. There was no sign of anyone following us. I didn't think there would be, but I wasn't taking any chances. Aseeb would be very angry with me and I didn't doubt he would want some form of revenge. Afghans were good at revenge. But for now we were on our own. I relaxed a little and let the speedometer drop back to something like a legal speed. Adeena was still pale, but otherwise she looked as she had done the last time I saw her.

'Are you all right?' I asked.

'Yes.'

'Did they hurt you?'

'No, but when they found me in that shop they were very angry with me. They would have killed me if I had not gone with them. I am sorry, Richard.'

I waited for her to say more.

'They were angry with me for running away from them.'

I pulled the car into a lay-by and switched off the engine.

'Adeena,' I asked, 'did they take you, or did you go back to them?'

She turned away from me so that I could not see her face and said in a voice so quiet I could hardly hear her:

'Before you came they were talking about selling me.'

'Selling you?'

'Yes, they were going to sell me to a . . . to a house . . .'

She hid her face in her hands. I put my arm around her and waited for her to stop shaking. After a while she recovered some of her composure.

'They were going to sell me to a man Aseeb knows. He said I was of no further use to him after I ran away. This man has a house in the east of London where women have to lie with men who pay money. They have to do unspeakable things for these men. If they do not, they are beaten until they are so frightened they will do anything that is asked of them. It is worse than going to hell, this house. That is what Aseeb told me.'

'You're safe now,' I said.

'You came for me, Richard. I knew you would. They said you would not care but I knew you would come and find me.'

If I had known what Aseeb's plans for Adeena had been twenty minutes ago while I was still in the same room as him, I would certainly have shot him, no matter the consequences. Perhaps it was just as well I didn't know.

Sixteen

After that Adeena was silent all the way back to Oxford. We returned the rental car and got a taxi to take us to the station. She did not speak until we were on the train.

'Where are we going now?'

'Back to my flat.'

'Will it be safe?'

'I don't know. I do know that I'm not running away any more. Besides, where else can we go?'

Adeena looked tired and drawn, but she was still beautiful. I found myself contemplating her face: the bruised shadows under her eyes denoting lack of sleep, her pale complexion. Her sculpted features, the shape of her nose and mouth . . .

'Why are you staring at me?' she asked.

'I like to.'

Before she could say anything more my mobile phone rang. I pulled it from my pocket and answered it. It was Nick Davies.

'Where are you?' he asked.

'On the train to London.'

'Did you get the girl?'

'Yes.'

'Any collateral damage?'

'Not the sort you're hoping for.' There was an audible

sigh, but he didn't ask any further questions. Instead, he started issuing orders.

'Go back to your flat now.'

'That was the plan.'

'Good. Once you're there, stay there. If our friend is going to try to take the girl back, he'll look for her at your place first. We'll be watching. If he comes anywhere near you we'll get him.'

'OK,' I said. I didn't have a better plan. I ended the conversation before Nick could give me any more instructions, and put the phone away. Adeena was looking at me warily.

'Who was that?'

I saw no reason not to tell her. In fact, it might put her mind at rest.

'Someone from the British security services. They're looking for Aseeb. They will be watching us. If Aseeb comes anywhere near my flat, they will have him.'

'The security services? This is your secret police, yes?'

I shrugged.

'They are the people who were outside Hartlepool Hall a couple of days ago. They are interested in Aseeb.'

This was not the whole truth – Nick Davies was just as interested in talking to Adeena. But if he could get a warrant and get his hands on Aseeb, maybe he would leave her alone.

I asked Adeena: 'Did they feed you in that house?'

'Some fruit. A slice of bread. Not much.'

'Well, I'm starving. We must get some food. I think we'd better eat in my flat. Do you want me to cook something for us?'

Adeena's demeanour changed. The hunted look disappeared

and she smiled for the first time since I had rescued her from Aseeb.

'If you are hungry, then I should like to cook for you. Even if I am your wife only for a short time, I should like to do that for you.'

'Can you cook Afghan food?'

'Of course. We shall need a chicken. And some rice.'

By the time we got off the train I had quite a long list of things to buy. We bought most of them from Mohan's deli and a chicken from the halal butcher next door.

Once we were back in the flat she went into the box room and changed out of her burka into the European clothes she had been wearing the first time I had met her. Then she busied herself in my kitchen. Soon a smell of roasting chicken came from the oven, making my mouth water. I sat next door and drank a glass of wine while she prepared dinner.

Adeena could cook. She cooked fluffy white rice with sultanas in it that she called *chalau*, and a chicken *qorma* with onions and lentils and plums and cardamom. Besides that were salads of raisins and nuts, tomatoes and more onions, and some naan bread we had found in the deli.

'I am sorry,' said Adeena, as we sat at the kitchen table. 'This is not a proper meal in the Afghan way.'

'Why is it not proper? It is delicious.'

'At home in Kabul,' said Adeena, 'the preparation of the table is as important as the food. We call it *sofrah*. There should be many different things on the table to arouse your appetite. There should be different kinds of breads – *lavash*, *torshi*, naan – fresh from the baker, not out of a packet.' She sighed to herself and glanced at the feast with dissatisfaction. 'There should be copper bowls with water to wash your hands in. There should be yogurts, and many kinds of chutney, and different kinds of rice, and more salads. We did not have time. Another day I will do it for you properly.'

'You are a very good cook, Adeena.'

She was pleased.

After a while, I couldn't eat any more. Adeena cleared the plates from the table and then said, 'Now I will make some tea for you and we will sit and drink it. If we were in Kabul you could smoke a narghile. Do you know the narghile?'

'What is a narghile? Oh, I know – a water pipe.'

'You should smoke, you know. It is very good for men. It relaxes them and helps their digestion.'

After she'd made some black tea we went into the sitting room and sat on the sofa.

'What other skills do you have, apart from cooking?' I asked.

'I am very good with languages. Some languages.'

'Good English.'

'Yes, English and French, of course. I also speak some Pashto and Dari. I speak Arabic, my mother's tongue.'

'You are a very talented girl.'

'Yes, I had a good education in France. My mother taught me Arabic when we lived in Qatar. I learned Pashto and Dari when we moved to Waziristan.'

'You could easily get a job here in London with all those languages.'

'Maybe, if they let me stay. When I worked for the aid agency in Kabul I did most of the translation work.'

'They will let you stay, Adeena.'

'They won't. They will think I am bad because Aseeb brought me here. They will never stop watching me. Or they will put me in prison. Or they will send me back to Afghanistan.'

'Not if I can help it. I think Nick Davies might do a deal.

Let me talk to him tomorrow. He might agree to leave you alone if you tell him whatever you know about Aseeb.'

'But I know nothing about that man.'

'You must know something,' I said. 'You probably know more than you think. You might have heard him say something, or seen something that means nothing to you but might mean something to Nick Davies. Help me do this, Adeena, and I swear I'll do my best to get Nick to allow you to stay. I'm sure he can agree our marriage was legal, and not a sham.'

I wasn't sure, but I knew that co-operation with Nick Davies was our best chance.

'Even if they let me stay here for a while, where shall I live?' asked Adeena. 'I know nobody. I have no friends in this country. You have been so kind to me, Richard, but I cannot ask you to look after me. You have your own life to live. I am lost.'

'You aren't lost,' I told her. 'You're with me. I will take care of you.'

'Yes, tonight you will take care of me.' Suddenly her eyes were wet. 'But later you will become bored. You will find me too strange; too different to all the English girls you have known. You will want to marry an English girl, not a mongrel half-French, half-Arab like me. And what will I do then? I can never go back to Kabul.'

I put my arm around her and pulled her to me.

'I'll look after you,' I promised. As I said it, I meant it. A feeling so profound I could not identify it swept through me. 'I'll look after you. Don't worry.'

She leaned her head against my shoulder.

I kissed her on the eyelids and then on her cheeks and forehead, and finally on her lips. She kissed me back. In a moment we were in a tight embrace. Then she broke free, saying: 'I am going to bed now. I am very tired. I have been frightened for too long.'

'I will sleep in here,' I said, indicating the sofa with my hand. She heard the lack of conviction in my voice.

'No, you will sleep next to me. I don't want to be alone.'

I waited until she had gone next door and got into bed. Then, very quietly, I opened the bedroom door and went in. I looked down at her as she lay there. She was asleep already, her face exhausted, but peaceful. At least I had put her fears to rest for the moment. I took off my shirt and jeans and lay down chastely on top of the bedspread. After a while I too went to sleep.

In the middle of the night I was awoken by a sound. I was glad to be awoken. I had been dreaming again. In the dream I was by the side of the road outside Musa Qala, noise and screaming and shouting coming at me from every direction. At first I couldn't make out why I was awake. Then I heard Adeena mumbling in a language that sounded familiar but which at first I didn't recognise. I realised she was speaking in French again.

'*Je suis aux fonds du désespoir.*' She sounded so anguished. I grasped her by the shoulder and she turned and blinked, then shook her head.

'What's the matter?' she asked. 'Why did you wake me?'

'You were having a bad dream. You were talking in your sleep.'

She raised herself a little from the pillow, pulling the blankets around her.

'What did I say?'

'You spoke in French again. You said you were in the depths of despair. Why did you say that?'

'I don't know.' She rubbed her eyes with one hand. 'I can't

control what I dream about. I can't even remember my dream. Why are you so angry?'

'I'm not angry,' I said. 'I just don't understand you at all. I don't know why you're here.'

'Then why did you take me away from Aseeb? You could have left me there.'

'Because I care about you,' I said angrily. 'And I need you, and I don't know who you are or what you want.' I hadn't known I was going to use those words, and as soon as I spoke them I knew that they were true. What the hell am I doing? I thought. I have no control over my life at all.

She was sitting up straight now. The sheet barely covered her breasts and her hair fell over her bare shoulders. I wanted her so badly at that moment I could hardly stop myself from taking her in my arms again.

'Don't talk any more, Richard,' she said. She looked straight at me. She was so much stronger than me. She could face anything, bear anything. All my courage had been used up a long time ago.

'You ask all these questions,' she told me. 'Why ask? *Inshallah*. You think too much.'

'I don't want to lose you. I want you to stay,' I said.

'Come here.' She let go of the sheet and reached out across the bed and gently pulled me towards her. Her skin felt like silk. I was lost.

We made love and then we talked and then we made love again. I said lots of things to her, and made many promises I knew that, even as I gave them, I would never be able to keep. And I called her 'darling'. She held me tight and said: 'I like that word. I have never heard it spoken before. Call me by that word again.'

Afterwards we slept.

Seventeen

I remember Emma waking me up in the middle of the night.

'Dick?' She tugged at my shoulder. I pushed her away and groaned, still half asleep.

'Dick, are you all right?'

I sat up in bed. She had switched on her bedside lamp.

'What's the matter?' I asked.

'You're soaking – you're absolutely dripping with sweat.'

It was true. I suddenly felt chilled to the bone.

'I'll go and have a shower.'

'It's half past three in the morning,' Emma pointed out.

'I can't go back to sleep like this.'

The hot water woke me up, and the cobweb of dreams vanished beneath it. I had been dreaming about a man we had found when I was working in Baghdad. He was a Swiss electrical engineer who had been kidnapped by insurgents. They had decided he was an American spy and had hidden him in a spider hole, a space that would have been cramped even for a large dog, with a tiny aperture which let in just enough air to stop him suffocating and light for about five minutes a day. When we found him, he had been gone for two weeks and was barely alive, but he was no longer sane. I often dreamed about being in that spider hole myself, slowly suffocating, trying to claw my way back to the daylight. I stepped out of the shower and towelled myself dry. Then I went and lay down next to Emma.

'You should see someone about that,' she murmured into her pillow.

'See someone about what?'

'About these nightmares you keep having. It's every other night.'

'I think we probably ate too late,' I said. 'It's going to sleep on a full stomach that does it. I'm sorry I woke you.'

The next morning she either didn't remember, or chose not to talk about my nightmares. Of course, I did nothing about them. Emma kept telling me I ought to talk to someone. I knew, if I was being rational, that it was good advice. But it was easier said than done: to whom could I talk? Any normal person would conclude I was a fantasist if I told them half of the things that had happened to me, the places I had been, the things I had seen. If Sergeant Hawke had still been around I would have gladly talked to him. But he was a long way away.

The restaurant had settled into a rhythm. We weren't full every night, but at weekends people who hadn't booked a table were usually turned away. We had a good chef: Mary, who had helped us at first, had not wanted a full-time job so we had recruited a young man called Michael who had trained at one of the top London restaurants. He was fond of classical French cookery: lots of cassoulets and confits and regional French dishes that filled the restaurant with a delicious savoury smell and made you feel hungry even if you had just eaten. When he came, he brought new customers with him.

Charlie the barman doubled up as the wine waiter.

Although rather too fond of filling his tasting cup from almost every bottle he opened, he was popular and had that nice ability to appear astonished at the foresight and sophistication of his customers in choosing their wine, even if it was the house red. He improved our list, got rid of some of the overpriced New World wines and concentrated on good-quality, middle-of-the-range Bordeaux and burgundies. And he mixed excellent cocktails.

We had a good lot of waitresses. They were competent and welcoming. Giulia, the Italian girl, was almost too friendly, verging on the flirtatious. But that did no harm. I thought she was easy on the eye and good for business.

Lunchtimes were busy, too, and we started to receive group bookings. The biggest struggle was recruiting staff to keep up with the volume of business we were getting. For the first few months we exceeded our forecasts, and managed to pay off a slice of the bank loan ahead of schedule. The staff seemed quite settled too. That was Emma. She enthused people, and led by example: no one worked harder than she did, and she would pick up the phone to take a booking, or serve drinks, or even help with the washing up if necessary. Our employees were wary of me, however. They couldn't really understand what I was doing there. Nor could I, if I was honest. I met people at the door, and tried to make them feel welcome. I took their drinks orders, handed out menus, and then my job was done. Sometimes Emma tried to coach me.

'Dick, darling, try not to give the customers your thousand-yard stare when they come in.'

'What thousand-yard stare?'

'As if you are sighting your rifle on them. Remember the warm and friendly smile?'

I practised my warm and friendly smile in the mirror. I thought it made me look deranged. If Emma noticed any change in my demeanour she did not comment. Now and then I would catch her giving me an anxious glance as I chatted to customers. Sometimes I know I was a bit abrupt. I didn't mean to be, I just lost it.

One evening Emma took me by the elbow and steered me into the little vestibule where we hung up people's coats.

'Darling heart, one of the customers has just complained that you spoke to him a little sharply.'

Whenever Emma was really worried about me, or annoyed with me, or both, she spoke to me in a particular way, as if I were made of glass and might shatter if she talked too loudly.

'I just told someone to be patient.'

'He says you told him to "wait his bloody turn".'

Oh, that man. He had come in with a party of three. Spectacles, a pinstriped suit, and a pompous manner. He had called me 'waiter', and asked me how much longer they would have to wait for their table.

'Sorry. I probably did say that. Shall I go and apologise?'

'They've left now.'

'Oh dear. Well, I'm sure the table will be taken by some-one else once it's free.'

'That isn't the point, darling. We need to talk, but not right now. Please try to keep your temper. For me?'

But we finished work late that night. By the time we got back to Emma's flat it was after midnight. I switched on the television in the sitting room and poured myself a large whisky. I could hear Emma moving about in the bathroom, getting ready for bed, and waited for her to come back in and challenge me about my behaviour earlier in the evening. I frowned at the television and poured myself another drink.

Then I heard her shut the bedroom door and knew that she had gone to bed.

A couple of weeks later, I attended a memorial service for someone I had met a few times in Baghdad. He had been working at the Coalition headquarters in the International Zone. I didn't know him very well, but had liked him enough to want to see him off. The poor sod had died at the age of thirty-four of a heart attack in his house in Guildford, having survived God knows what in Iraq. Maybe the war had been responsible for his heart condition, but it was probably just one of those things.

After the service I bumped into a couple of people – well, four of them – I had met out there and one of them asked me what I did for a living now. When I told them I was a restaurateur, there was a lot of laughter.

'Do they make you wear a pinny and a chef's hat?' asked one.

'Always thought you would make a good waiter,' said another.

'It's a bloody good restaurant,' I said indignantly. 'You won't find many better places in London.'

'We'll come and try it,' said the person who had spoken first, a captain who had been well known for the size of his mess bills, which often included quite a few breakages.

'Be my guests,' I suggested, not really thinking they would accept. The captain, in civilian life Ned Taylor, was not going to pass up an invitation like that. He took out a diary, and after consulting with the others, named an evening when they would all come. I felt apprehensive for a moment, and wondered what I would say to Emma. Then I promptly forgot all about it.

They turned up at the restaurant just over a week later.

'Oh God, Em,' I said. 'It's some old army friends of mine. I forgot to tell you. I offered them dinner on the house. I never thought they'd come.'

For once, Emma was really annoyed.

'*On the house?* Darling, you must be mad. We simply can't afford to run the place like that. And quite apart from that, once the staff see you treating your chums to free meals, they'll start wondering why they can't put their own hands in the till.'

'I don't see why they should think that.'

'It's just the same.'

She was very angry. I was seeing another side to Emma now: her old-fashioned, Presbyterian upbringing. I knew all about that inner toughness: it was one of the reasons I had taken to her in the first place. But I didn't like being on the receiving end of it.

'I'd better go and look after them,' I suggested.

'Yes, you better had. Go and sit with them for a while.'

The captain saw me crossing the room as he and his party sat in armchairs waiting to be given drinks and menus.

'*Waiter!*' he shouted at me in a high, whinnying voice intended as a parody of Bertie Wooster. Heads turned. I groaned inwardly. This was going to be a difficult evening. I sat down with them and waved at Charlie the barman to come and take their drinks orders.

'How are you all?' I asked.

'Never better,' said Ned. 'Andrew has just been telling us about a friend of his who was mentioned in dispatches for being shot in the arse while running away to hide behind the wall of a house in Basra. Caipirinhas all round, don't you think?'

Caipirinhas were all the rage at the time: a cane spirit and fruit mixture that could do serious damage to your powers of reason in a very short time. I had the impression that Ned and the others might already have had a drink or two. Emma came over and they all jumped to their feet.

'I'm Emma,' she said. 'You must be Dick's friends – how nice to meet you.'

'The pleasure is all ours,' said Ned, taking her hand and kissing it in a way that annoyed me. Perhaps it was intended to. Emma stayed for a moment, chatting, then said, 'I must go and look after our other guests – have a lovely evening.'

'Smashing bird,' said Ned, while Emma was still within earshot. 'Well done, Richard. I never thought of you as a ladies' man, but there you are, pulling a smart-looking piece like that.'

The menus arrived. Everybody chose what they wanted to eat, and a second round of drinks was ordered. I decided to enter into the spirit of the occasion and had another drink as well. And why not? This lot weren't really my friends: just people I'd had some beers with a few times in Baghdad.

When their table was ready, I sat with them for a while: as much to keep an eye on them as to be friendly. I watched them being served their starters. I wasn't eating with them as I never felt hungry in the restaurant: being around all that food all night every night put me off the idea, even though I knew it tasted very good. Wine was ordered, and then more wine when the next course arrived. The noise level at our table was becoming quite high. Andrew and Ned were the noisiest. Ned had one of those voices that penetrated the entire room, which was unfortunate because his language grew riper as the evening went on.

Eventually I said, 'Ned, could you keep your voice down a little?'

'Why?' he asked. 'Oh, I see: walls have ears, don't they? Careless talk costs lives. I forgot you used to belong to a hush-hush outfit, Richard. Whispering must be second nature to you. Still, don't want to upset the gorgeous Emma, do we?' He started hissing at the other three in an exaggerated whisper. I decided it might be better if I left them to it.

'I'd better go and see if Emma needs a hand.'

'Well, if she doesn't like yours, I've got a free one.' He turned to see where Emma was, and found her a few tables away, looking at us anxiously.

'Hey, babe,' Ned shouted, 'if you don't want Richard's hand, then come and try mine!'

The next moment he was lying on the floor, blood coming from his mouth where I had hit him. I didn't even remember doing it, except that my knuckles were scraped where they had caught his front teeth. Ned lay there for a second, looking stunned. Then he smiled and wiped the blood from his face with the back of his hand and started to climb to his feet. Andrew bent over and helped him up.

'Well, well,' said Ned. 'You and I are going to have a bit of a chat about things, Dicky boy.' He started towards me but Andrew and one of the other two – I couldn't remember their names – held him back. He didn't seem too steady on his feet. Someone righted his chair and he sat down heavily. The entire population of the restaurant was watching our table and every single conversation in the place had stopped. I could see Emma a few feet away, her hand to her mouth.

'You were a bit over the top, old boy,' Andrew told Ned.

'I think you'd better leave,' I said. There was no

opposition to this idea. One of the other two men reached for his wallet, but I told him:

'Forget it. No bill. Just leave, please.'

'I'm sorry about Ned's language,' Andrew said. 'He gets a bit overexcited at times. Misses the action.'

I didn't reply. Ned was using a corner of his napkin to stem the flow of blood. He left the restaurant still holding it to his mouth, and clutching a half-full bottle of burgundy. Gradually conversation in the restaurant started up again. A waiter came across to the table. He cleared away the plates and glasses, removing any trace of the unpleasant little scene that had just taken place. I went across to Emma to apologise. She shook her head and went into the kitchen. She almost ran there. I followed her through the swing doors. Beyond them was a hubbub of noise and activity. No one in there had heard about the incident outside, but they soon would do, and then every eye would be on me.

Emma was in a corner of the kitchen, bending over a dishwasher, as if she were loading it. But she wasn't. As I approached she turned and I could see tears on her cheeks.

'You'd better go home, Richard.' It was not good news when she called me Richard instead of Dick. I started to apologise but she cut me short.

'Just go home, for Christ's sake. Haven't you done enough damage for one evening?'

'Fine,' I replied, and left without saying another word. When I got back to Emma's flat, it was still only half past nine. The prospect of sitting there for the next two hours waiting until Emma came back, followed by yet another heart-to-heart – we seemed to be having those more frequently these days – did not appeal to me. Rather than sit in the flat on my own, I decided to go to a pub I knew, about half a mile away.

I had a couple of drinks and then walked about the streets for another hour. I told myself that I just wanted to calm down, and make sure I wasn't angry when I talked to Emma. I was angry. OK, it was my fault for having invited those idiots to eat at the restaurant and my fault for offering them dinner on the house. They wouldn't have come, otherwise. But then, what did she expect me to do when Ned Taylor behaved like that? Was I supposed just to stand there while he yelled offensive remarks at me, at Emma, and no doubt everyone else in the place? How could people behave like that?

I suddenly stopped in the middle of the street. I knew why people behaved like that. They were sick in the head. I was sick in the head. We had all seen things we should never have had to see, done things we should never have had to do. And all of us, when we came back from Iraq or Afghanistan, were constantly being reminded, every time we opened a newspaper or switched on the television, that we had done it for a cause the grateful public did not believe in any more, if they ever had. In the old days, it was 'my country right or wrong': when things happened that seemed to cross every boundary of human morality or decency you could always tell yourself, I suppose, that you were serving your country. But we had fought in wars that few people at home really cared about. No wonder some of us behaved badly.

By the time I got home, Emma had put herself to bed. There was a note on the kitchen table. It said: 'Sorry I was cross – love you. xxx'. *She* was sorry. I was almost angry with her for being sorry when everything was so very much my fault.

The next morning Emma woke me with a cup of coffee. She was wearing her dressing gown.

'You slept right through,' she said cheerfully. 'No bad dreams. Isn't that good?'

I took the coffee from her and sipped it.

'Look, about last night . . .' I said.

'I understand about last night, darling. It wasn't your fault. Those men behaved abominably.'

'It was my fault for asking them.'

'You weren't to know.'

There was another pause. I knew there was more to come.

'Only, one bit of not so good news, darling,' said Emma. 'Michael has handed in his notice.'

'Michael? Our chef?'

'Yes. He said he couldn't afford to work for employers who got themselves into fistfights with the customers. He said that sort of thing gets around the trade pretty fast, and much as he liked working for us, he thought it would be better if he moved on.'

I was silent for a few moments. This news wasn't just 'not so good'; it was very bad indeed. A lot of our customers came to us because of Michael and for no other reason. With him gone, business would fall off and who knew when, if ever, it would recover.

'Where's he going?' I asked. 'Some bastard has doubled his salary, I expect.'

'He doesn't have a job to go to,' said Emma. 'But he won't change his mind. You know what he's like.'

After a pause I said, 'I'd better not come in for a day or two, let things calm down.'

'I was just going to suggest that, darling.'

'And you don't suppose, if you rang Michael . . .'

'No,' said Emma. 'It wouldn't do any good.'

Business did fall off at the restaurant after that. The change wasn't dramatic at first – the occasional empty table on a Friday evening, when normally we would have been full – but after a while it became more noticeable. The restaurant no longer had that indefinable 'buzz' about it and we had difficulty getting a permanent replacement for Michael: we had to make do with a series of agency chefs, some of whom were adequate, but some of whom were mediocre. None was a patch on Michael.

I went into the restaurant less frequently. At first it was just because I felt I ought to keep a low profile. Then it was because there really wasn't that much for me to do. Instead I used to sit and worry about the numbers. There was a big slug of loan repayment due at the end of the quarter. A month ago, repaying it had seemed quite straightforward; now it looked like a challenge. It wasn't just that we had fewer customers: the kind of customers who were coming in now spent less on wine and drinks.

Emma was worried, too, and I wasn't much help. The truth was, I had never been that interested in the restaurant. It had just seemed like a good idea at the time. Now it was becoming a drag. There was no chance that either of us could take a half-decent salary from it with business the way it was.

Emma's answer was to work even harder. She let one or two staff go, to cut down on our outgoings, and tried to do their jobs as well as her own. She would come back to the flat late and too tired to speak. Then she would be up early the next morning in order to go to the markets to buy fresh produce and meat for the restaurant because without Michael she could no longer trust anyone else to do the job properly.

Her good temper, which was close to saintly, began to fray around the edges.

One afternoon, before she went out to work, I suggested she take a break.

'We'll go out to supper somewhere,' I said. 'Someone else can serve you for a change, rather than the other way around.'

'Oh no, I don't think we can do that. We're very short-staffed tonight. I had to let another of the waiters go: the Romanian one. We couldn't afford him and I'm not entirely sure he was honest.'

'We used to have three waiters on weekdays,' I said. 'You can't expect to do everyone else's job as well as your own.'

'Well, do you have any bright suggestions?' said Emma fiercely. 'You're not much help yourself, you know.'

There was a silence, then, 'I'm sorry. I didn't mean to snap at you, Dick. Only . . .'

'Only I'm not much help.'

'Well, if you want me to be honest, you aren't. You seem to think waiting and washing up are beneath you. But we wouldn't be in this fix if you knew how to keep your temper and be pleasant to people.'

'I knew you'd bring that up again,' I said. 'What did you expect me to do when that man started shouting obscenities at you?'

'You didn't have to hit him. But it isn't just that. You don't seem to be able to get on with people, darling. I can't understand it. You used to be so easy with everyone. Now all you do is bite their heads off.'

I could feel my face setting into a grim mask. I knew this was the moment to say something conciliatory. Instead I said:

'This whole bloody restaurant was your idea in the first

place. Neither of us knew anything about running a restaurant, and now it shows.'

Emma looked very hurt.

'The point was to find something we could do together,' she replied. 'You know that. How can you be so unkind?'

She burst into tears. I didn't feel like comforting her. Instead I stared at her until the sobbing had stopped.

Then I asked, 'What will you do if the place goes bust?'

Emma dried her tears with a handkerchief.

'I'll have to sell this flat, I suppose. I took out a second mortgage on it when we started the restaurant.'

'Well, looking at last week's figures, I'd say our luck is running out.'

Emma didn't reply. Instead she started getting ready to go out.

'What are you doing?' I asked.

'Going to work, of course.'

'But it's early.' It was only four o'clock in the afternoon and she didn't need to be there until six.

'We haven't got a cleaner at the moment,' she replied in a weary voice. 'I need to give the place a thorough going over. It's beginning to look grubby.'

'Fair enough. I'll see you later.'

I picked up the newspaper as Emma continued to get ready. I had already read it, but I felt it was best to have some form of occupation.

'I'm going now,' Emma said.

'OK.'

But she wasn't quite ready to go, after all. She went as far as the door and then turned.

'Richard, when you came to me from your parents, I did everything I could to help. I could see how difficult you were finding it to deal with life. I could see how difficult it was for you to be around people – your family, even me. You treated us all like strangers, even as if we were enemies. But I stuck with you. I'm still sticking with you, because it hasn't got any easier to live with you, believe me.'

'OK,' I said again. 'What do you want me to say?'

Emma stared at me. Her large eyes became even rounder. 'I don't expect you to say anything.'

'Then what do you expect me to do?'

'I want you to help me, Richard. Just help me.'

Eighteen

A week or two passed and things calmed down. Emma became her old, cheerful self again: although a pale ghost of worry settled on her face from time to time when she thought I wasn't looking. I was worried, too: the restaurant wasn't doing well at all. Even though the whole place had been refurbished and re-equipped only a few months ago, it was already beginning to look tired. When Michael left there hadn't been a mass walkout, but staff seemed to come and go more frequently. I tried to support Emma. I helped with the paperwork and the stocktaking. I went with Emma to see her bank manager to explain why we might be a little late with the next quarterly loan repayment. He agreed to re-schedule our payments, and charged us a new arrangement fee while he was at it.

There was a sensation of trying to walk up an escalator that was going down; no matter how hard we tried, we were being carried remorselessly in the wrong direction. I tried to talk to Emma about it. We needed to have a plan in case the business got into serious trouble. But she wouldn't hear of it. Her answer was to work even harder.

Around this time I took an evening off – one of several in recent weeks – to have dinner with Ed Hartlepool. I'd seen him once or twice since joining the army, but we hadn't spoken for a year or two at least when he rang me.

'I heard you were back in London,' said Ed. 'And with Emma Macmillan, too. Are you married yet?'

I experienced a slight feeling of guilt. I'd always said I'd marry Emma as soon as I was out of the army and in employment. Well, it had been several months now. Why hadn't I done anything about it?

'No. We're living together, though. And we've bought a restaurant.'

'Yes, I'd heard that too,' said Ed. 'Now someone was telling me something about your place – something funny happened there. What was it?'

I guessed that he had heard some gossip about the night Ned Taylor and his friends had visited. I didn't reply.

'What about you?' I said, changing the subject. 'Are you up at Hartlepool Hall at the moment?'

'No, I'm not,' said Ed. 'I've had to move to the South of France. After my father died and I inherited, there was some tremendous cock-up with a family trust and there's been a row with the taxman. So I have to live abroad a lot of the year to avoid being a UK tax resident. I get back to Hartlepool Hall now and again. But I'm in London at the moment, at our flat in Knightsbridge.'

I couldn't imagine Ed living in the South of France, and said so.

'Oh, it's all right,' he said. 'There are a lot of other expats around, so there's a bit of social life. But I like to get back to London once in a while. I'm allowed to spend a certain number of days a year over here without losing my non-dom status. And I've joined a gambling club in London. You ought to come and have a drink with me there. It's the most awful dive, but the drinks are good, and some of the members are hilarious.'

It didn't sound very tempting. But the alternative was yet another grim evening at the restaurant, waiting for customers to come in, while the waitresses hung around by the door to the kitchen. I needed a night off from all that and Emma wouldn't miss me. Tonight less than half the tables were booked, and we didn't expect many walk-ins.

'Well, yes, that might be different,' I said. 'I'm free tonight, if that's what you had in mind.'

'Yes, tonight would be good,' said Ed. 'Come to my flat about seven and we'll have a sharpener there and then go on to this joint. It's called the Diplomatic.'

That was how I started going to the Diplomatic.

When I told Emma I was taking the evening off she said, 'Yes, do that, darling – it will be good for you to have a bit of a break. Give my love to Ed. He probably doesn't remember me.'

She wasn't being a martyr as she said this, but her smile was weary. She was working too hard, but nothing I could say or do would persuade her to take any time off herself.

To my surprise, when I met Ed at his flat, he had put on evening clothes.

'It's the rule there for members,' he said.

'Seems like a lot of effort just to play cards,' I suggested. 'Anyway, won't they bar me from entry for being improperly dressed?'

'No,' said Ed. 'I'll tell Eric you're a potential new member. They make allowances for guests.'

'Who's Eric?'

'Wait and see.'

Eric, the hall porter, was a big man with the complexion and figure of a huge tuberous root. He had a large pale face, and a dome-like skull covered in a few strands of well-oiled hair. His eyes were small and dark and he had a rosebud mouth. He must have been six foot six but he had managed to insert himself behind a tiny desk. He checked Ed in and gave me an unfriendly nod when Ed introduced me. Then we went through to the bar, where Ed ordered champagne cocktails. Refreshed by these, we wandered upstairs, and before I knew what was happening, Ed had pulled up a chair at a table where a card game was going on, and waved at me to do the same.

'This is Bernie,' said Ed, introducing me to a large dark-haired man who was dealing out the cards.

'Hello, Bernie.'

Ed then gestured towards a tall, thin man with a cadaverous face and wispy blond hair plastered across the top of his head.

'And this is Willi Falkenstein.'

Willi Falkenstein stood up, clicked his heels together and gave a sharp nod. I shook hands with him.

'Everybody, this is a *very* old friend, Richard Gaunt. He used to be a soldier and now runs a restaurant. He's thinking of joining the club, so please, don't take too much money from him tonight.'

There was a general murmur of greeting and I was dealt a hand of cards. The game at that moment was five-card draw poker, which I could just about cope with: we'd played a bit in the army. At first I won a little, and then I lost a little and then a little more. By midnight I was down a couple of hundred pounds, which was far more money than I was carrying on me. But Ed was relaxed when I explained I had to leave, and would have to give everyone a cheque.

'Don't worry. No one carries cash around these days. All you need to do is sign a note saying how much you owe and to whom. Anyway, I'm your main creditor tonight. We'll give you a chance to win back your money next time you come.'

'Next time?'

'I've put you in the membership book,' explained Ed. 'Bernie and Willi will second you. It's only a hundred pounds to join, and I get something off my bar bill every time I introduce a new member.'

So that was how I joined the Diplomatic. Emma didn't mind, although I could see that she felt that me becoming a member of a gambling club in Mayfair while our business venture was struggling wasn't an obvious priority. But that was Emma. She always thought about me first, herself second. She was so good-natured it was beginning to irritate me.

After that, the weekly game at the Diplomatic became an accepted fixture in my life. I tried to make up for it by being – as I thought – extra helpful in the restaurant. Then Emma caught me taking two hundred pounds from the till just as I was about to set out for an evening's card play. It was five o'clock in the afternoon and there was no one else in the front of the restaurant except the two of us. Our current chef was organising himself in the kitchen and the other staff were not in yet.

'What on earth are you doing, Dick?' Emma asked when she saw me filling my wallet with twenties.

'I just need some stake money for tonight,' I explained. 'It's all right, I've put an IOU in the till to keep the books straight. I've only taken two hundred pounds.'

Emma looked appalled.

'Two hundred pounds? But that must be practically all the money in the till. We won't have any cash float left.'

'Sorry,' I said. 'Anyway, most people pay with credit cards, don't they?'

I started towards the kitchen, intending to let myself out through the fire exit, but Emma hadn't finished with me.

'*Two hundred pounds?*' she repeated. 'What kind of money do you play for in that place?'

I didn't want to admit to Emma that I was over a thousand pounds in debt, and that the two hundred pounds was meant to help me get back into the game and recover some of my losses.

'Oh, the stakes vary,' I said vaguely. 'Nothing sensational.'

'But that's more money than we have to live off for an entire week.'

'Don't worry,' I said rather more snappishly than I intended. 'I'm not going to bankrupt myself. I thought you didn't mind me having a bit of fun now and again. I can't hang around this place six days a week, even if you can.'

The sound of someone rapping on the glass door at the front entrance interrupted the beginnings of a nasty row. Emma went and opened the door, and Giulia came in. Emma had already complained about the shortness of her skirts and the amount of cleavage she sometimes displayed, but I told her it cheered up the customers. She certainly cheered me up. She brushed against me as she walked past on her way to the kitchen.

'Oh, good evening, Giulia,' said Emma rather curtly, then turned back to me. But I already had my hand on the door.

I went out saying: 'Don't wait up for me, darling. I might be a little bit late tonight.'

That night I recouped most of my losses and returned home feeling rather virtuous. In the morning Emma brought me a cup of coffee, as usual, and then sat on the edge of the bed. That meant we were going to have A Talk. I wasn't in the mood for a lecture, or for pouring my heart out to Emma, or for listening to her pour her heart out to me. But it was her flat, her bed and her coffee.

'How did you get on last night?' she asked.

'Oh, quite well. I won a bit. It wasn't a bad evening. I'll put the two hundred pounds back in the till when we go in this afternoon.'

Emma fiddled with the edge of the bedspread. She wasn't really listening.

'Was it busy in the restaurant last night?' I asked.

'So-so.'

I sipped some coffee.

'Darling, what are we going to do?' she asked suddenly.

'About what?'

'About the restaurant. About us. About our life together.'

I thought for a moment.

'Well, while the restaurant isn't that busy, I suppose I really ought to try to find another job and bring in some extra income.'

'Doing what, exactly?' asked Emma. 'Do you have anything in mind?'

'I'd need to give the question some thought,' I said, and smiled. Emma didn't smile back. She wasn't even looking at me.

'You know, I used to think we would be married by now. After all, we've been engaged for nearly three years.'

'I do want to marry you,' I said quickly. 'You know that. But I didn't want us to be married until I came back home and got my promotion.'

'But you're not in the army now. No one's going to promote you. You have to do it yourself.'

I didn't answer.

'So what's the plan now, Richard? When will we get married? Next year? In ten years' time? I'm twenty-seven, Richard, and I've been waiting a long time for you to decide what to do with your life. I've put nearly all my savings into this restaurant, *and* taken out a mortgage. Now the restaurant might go bust if business doesn't pick up. And as far as I can see, we're no more likely to get married than we were the day we met.'

I could see her point. But the trouble is, when someone speaks to you like that, it doesn't exactly encourage you to get down on your knees and make a declaration of undying love. That's what I thought at the time, anyway. Since then I've often wondered whether – had I done just that – things mightn't have turned out differently. I tried to explain how I felt.

'It's just that since I came out of the army, I've been feeling very unsettled. It's not you, darling. I just can't seem to get my life together.'

This was truthful, as far as it went. Emma was unimpressed.

'Some of my friends think you're just using me. You live in my flat, you get free meals and drinks at the restaurant, and you get me. All for nothing.'

'I'm sorry if some of your friends think that,' I said stiffly. 'I can't help what they think.'

'Is that all you can say? Dick, I really worry about us. You know I love you. The trouble is, I don't know if you love me any more. I used to be so sure, but you've changed. You used to be so straightforward and fun to be with. Now I don't know who you are. I feel shut out of your life. I'm not sure how much longer I can cope with this.'

I set my coffee cup on the bedside table and tried to put my arm around her, but Emma shrugged me off.

'I've got to get dressed,' she said. 'I need to go to the market and buy the meat and vegetables for tonight.'

Presently I heard the front door of the flat slam as Emma went out. I tried to discern what I felt about Emma, about what she had just said. I knew it was important. I knew I had to reply to her somehow, to say or do something, and soon. But I couldn't concentrate on the problem.

That evening at the restaurant I was determined to be helpful. First of all I put the two hundred pounds back in the till, making sure that Emma saw what I was doing. Then I went and got the stock file from behind the bar.

'I'm just going to do a stocktake in the wine store, see what needs reordering.'

She was moving across to greet a customer as I spoke. She simply gave a brief nod and said, 'Fine.' Then I heard her saying hello to the customer, as if they were her oldest and best friend. She was good at that. Her warmth was quite genuine, too, which was why I had fallen for Emma in the first place. I went into the wine store and started checking off bottles against the list and making notes of what we were about to run out of. I became absorbed in the task, and almost jumped when the door suddenly opened and Giulia came in. She was, as usual, wearing clothes at the limit of what Emma would tolerate in a waitress: a short black skirt and a tight white blouse. She carried a napkin in one hand, to dust off the wine bottle she had come to find. She gave me a smile.

'I need a bottle of the' – she looked at her notepad – 'Château Méaume.'

I pointed to the top rack.

'It's up there. Shall I get it down for you?'

'No, Mr Reechard, I can manage.'

She stood on tiptoe and stretched.

'Oh, I can't manage after all,' she said. I thought she could have if she'd tried a little harder, but I stood next to her and reached for the bottle. She brushed against me and I was suddenly very conscious of the curve of her breast inside the blouse, and the way her already short skirt was riding up on the back of her thighs. I was instantly aroused, as if I had slipped into an erotic dream. But this wasn't a dream: something was happening and I needed to be very careful.

'You know, Giulia, you really ought to wear longer skirts,' I said.

'Do I? But I am wearing something underneath. See?'

She flipped up the back of her skirt with a wicked smile. I saw her bottom, its nakedness emphasised rather than concealed by a pair of knickers not much bigger than a thong. I remember thinking: I can back out of this, it needn't happen, all I have to do is tell her to get on with her work.

Then I thought: why not?

The coupling that followed was almost instantaneous and so intense that I lost consciousness of everything except the physical act that took place. It was achieved standing up. Somehow no bottles were broken, and we made very little noise, although Giulia bit my shoulder in order to conceal a muffled cry of pleasure. Then it was over. With absolute composure she used the napkin to clean herself up, then straightened her clothes and picked up the bottle she had come for.

'That was very nice, Mr Reechard,' she said. 'You can do that again some time, if you like.'

Then she was gone. The whole thing, from start to finish,

had been a matter of minutes. I stared at the door as it closed behind her with absolute dismay. What had I just done? How was I going to conceal what had happened from Emma? I couldn't believe my own behaviour: the knowledge that I had betrayed so many years of goodness for a moment of – what? Not even real pleasure, but the act of an animal. I stayed in the wine store for a moment or two longer, trying to compose myself and making sure that there was no visible trace of what had just happened in the room or on me. Then I went back into the restaurant, hoping that Emma would not notice anything.

As I came into the dining room Emma was standing beside the bar, loading a round of drinks on to a tray. She glanced at me. And in that single glance I saw that she knew. My face felt as red as fire. I couldn't hold her gaze. I brushed past her, and put the stock book back in its place. I wondered whether she could smell Giulia's musky perfume on me. At that moment I saw Giulia herself come through the double doors that led into the kitchen. She, too, gave me the briefest glance: haughty and complicit at the same time.

I tried to appear busy for a while, handing out drinks and chatting to customers waiting to be served. I sounded forced and uneasy, even to myself. After half an hour the restaurant quietened down. Most of the customers had now been seated and were eating. Emma walked over to me as I stood by the bar.

'Come into the wine store with me. I want a word with you in private.'

I followed her dumbly into the room. She shut the door and turned to face me.

'Is this where it happened?'

'Where what happened?'

But Emma wasn't in any mood to bother with my evasions.

'You had that slut Giulia in here, didn't you? I saw it written all over her face the moment she came back into the restaurant. I wondered what was taking her so long. Then I realised it was the boss, screwing her. I should think everyone in the restaurant knows that by now.'

I tried to think of something to say. I could hear the anguish in her voice and see it in her face. But I couldn't do anything about it.

'How could you?' asked Emma. 'How *could* you?'

I tried to explain that I hadn't meant for it to happen. I tried to say that I was sorry. I might as well not have spoken; she wasn't listening. I could see tears running down her face. When she finally managed to speak, though, her voice was firm.

'Go back to the flat,' she told me. 'Take your stuff, and go. Leave your keys on the hall table. I don't want to see or hear from you again.'

'Em,' I said, pleading. 'It can't end like this.'

'*You* ended it,' replied Emma. She looked at me with contempt. 'Now just go. Please just go.'

Of course, life isn't that simple. I did go back to the flat, and I hung around for an hour or two, hoping that Emma would come back and we could talk. But she didn't: later I found out that she had gone to stay with a girlfriend that night. I stayed up waiting for her. At three in the morning I could stand it no longer so I packed a suitcase full of clothes and by six in the morning had found a hotel that was prepared to let me in at that time of the day. I stayed there for the next few nights until I found the flat I now live in.

For the first few weeks I tried to ring Emma, but when she heard my voice, she just hung up. Then I tried emails. Finally I started writing letters: long and desperate; short and angry. Neither style worked. I didn't have the nerve to go round to her flat and confront her. I knew that one look from her would fill me with such shame I would lose all power of speech.

Who knows? Perhaps if we had seen each other again, she might have relented. But I doubt it. The betrayal had been so instant and so complete.

A couple of months later I heard that Emma had closed the restaurant. Or the bank manager had. She left London.

It shouldn't have ended like that, but Emma was an old-fashioned girl: for her black was black and white was white and there was not much room for grey in her life. Well, that was her problem, I thought at the time. If she wanted to dismiss the last few years as if they had never been, that was her choice. I knew that there was nothing I could say to change her mind. My long affair with Emma was over: the only worthwhile thing in my life had ended.

I remember how, when she was still a teenager, my little sister Katie used to close down an argument when she knew she was losing. She would just stare at me defiantly and say, 'End of story.' That was how it was now. End of. I told myself it was all for the best. I told myself that if it hadn't been one thing, it would have been another. I told myself that that's how it was. And all the while another thought was running on at the back of my mind.

If only there was a rewind button you could hit. If only – when you got to a certain point in your life – you could just say: 'I didn't mean things to turn out like this' – and then press the button. It was what you might think after a car crash: if only I hadn't been doing sixty miles an hour in a thirty-mile-an-hour zone. If only I hadn't had another drink. If only. Pause. Rewind. If only.

Nineteen

I awoke to bright daylight. There was nobody next to me in bed. It seemed only moments ago that we had been in each other's arms. I stretched and sat up and looked at my watch. It was nearly ten o'clock. I could hear Adeena's voice. She was talking to someone. I got out of bed, pulled on some clothes and went through into the kitchen. As I came in, she put down the phone.

'Good morning,' I said.

'Good morning, *darling*.'

I smiled and put my arms around her. She smelled so good. Then I released her and we stared at each other with the momentary awkwardness that sometimes overtakes new lovers.

'Who was that on the phone?' I asked.

'My brother in Kabul,' she replied. 'You don't mind if I use the phone? I know he worries about me.'

I sat down at the kitchen table and Adeena sat opposite me.

'You remember what I said last night?' I asked her.

'You said many things last night.'

'I mean about going to see Nick Davies. About doing a deal with him. Will you help me do that?'

'Of course. If you think it is for the best.'

I was slightly surprised. Last night she had treated the idea with a mixture of suspicion and despair. Now she seemed much calmer.

'Good,' I replied after a moment. 'That's good. I'm going to have a shower and get dressed. Don't go anywhere.'

When I came back Adeena was standing at the kitchen worktop where I had piled all my unanswered letters. She was looking at a card. She held it up so that I could see it.

'What is this?' she asked. 'It says it is about Afghanistan.'

Christ. I'd forgotten all about it. And I'd accepted the invitation too.

'It's just a thing for veterans of the Afghan Campaign,' I told her, 'and this state visit that's coming up. Don't tell me it's today.'

'It says so here.'

She put down the card.

'Will you go?' she asked.

'Let's see what Nick Davies says first,' I told her. 'If he'll see me today, that's more important.'

I rang Nick on the mobile number he'd given me. After a couple of rings he answered.

'Richard? I was just about to call you. We need to talk but I'm stuck in my office. I'll send a car for you. The driver should be with you in about twenty minutes and he's been told to bring you here. Is the girl with you?'

'Of course.'

'Make sure she stays in the flat.'

'I thought you were watching it,' I said.

'I can't – I haven't got the manpower today. I'll explain when I see you. I have to go now.'

He hung up, and I flipped my phone shut.

'I have to go out soon,' I said to Adeena. 'Nick's sending a car for me.'

'I don't like to stay here alone,' said Adeena.

'I'm sorry, but it's best if I do the talking without you being there,' I said. 'Keep the door locked, and don't answer to anyone.'

Adeena embraced me.

'Yes, you must go. I understand. I know you will try to help me.'

'I won't be long, I promise. Maybe two hours.'

'Richard . . .' said Adeena. She clung to me for a moment longer, then she let me go and nodded.

'I will wait for you.'

I left the flat, locking the front door behind me. It was much colder that morning than the day before. The sky was grey and the streets were damp. As I came into the main road a red minicab flashed its headlights at me twice. I went across to the driver's window and a ginger-haired man in his twenties sneered at me.

'Party by the name of Gaunt?'

'That's me.'

I got in and we drove south through the heart of London and across Vauxhall Bridge. At first I wondered whether we were meeting Nick at the huge palace that houses the intelligence services on the south bank of the Thames. I was curious to see inside that enormous building, but we drove straight past it and then dived into the network of anonymous streets to the south of Wandsworth Road. We stopped outside a small parade of shops.

'Here?' I asked the driver.

'Yes, mate. Fare's paid for. Tip is up to you.'

I climbed out and gave him a pound. He took it wordlessly then shot away with a screech of tyres. While I was trying to work out where I was supposed to go, a door at the end of the row of shops opened and Nick emerged. He looked as dishevelled as ever. I wondered whether he ever slept, or changed his clothes. He certainly hadn't shaved in a while.

'Come upstairs,' he said. 'That's where our office is at the moment. Temporary quarters, apparently. The usual re-organisation of the department. Every time it happens we're given new offices, new organisation charts and a new internal phone directory. Then we're told to get on with it. It's extra-ordinary that any real work ever gets done.'

We climbed a steep flight of stairs and came to a landing with a glass door. Nick pressed the keys on a pad next to it and the door clicked open. A moment later we were in a large, dingy space that ran above the shops. About twenty people were sitting at rows of desks on either side of a central aisle, staring at computer screens and talking into phones. It could have been a call centre for selling life insurance. Nick led me along the centre aisle towards a glass-partitioned office at the far end. He sat down behind a desk and beckoned me to take a seat, then shouted through the door: 'Coffee. Two.'

Then he sat back and gazed at me.

'Thank you for coming,' he said at last. A girl brought in two plastic beakers of black coffee, and a handful of sachets of dried milk and sweetener.

'Did I have any choice?'

'It's a free country,' said Nick. 'But no, you didn't. Where's the girl?'

'Still at my flat.'

'Married life OK? How was your friend Aseeb? Didn't he object to you taking the girl away with you?'

'We agreed to differ on the point.'

'There was a man admitted to the Radcliffe Infirmary in Oxford yesterday with a gunshot wound to the leg. Know anything about that?' Nick continued.

It must have been Kevin.

'No,' I replied. 'Nothing at all.'

'He'll live,' said Nick. 'But he'll never run the one hundred metres. Name's Kevin. You might have met him?'

'Cut the crap, Nick,' I said. 'Will you help Adeena get permission to stay here if I make sure she talks to you?'

Nick Davies sipped his coffee.

'Christ,' he said. 'That's dishwater. You're lucky you got away with it. Where did you get the gun? I don't suppose you'll tell me that either. I honestly wasn't sure you'd get out of there, let alone with the girl. I can't think why Aseeb let you take her away. Doesn't he *want* the girl?'

I wondered what new information had come in. If I waited long enough, Nick would get around to telling me.

'We received a warrant to pick him up yesterday evening,' said Nick. 'Issued by the department that closes doors after the horse has bolted. By then Aseeb had vanished. The house was empty.'

'Then what's all the panic? Why did you send for me?'

'State visit. The president of Afghanistan arrives here this afternoon. I've lost practically all my staff for the next couple of days. I might have to join a conference call shortly, so let's press on. You want to do a deal with me on behalf of Nadine Lemprière?'

'I call her Adeena,' I said.

'Well, her file says Nadine Lemprière.'

Before Nick could say any more, his phone rang, and he answered it, at the same moment pushing a photo across the desk towards me. It showed a much younger Adeena. She was wearing a black gown and a headscarf. She looked different: younger, and wilder. Cruel, inhospitable ridges of rock filled the background of the picture and in the foreground was a dusty hillside, strewn with boulders and other objects I could not make out. Adeena was staring up and the shot had been taken from somewhere above her. Behind her was an area of charred ground. The photograph was grainy and blurred, as if it had been reproduced many times. But it was Adeena, no question about it.

'Ask someone else. I'm in a meeting.' Nick slammed the phone down and turned his attention back to me.

'This photo was taken at an al-Qaeda training camp in the Safed Koh mountains. That's on the border between Afghanistan and north-west Pakistan.'

I felt myself go cold, as if my blood temperature had dropped a couple of degrees.

'What training camp? Where did you get this picture?

'It was in her file,' Nick told me.

'What file?'

'The file that we eventually got from our allies: the Combined Security Transition Command in Kabul. The file of Nadine Lemprière, daughter of the late Jean-Paul Lemprière.'

Nick smiled at me, as if he'd laid down a particularly good hand of poker. I wasn't sure I wanted to hear any more.

'She told me her father was a journalist based in Qatar . . .'

'That's bollocks.' Nick paused and watched me to see the effect his words were having. 'Her father got his first entry on the files as a radical student. That was in 1968, during the student riots in Paris. He was right at the centre of the violence, a real hard-case anarchist. Then nothing was heard from him for quite a few years, until the CIA station in Beirut ran a check on him. By then he was working in the city, lecturing on journalism at Beirut University – on the days when it was open for business, that is. He had a reputation as an anti-Zionist, and an anti-American. While he was there he married a Palestinian girl from one of the camps in south Beirut. Nadine was the result. They lived in Paris for a while and then disappeared off the map.'

He paused, sipped his coffee again, and pushed the photo forward an inch.

'This was taken six years ago from a Predator drone. It was overflying a camp in the Safed Koh mountains. Everyone was after Osama bin Laden and Mullah Omar at the time, so the air was thick with flying cameras and missile platforms like the one that took this picture. Nadine and her parents had been living there for a while.'

He paused and looked at me, wanting to determine how much of this I already knew. But this version of Adeena's story was very different to the one she'd given me.

'Of course, Jean-Paul called himself a freelance journalist,' continued Nick. 'Of course, he said he was based in Qatar. But he was never there. The CIA became interested in him again when his pieces about al-Qaeda started appearing on various so-called "non-aligned" news channels. It was like he was the AQ in-house public relations department. The CIA – or someone – decided he had the wrong sort of friends and knew too much to be just a journalist. Eventually they picked up his image on the same flight that grabbed this picture of Nadine.'

Outside in the main office several phones started ringing at once but Nick was concentrating on his story.

'The people operating the drone checked and confirmed the image. They knew if Lemprière was in that camp then

231

some of the really bad guys would be there too. Luckily for them the kill chain was short: they were sitting looking at the pictures in real time in Nevada, and the senior officer they needed to talk to was in the same time zone and awake, for once. They got the heads-up to launch a Hellfire missile at the camp. I'd guess it was a few minutes after that photo was taken. It hit the target: parents both killed, as well as a dozen other interesting individuals Jean-Paul had presumably been interviewing for his next big scoop. The CIA got a result but they didn't get Nadine.'

There was a silence. At last I felt able to speak with a steady voice.

'So what happened to Adeena?'

'You tell me. Someone got her out of there. Someone got her a job as a translator for an aid agency in Kabul. That bit's true. She did change her name to Adeena before she applied for that job. For all I know, Adeena Haq may now be her legal name, at least until she married you. But that's not the issue here.'

'Does she have a brother? A brother who lives in Kabul?' I said.

'No,' said Nick. 'No brother. Why do you ask?'

I thought about the phone calls to her 'brother' that Adeena had made from Hartlepool Hall and then from my flat. If there was no brother, then to whom had she been talking, and about what?

'So what is the "issue"?' I said, not replying to his question.

'The issue is Aseeb's motive. Why did he bring Nadine here? It must have involved considerable personal risk. It's not what he normally does, which is money laundering for his paymasters in Afghanistan and elsewhere. He didn't bring her all this way just to sell her for a few hundred pounds or use her as a sex slave. He might have used her as a mule to carry money or drugs, but then why bother with all that marriage business?'

'I don't know,' I replied.

'You're not the thinking type, are you?' said Nick. 'A beautiful girl of mysterious Middle Eastern origins falls all over you, and you don't even ask yourself why? You must have a very high opinion of your charms, Mr Gaunt.'

'Of course I don't,' I said angrily. 'They just picked me up off the street.'

'Yes,' interrupted Nick. 'They picked you up off the street. That's where it all went wrong for a moment. We've been talking to the lad Kevin. Instead of getting hold of some drifter, he picks up a slightly pissed ex-army officer who is trained to kill. Probably not what was in the original job specification. All they wanted was some poor bastard who was desperate enough to give his name to a marriage in return for a lump sum, very likely a lot less than they paid you in the end. But you went along with them anyway. Why was that?'

There wasn't an easy answer to that question. The Richard Gaunt of two weeks ago now seemed like someone from another age. Then I had been indifferent to anyone and everyone, living a life without meaning or purpose. I had been walking to Oxford for a bet when I was kidnapped, hadn't I? That alone was a fairly stupid thing to do.

Nick Davies was right. I didn't think deeply: thinking deeply led me to places I didn't want to go to. And now, everything had changed.

'Why was that?' repeated Nick. 'Well, I don't suppose you've got much of an answer anyway. You helped them get what they wanted: Nadine was recreated as Adeena Gaunt, given the right to stay in this country, and was one step away from full UK citizenship, thanks to you. But Aseeb wasn't really interested in you at first. He wanted to create a new identity for the girl, and you would have been discarded as soon as you had done what was asked of you. When you left, that should have been the end of it. But it wasn't.'

Basil put his head around the door.

'The minister's on the phone. He wants you to join a conference call shortly. What do I say?'

'Say what you like,' Nick snapped. 'Tell him that if I spend my entire time reporting to him and joining pointless conference calls, I'll never get anything done. He wants me to keep the president of Afghanistan alive while he's in London, I suppose? Then why doesn't he let me get on with it? Tell him "Yes", Bas, but have a car ready and get a dial-in number so we can join in on the call on a mobile.'

Nick turned back to me.

'Nadine is a sleeper, Richard. She's a terrorist, with a more or less legitimate UK identity, waiting to be pointed at an opportunity. So why did she come back to you when you left? Suddenly their long-term plan had become a short-term plan. They must have seen something. Or you told them something. What was it? Try and think, for once. It could be really, really important.'

I had no idea what he was talking about.

'You said something,' persisted Nick. 'Or else they saw something when they went to your flat. Or something else happened that rang a few bells. They sent Nadine after you. What was it that changed their minds?'

I wasn't on Nick's wavelength at all. He was talking about someone called Nadine, and all I could think about was

Adeena: a girl who had run away from her captors in search of help, who had come to me because I was the only person in the United Kingdom whose address she knew. Now I had promised to look after her, no matter what. But *who* had she been calling on the phone?

'Why don't you ask her yourself?' I suggested.

'Good idea,' agreed Nick. '*Cherchez la femme*. We'll ask the lady herself. Call her to tell her that you're on your way home.' He held out the handset towards me so that I could punch in my number. After a moment the line connected, and I could hear the phone ringing. No one answered.

'She won't pick up,' I said.

Nick frowned. Then he stood up and went to the door of his office and shouted:

'Right. *Basil!* Car.'

Basil was bending over a desk, talking into a phone. He raised his head.

'Car's downstairs, Nick.'

'I want your guarantee that she won't be arrested,' I told Nick.

'No deals. No guarantees,' he said. 'We're way beyond that. You know that. Let's go.'

Feeling sick, I followed Nick through the office and down-stairs. There was a black Audi A6 parked outside, with a driver at the wheel. Nick gestured to me to get into the back, then walked around the car to sit on the other side. A moment later Basil came flying down the stairs and jumped into the front passenger seat. As the car took off, Nick leaned forward and gave my address to the driver, then asked Basil:

'What time's that conference call?'

'It's been put back half an hour, Nick. The minister's in with the prime minister, reporting to him.'

'Jesus,' said Nick. He checked his watch and stared out of the window.

'I don't want Adeena to be locked up, or sent back to Afghanistan,' I said.

'You're not in a position to ask for anything. Don't even bother trying.'

The driver drove fast, but well, and we arrived at my flat in a surprisingly short time. I got out, wondering whether Adeena was watching. I looked up but did not see her face at the window. I ran up the steps to the entrance to the flat, with Nick and Basil close behind me. The door was still locked. I found my key and opened it, my hands trembling slightly. I stepped through the small hallway into the kitchen. It was empty. I called out.

'Adeena!'

Nick and Basil pushed past me and looked in the sitting room, the bathroom, my bedroom and the box room. Then Nick came back into the kitchen. Basil was already on his mobile, talking to someone.

'So what's the story, Richard?' asked Nick. 'Where is she? Is she having her hair done? Or has she gone to be with Aseeb? What's your best guess, Richard?'

I stared at him. Then I sat down at the kitchen table and put my head in my hands.

'Come on, Richard,' said Nick. 'Let's not fuck about. Something's gone wrong, hasn't it? Where is she?'

Twenty

'Sir, the conference call is open. We can join in now.'

Basil waved the mobile phone in Nick's direction.

'Put the bloody thing on speaker and let's hope the battery doesn't run flat halfway through,' said Nick. For a moment the two of them had forgotten about me. I heard some static and then a voice: 'You are joining a secure conference call. Please identify yourselves.'

Nick and Basil gave their names and a pass code. There were some clicks, and then a booming voice came across the line. I recognised the clipped tones of the minister David Longtown. He was fond of making television and radio appearances and one heard his voice with great regularity, whether one wanted to or not.

'David Longtown here. Commander Verdon is in the room with me. Stand by. Is Cheltenham on the line?'

Another voice said yes, GCHQ at Cheltenham was standing by.

'It's two o'clock,' said David Longtown. 'I'll just run through the main points of the timetable. The president is touching down at Heathrow about now. He'll be picked up by car. That's the Foreign Office, plus standard police escort. He goes to Buckingham Palace for an audience with Her Majesty at three. Three forty-five he leaves the Palace and they drive down the Mall to St James's Gate, turn into

Lancaster House. Four to four thirty he has a reception at Lancaster House. After that the convoy goes down the Mall, turns right into Horse Guards, along George Street and then to Number Ten. That's where I'll meet the president, along with the prime minister. OK so far?'

Everyone said yes.

'Commander Verdon, can you introduce yourself?'

A new voice announced itself. The minister said, 'Commander Verdon is from Counter Terrorism Command and he is Gold Commander for this operation. In any emergency, he is in charge. Everyone got that?'

Various noises of assent sounded over the speaker. The minister continued: 'This line will stay open until the president and his escort arrive in Downing Street. Any problems, anything at all that doesn't seem right, call it in on this number. Anything new on threat status, Cheltenham?'

'The usual increase in activity in Internet chat rooms,' said a voice. 'Threats to blow up the president, cut off his head and so on. Some mobile chatter. Nothing specific. We'll keep listening.'

'Do that,' said the minister. At that moment Nick realised I was still in the room. He turned and mouthed, 'Get out.' As I left the kitchen I heard Nick say, 'Minister, Nick Davies speaking. We may have a situation here.'

Bas closed the kitchen door, cutting off the sound of Nick's voice. I stood in the sitting room. An awareness was growing within me: not all at once in a flash of revelation, but creeping up on me like a poison injected in my veins. I'd been had; I'd been played like a fish. Adeena's appearance outside my flat, calculated to arouse my sympathy, had been the hook. Her apparent abduction in the supermarket had set the hook within me. I felt compelled to go after her and release her, as they knew I would. And how easy they had made it for me! Two hardened members of al-Qaeda had let me walk all over them at the house in Oxfordshire. It was obvious to me now that the whole episode had been a set-up. I had done exactly what they wanted me to do – with the possible exception of shooting Kevin in the leg. I had brought Adeena back with me and . . . Adeena had brought a bag with her.

I went into the box room and looked for Adeena's bag. It was still there. I opened it. It was empty. I went into the bedroom. The clothes she had been wearing at breakfast had been thrown on a chair. I could see no sign of the burka, either in the wardrobe or anywhere else. A feeling of panic was rising in me. I opened my sock drawer and dug out the Sig Sauer once more and checked the clip. There were still seven rounds left. I stuck the pistol in the belt of my trousers. Then I went back to the kitchen and opened the door. The conference call was still going on but I ignored it. Nick and Bas rose from the chairs the moment I came in but I ignored them too. I went straight to the pile of post that lay on one of the worktops. As I leafed through it Bas took me by the arm.

'It's gone,' I said.

'Come on, sir,' said Bas, trying to steer me out of the room, but Nick stopped him. He hit the mute button on the phone.

'What's gone?'

'My invitation,' I said stupidly.

'Your invitation to what, exactly?' I could see Nick was trying to keep his temper.

'My invitation to the veteran soldiers' reception to meet the president of Afghanistan: the reception at Lancaster House. It's gone. Adeena must have taken it.'

Nick sat motionless as he took this in. Then he said: 'Oh,

shit,' and ran his hands over his face and through his hair so that it stood up in spikes. 'Oh, God. You couldn't have told us this sooner, could you? That's the answer. That's why she was here. She wanted access.'

He waved at me to sit down, then turned off the mute button to rejoin the conference call.

'We lost you there for a moment, Nick,' the minister said, 'please repeat what you were saying?'

'We have new information. We believe that there will be an attempt on the president at the Lancaster House reception. We have a female suspect who has a security pass issued in the name of Gaunt. Commander Verdon, have you got that?'

There was a chaotic noise on the other end of the line as everyone talked at the same time.

'We'll advise security at Lancaster House,' Commander Verdon's voice drowned out the others, 'but your suspect may already have got in. We must abort the president's visit there. I will contact the Foreign Office and ensure the reception is cancelled. The convoy will go straight from the Palace to Number Ten. Minister, I assume you will keep the prime minister's office informed? Nick, can you give me a physical description of the woman we are looking for?'

Nick turned to me, the question in his eyes.

'I think she's wearing a burka,' I told him, 'but she looks European. She may have put on a veil as well.'

Nick looked at me in horror.

'There's no time to get a photograph circulated. Can't you do better than that?'

'I'd be able to recognise her whatever she was wearing,' I said.

'Nick, who is the new voice on the line?' asked Commander Verdon. Nick turned back to the phone and explained.

The commander spoke again: 'Give me your address, and I will send a car immediately to collect Mr Gaunt. We need him to go to Lancaster House to identify the target, if she is still there. Nick, it would be best if you could return to your office and then rejoin this call from a secure line. We have a possible terrorist event in progress.'

'If this is an AQ event then there will almost certainly be more than one incident,' said Nick. 'Their signature is multiple attacks.'

'I agree,' said Commander Verdon. 'I am raising the threat level from "Severe" to "Critical". I repeat: the threat level is "Critical".'

The minister spoke. 'I'm leaving this call now and handing over to the Gold Commander. He is in charge. Call in with any developments, especially you, Nick. This is your department's responsibility.'

I saw Nick mouth an obscenity at the mobile.

'And remember,' the minister continued. 'We don't want a repeat of July 2005. We don't want to shoot another innocent passer-by. Dead civilians do not make good headlines. Any mistakes and the officers responsible will be held fully accountable. That's you, Commander Verdon; and you too, Nick.'

The call ended. Nick stood up.

'There you are. That's how to say "You're damned if you do, and you're damned if you don't." I'm going back to the office. Bas, you stay here with Mr Gaunt until CO15 pick him up. Richard, if you remember any other details that might have slipped your mind, perhaps you'd be kind enough to let us know.'

He was halfway through the door when I said: 'There was something in the bag.'

Nick turned so suddenly he almost fell over.

'What bag?'

'She came back from Oxford with a canvas bag. It was heavy. She told me it contained her personal belongings.'

'Did you look inside it?' asked Bas.

'I did just now. It's empty.'

'Get down there to Lancaster House,' said Nick furiously. 'Find her. Stop her. Do something. Wake up to what's been going on under your nose.'

Adeena was an associate of terrorists and was probably a terrorist herself. Deep down, I'd known it all along – I just hadn't wanted to admit it to myself. I'd been taken in by her beauty; by the air of desolation that surrounded her. I felt sorry for her. I wanted her. And last night she had made quite sure that all I was thinking about was being in bed with her.

But for me, it had been much more than that: it was fuelled by my own longing to fill the hole in my life that had been there for the last two years since Emma left. I had to accept Adeena had used me. It was no use hating her for deceiving me: the only deception had been the one I'd practised on myself.

'Are you all right, Mr Gaunt?' asked Bas. He was staring at me. I looked down at my hands and saw they were both balled up into fists, my knuckles white.

'I'm all right,' I said, without looking at him.

'The coppers should show up any minute.'

Adeena. Nadine. She wasn't called Nadine, I told myself. That name was taken away from her when they blew up her father and mother in a camp in southern Afghanistan. Now she was Adeena Haq. No: she was Adeena Gaunt. And she wanted to make us pay for what had been done to her family. The truth was I didn't know her and I had never known her. I remembered her talking about the war in Afghanistan with a passion that was different to her normal calm. Normal? I'd known her only for two weeks.

The doorbell rang.

Bas said, 'I'll answer that, if you don't mind.'

He went to the door and opened it cautiously, then widened it to admit two very large men in jeans and fleeces. They had to duck their heads as they came in. I was over six foot tall and I didn't need to do that, but these two men made the room seem very small indeed. There was a little courtship ritual while Bas and the men showed each other their warrant cards, then the older of the two looked at me.

'You're Gaunt?'

'I'm Richard Gaunt.'

'We're from Counter Terrorism Command. You can call me Arthur.' He jerked a thumb at the other man. 'And you can call him Martha. Let's get going.'

'Good luck, Mr Gaunt,' said Bas. I muttered something in reply and followed the two men down into the street and over to their car.

As we screeched off down Camden High Street, Arthur turned on a radio and picked up a mike from its cradle.

'C5 reporting in to Control. We have the guy who can make the eyeball in the car and we're on our way. There in twenty. Standing by for instructions.'

There was a burst of static and a garbled voice said something entirely unintelligible.

Arthur looked at Martha. 'These new radios are no better than the last ones. Can't hear a word.'

The car took a corner at unnerving speed. Ahead of us was heavy traffic. I heard the siren start up and the cars in front of us pulled over to the side of the road to let us past. I checked my watch: it was 3.20. Adeena might already be through security at Lancaster House. We hadn't been asked to bring any identification, just the invitation itself. She would be admitted, along with all the other wives. The burka would even help her. Security would be terrified of doing or saying anything that could be construed as politically incorrect. Adeena would be waiting for the arrival of the guest of honour. What would she do when the news got out that he wasn't coming? My job was to get to her first, make sure she was safe and that she didn't get shot by Arthur, Martha or anyone else.

The next thing would be to find out where Aseeb was, and deal with him. Adeena would know. She must know. He must have picked her up outside my flat and taken her as close as he could get to Lancaster House. The car ground to a halt. Ahead of us the traffic was absolutely solid. Horns were sounding and there was the noise of an ambulance in the distance.

'Christ,' said Arthur to Martha. 'Try and find a way round this, will you?'

Martha reversed, causing the driver of the car behind to lean on his horn. Then he did a U-turn in front of an approaching taxi, bumped on to the pavement and shot the wrong way down a one-way street, weaving between the oncoming cars. Luckily we didn't hit anyone. We turned south again. The traffic was only slightly less solid than before, but with lights flashing and siren going, we were able to make some progress. Arthur tried the radio again.

'Control,' he called over the mike. 'When we make the eyeball, what are our instructions?'

'. . . ake . . . op . . .'

'Did he tell us to make the stop?' Arthur asked Martha.

'I can't bloody well drive in this mess and listen to the radio,' complained the driver. 'You tell me.'

Arthur tried again, but the words were no clearer.

'What's "make the stop" mean?' I asked.

'You don't want to know,' said Arthur, briefly. As soon as he said that, I knew exactly what it meant. Every unit has its own slang and this was theirs. They were asking about instructions to kill Adeena on sight.

Arthur started fiddling with the radio to find a better frequency.

A voice said: 'Pick up in ten minutes at number forty-three, Nelson Crescent, to go to King's Cross. Anyone?'

'Jesus Christ,' Arthur swore. 'I thought this was supposed to be a secure radio network.'

'These minicab outfits don't care,' said Martha. We were now weaving through thick traffic down Upper Regent Street. 'It's always the same when they shut down the Mall,' he continued. 'The whole of London grinds to a halt. What time are we due there?'

'Five minutes ago,' said Arthur. 'Get a move on.'

'You should tell Control to look out for a black Range Rover,' I said suddenly. Multiple attacks, Nick had said.

Martha muttered something and then did a hair-raising crossing of Oxford Street between two buses that were coming at us from opposite directions. Arthur picked up the mike and started trying to talk to Control, to pass on my message.

'Use a mobile,' I suggested. 'We did.'

'We're not supposed to once we've gone operational,' said Arthur. 'They're not secure. But that's exactly what I'll have to do if I can't get this heap of shit to work any better.'

We swerved down Regent Street towards Piccadilly. Arthur gave up on the radio and used his mobile. He got a connection at once, and tried to pass on my message. Someone at the other end was obviously more interested in telling Arthur what to do than in listening to him.

I heard him say: 'I can't make out what you're saying. There's a lot of noise in the background. Yes, sir. Yes, sir. I understand. If you say so, sir.'

He hung up and turned to Martha.

'They think there's going to be an attack on the motor convoy. We're stood down until the situation is clearer. We have to proceed to Lancaster House, make the eyeball, and then await further instructions. Can you believe it?'

It was now ten to four. For a frustrating ten minutes we fought our way through thick, almost static traffic around the streets of St James's until we managed to turn into Pall Mall. Just after four o'clock we, and everyone else in that part of London, heard a huge explosion. I thought I felt a faint shudder travel through the car ahead of the bang. I saw car brake lights come on everywhere along Pall Mall. Pedestrians flinched, or ducked, or put their hands over their heads as they tried to work out what was happening.

Later we learned that a moment or two after four o'clock, a black Range Rover packed with explosives and driven by Amir had gone through the police barriers at Admiralty Arch.

On the roof of the vehicle was an emergency flashing light, which Aseeb had bought on the Internet using a credit card in the name of Khan. The lights had caused just enough confusion for the vehicle to be able to force its way through the police cordon and make a headlong run at the approaching motor convoy.

'That was a big bang,' said Arthur.

'Not from the direction of Lancaster House, though,' said Martha.

They were right, as it turned out. The point of impact between the Range Rover and the convoy was just opposite the Duke of York Steps. The first car in the convoy, an escort vehicle containing three police officers, pulled sideways in front of the car carrying the president to block the approaching Range Rover, which detonated just before it hit the police car, obliterating the occupants. Not a trace of the three police officers remained, nor of Amir, and not much was left of either vehicle.

Fragments of metal were strewn across the Mall, beheading one bystander and wounding several others. The visit of the president of Afghanistan was not a big-ticket event, and the few people who had lined the pavements probably didn't even know which country's flag it was that was flying overhead, and had simply stopped to watch in case the convoy contained a member of the Royal Family. Two shards of metal went straight through the windscreen of the president's car. A permanent under-secretary and the driver were killed instantly. The president and the foreign secretary, sitting in the rear seats, were miraculously unscathed although, deafened by the explosion, they could hear little or nothing of the prime minister's sympathetic remarks when they finally arrived in Downing Street.

As our car raced into the courtyard outside Lancaster House I could see dozens of people coming down the steps. Police officers were trying to control the crowd until they had found out where the threat was. There were several wives in frocks and hats but I could not spot the person I was most anxious to see. I leapt out of the car before it had stopped moving.

'Make the eyeball,' Arthur told me, leaning out from the passenger seat. 'Martha will follow you. I'll try to get confirmation of our instructions.'

As I stared across the courtyard a honking sound overhead made me look up. In a darkening grey sky I could see skeins of geese and ducks circling, startled from their ponds and reed beds in St James's Park by the sound of the explosion.

Behind me I heard Arthur shouting into his mobile.

'What are our instructions, for Christ's sake? I can't hear what you're saying!'

It wasn't surprising. The courtyard was a melee. Two more police cars had arrived and there were officers everywhere, shouting at each other and yelling instructions. Radios crackled. Sirens were going off all over this part of London: ambulance, fire, police. A column of black smoke was drifting down the Mall, behind Lancaster House. Then at last I saw Adeena, standing in the middle of the crowd of soldiers and ex-soldiers. Her black-clad figure was so still among the moving crowd that it seemed as if she was lost in thought. She wore no scarf or veil: her blonde hair fell to her shoulders. She was half turned away from me so I couldn't see her face. I started to push my way through the crowd towards her.

Martha followed me, muttering. 'Which one is it? Is that her in the black gown?'

I didn't reply. I was intent on speaking to Adeena. I needed to explain to her that whatever she was planning to do she must not go through with it. She needed to stay alive. As I pushed through the crowd one or two voices called my name:

'Gaunt? Is that you, Gaunt?'

'Do you know what's going on, Richard?'

I bumped into a man, who staggered and nearly fell over. I saw from his movements that he had a prosthetic leg. He was wearing a dark suit with a campaign medal pinned to the lapel and he swore at me as he fought to regain his balance. Martha stopped to help the man, and fell behind me in the confusion.

'Sorry,' I said over my shoulder. I elbowed past another man, a colonel whose face I thought I recognised, but I ignored him too. Adeena was only a few yards away, standing erect and looking towards the house, where yet more people were emerging: senior officers, and a couple of suits who looked like politicians or civil servants. Even though her back was to me, I would have recognised her slender figure anywhere, even in that black gown.

Except she wasn't slender any more: I thought that there was a thickening around her waist. I remembered a spindly boy coming around a corner in a street not far from the Green Zone in Baghdad. A spindly boy: thin-faced and narrow-shouldered, with spindly legs poking from the bottom of his gown. Around the middle he was as plump as a partridge. Just like Adeena. At that moment I finally knew beyond any doubt what was about to happen.

She was a suicide bomber. The realisation almost overwhelmed me and at the same time I was unsurprised, as if I'd always known it. But there was no time for thought. There never is, when you most need it. I opened my mouth to yell

'Everybody down' just as I had once before, but no one would have taken any notice. So many people were already shouting instructions, contradicting each other, that one more order would probably have made little difference. By now I was only two or three yards behind Adeena. I called out her name. I did not use her new name.

'Nadine,' I said. Somehow the frenzied activity and noise around us seemed to fade. She heard me, and turned around. Her eyes were wide and she was smiling at me, that smile she had that melted my heart. She mouthed a word. She may have spoken it aloud, but she did not need to. I knew what she had said.

'Darling.'

Her left hand gripped the edge of her burka and now I saw her slip it inside the folds of cloth. I had already pulled out the pistol. Holding it with both hands I fired twice, straight at the centre of her forehead. She crumpled backwards without a sound.

I can't remember much of what happened after that. I don't want to remember. Martha grabbed me from behind as I knelt by Adeena's body, and then Arthur arrived. Between them they half dragged, half walked me back to the car almost before anyone else had realised what was going on. Uniformed policemen crowded around the car and there was a brief conference, or perhaps it was an argument. Then I found myself slumped in the back of the car and it was reversing at speed out of the courtyard, before driving away, away from the black-clad body still lying on the tarmac.

I was in a lot of different places that evening. First we went to an underground crisis management centre, somewhere off Whitehall. Then we spent hours going from one office to another at New Scotland Yard. At last Arthur and Martha and two uniformed officers took me back downstairs and put me in another car and I ended up in the rooms above the parade of shops in Wandsworth.

All that long and weary evening, people kept pushing their faces into mine, asking questions I couldn't understand. At first tears leaked down my cheeks, and I could not stop them, but I don't remember making any sound. I felt trapped inside a bubble of silence. It wasn't grief or anger. I was so numb that the events of that afternoon seemed like bright images seen through the wrong end of a telescope: remote and unreal. From time to time fragments of conversation penetrated my mind.

'He's in shock.'

'Did anyone get a picture of him?'

'Not that I know of – we got away clean, I think.'

Then, later on, a man with a pompous voice that was somehow familiar turned up. He didn't bother talking to me but addressed the other people in the room.

'We don't want another trial. Make him disappear.'

None of this made any sense to me at the time. As the evening turned into night, I found the energy to speak at last. We were sitting in Nick Davies's office with Bas. Arthur and Martha had disappeared and Nick was gazing at me while I drank neat whisky out of a paper cup.

'Tell me,' I said to Nick. I thought he looked even more tired than usual, but his expression was slightly less hostile.

'Tell you what?'

'About Adeena. She was wearing a suicide vest underneath the burka, wasn't she? I thought she was about to detonate it.'

Nick and Bas stared at me.

'That's why I had to take the shot,' I explained. 'There was no time to ask questions.'

Bas looked away from me and stared at the floor. I repeated my question: 'She was wearing a suicide vest, right?'

Still no one said a word.

Twenty-One

A suicide vest is often a simple garment. You can make them at home. People do just that. I had seen a few in Iraq, when we raided bomb factories. The vest is usually constructed from heavy-duty polythene, or canvas, with two flaps. There is a hole in the middle to put your head through. Sophisticated versions have tapes so you can tie the garment around you. Stitched around the vest are pockets of webbing or some other material, which are used to hold the sticks of explosive. In the deluxe versions these are also packed with ball bearings, to increase lethality. The explosives are joined by wire to a detonator, which is activated either by the bomber himself – or herself – or in some cases by a kind friend using a garage remote or a mobile telephone. That was what I thought Adeena had been wearing.

After a moment's silence Nick replied.

'Yes. She was wearing a bomb vest but it was not well made. It might not have gone off. If it had done, there would have been one hell of a bang.'

Something like compassion flitted across Nick's features. Then he said, 'If you hadn't stopped her, she could have done enormous damage. You would have been killed, of course. And so would dozens of other people. It would have been a triumph for Aseeb if he had managed to pull off both attempts. He – or al-Qaeda – would have claimed the scalps of the president of Afghanistan, and a score of senior officers and campaign veterans.'

I remembered Adeena telling me: '*I know exactly what I believe in, Richard. And that is more than you can say.*'

Her belief had been strong and it had been quite clear. She was intent on martyrdom. For a while I hadn't seen her for what she was. I didn't understand her, because I didn't believe in anything any more. Belief had been knocked out of me. I was just a man with too many bad memories. As for Adeena, whether it was me who shot her – or someone like me – or whether she had achieved her death herself, the result would have been the same. The message would have been delivered.

'There's no point in reproaching yourself, Richard,' Nick added. 'She was a very clever lady. She fooled us all: she and Aseeb. It was a classic piece of misdirection. She had us all worrying about her – was she a terrorist, wasn't she? – and while we were busy doing that, Aseeb was getting on with Plan A. They both knew we would work out what she was intending to do, and would cancel Lancaster House and redirect the motor convoy down the Mall. The man in the Range Rover saw his chance and went for it. He came very close to killing everyone in that motorcade.'

Nick told me what they knew about Amir's suicide run at the president.

'He nearly succeeded,' said Nick. 'We picked up the threat when Cheltenham eavesdropped on a call which we think was the "Go" signal. Even then we didn't know where the threat would come from, except that Nadine Lemprière was probably Plan B, and not the main event.'

Aseeb. I had a strong desire to see him again.

'Was the call from Aseeb?'

'We think so.'

'Where is he?'

'The odd thing is that the call was traced to Middlesbrough. We only received that information about half an hour ago.'

'Middlesbrough? What the hell is he doing there?'

Nick paused, then said, 'We're not sure. Trying to go home, maybe? The UK Border Agency and the police all have descriptions of him so getting out of the country by plane or even road or rail will be a big risk for him. There are photo ID checks at most airports now. We nearly caught him at Heathrow a year ago. But Aseeb's style is to do the unexpected.'

'So why Middlesbrough?' I repeated. 'Why go north?'

Nick replied by asking a question of his own.

'What do you know about Middlesbrough?'

'Not much. It was once a big steel town . . .' I thought for a moment and then realised what he was getting at. 'Oh, I see. It's a port.'

'Yes, it's a port and quite a busy one, too. The actual harbour is called Teesport. Oddly enough – we don't know, but we think – Aseeb may have used it before. Because although it is still a large industrial port there are two interesting things about it as far as Aseeb is concerned. The first is that it was a soft entry point for illegal immigrants. The UK Border Agency has tightened up on that now, but it still goes on. The second thing is that it has a number of sailings to the Middle East: Port Sudan, Djibouti, Aden and so on. A ship might be slow, but it's the last thing he'd expect us to keep an eye on. And he'd be right, except that he doesn't know we spotted this as a potential route in and out a year ago. If he can get as far as Aden on a ship, the rest of the journey home would be a piece of cake for someone with Aseeb's connections.'

I stood up. I felt very weary and numb, but there was still work to be done.

'Let's go,' I said.

'Hang on,' said Nick. 'You're not going anywhere.'

'You need me,' I pointed out. 'I would recognise Aseeb in an instant if I saw him again. You don't have that advantage: you only have a fairly old photograph to work from. You have to take me. You can't afford to get it wrong.'

After a moment Nick nodded reluctantly.

'OK. But don't kill anyone. We want to catch Aseeb alive.'

'Then let's go,' I said again. Nick shook his head.

'There's no hurry. Either we're wrong about Middlesbrough and his intended method of departure, in which case he's probably left the country already, or we're right, in which case the next sailing he could possibly use leaves Teesport tomorrow night. There's plenty of time. Let's get some sleep. Bas will take you back to your flat and we'll pick you up tomorrow morning.'

That night I didn't sleep much. I lay on my bed fully clothed, grief bubbling inside me like acid. I tried to force it back down. Now was not the time to grieve. I thought a lot about Adeena that night, but in the end none of it made any sense.

I believe now that Adeena had taught herself to live more than one life. She was a terrorist or, as she would have put it, a martyr. That was one life. But the Nadine part of her, I am sure, pined for another existence: what she would have called a 'bourgeois' life. Terrorists sometimes destroy the things they most long to have themselves. She wanted a man, and a

256

family, and a life without fear. It was a life she knew she could never have, but that didn't stop her longing for it.

But that night I couldn't yet see how it might have been. I couldn't stop thinking about the moment when I had spoken her name, her true name, and she had turned and smiled at me. Uttering that final loving word had been her last conscious act before I shot her. I wished I had some sleeping pills or a bottle of whisky in the flat to drown my wakeful brain.

In the end I fell into a doze just before dawn and awoke late. I showered, changed and made some toast and a cup of coffee. Then I waited for Nick and Bas.

They arrived about ten o'clock in the same black Audi I'd seen them in the day before. Behind them was a large Toyota Land Cruiser with four men in it. They looked like serious people. As I walked towards the Audi with Bas, he jerked his thumb in the direction of the Toyota.

'The local police and the UK Border Agency are waiting for us but we're fielding our own team as well.'

I climbed into the car. Inside, Nick Davies was sitting in the front passenger seat eating a bacon and egg bun. Between mouthfuls he said, 'This is breakfast. I hope you've eaten too. This will be the last meal we have time for today.'

We drove north up the A1. By the time we reached our destination it was late in the afternoon, and the sun was sinking low in the sky. Middlesbrough is bisected by a dual carriageway that runs through the heart of the city and down to the coast, bending slightly south to follow the line of the Tees estuary. We drove in convoy, past the white spider's web of the Riverside Stadium, and the huge blue shape of the Transporter Bridge that carries cars and people in a gondola suspended above the river, then on to Port Clarence on the northern bank of the Tees.

After a while the town gave way to retail parks, and then acres of enormous sheds. I remembered from some dimly recollected geography lesson that this had once been the heart of the steel industry in northern England, with thousands of tons of ore, coal and potash being moved through the port. Now we passed a dereliction of railway sidings and old signal boxes, then the alien shapes of distillation columns and the cracking towers of a petrochemical plant.

'Where are we going?' I asked Nick.

'First stop is the UK Border Agency office at Teesport. We need to liaise with them, and the local constabulary, and check the sailing time of the ship we're interested in. Then we'll decide what to do. Some local advice would be helpful – this place looks enormous.'

We turned left at a roundabout and came to a security barrier that marked the main entrance to the port. After a few minutes an escort car turned up and we followed it to a small city of Portakabins.

'I'm not going to explain who you are, or why you're here, unless I have to,' said Nick. 'So keep quiet, if you can.' We got out of the car and followed the officer who had been sent to meet us into the nearest Portakabin. I noticed that the four men in the Toyota didn't bother to join us.

Inside the Portakabin was a small welcome committee consisting of a couple of senior policemen, an official from the UK Border Agency, and an older man from the Port Authority. They had obviously been briefed on why we were there because we got straight down to business.

'We could have done without this,' said one of the policemen. 'There's a match on tonight at Riverside. Kick-off is seven thirty. We're playing Newcastle. We were already stretched with crowd control before you lads turned up.'

'I'm sorry to hear that,' said Nick. He did not sound sorry. 'The man we're looking for is a major terrorist and was probably responsible for the explosion in London yesterday.'

'Well, we'll just have to do the best we can,' said the second policeman. He sounded as if he thought terrorists were a minor problem compared with football supporters at a north-east derby.

'What do you think your man will do?' asked the official from the Border Agency.

'You tell me,' replied Nick. 'What we do know is that there's a ship sailing to Djibouti from Berth Two at midnight, and we think he might try to get on it. He thinks we aren't paying attention to this route out of the country. He's expecting us to be throwing all our resources into watching the airports and the ferries and the Channel Tunnel. Which we are doing. But we have a feeling about this guy. He does things differently. He might just risk boarding the vessel here. Has anyone checked with the ship yet?'

'We've been on board and talked to the captain,' said the Border Agency official. 'There're no unauthorised personnel on the vessel. The crew won't start boarding until later this evening, and we've got tight security around this harbour already.'

Nick nodded.

'Have you got everything you need?'

'If my colleagues in the police can supply a few extra men, then we can make it more or less impossible for anyone to get near that ship without authorisation.'

'We want to catch this guy alive,' Nick said. 'We don't want to scare him away so we don't want any shooting. We want to allow him to get as close as possible without seeing any cause for alarm. Then we can take him.'

'Firearms?' asked one of the policemen. 'We'll need an Armed Response team, then.'

'He may have a weapon. It's possible,' said Nick. 'I have four specialists outside who are licensed firearms officers.'

'I'd rather have my own team,' said the first police officer.

'Talk to your Chief Constable, then,' suggested Nick. 'The minister has agreed to my plan, so you'd need him to change his mind.'

'I don't see how he can get into Berth Two without being seen,' repeated the official from the Border Agency.

'Well, I know what I'd do if I were him,' said the man from the Port Authority, speaking for the first time. His voice was soft and mild but he held everyone's attention.

'Do you, Mr Williams?' There was a measure of sarcasm in the official's tone, as if he very much doubted that anyone else in the room could tell him anything he didn't already know.

Mr Williams was by some way the oldest man there. He had a square face and faded blue eyes and was not very closely shaven. He had the look of an ex-mariner or a fisherman. But he sounded as if he knew what he was talking about.

'Tell me,' said Nick.

'Most of our illegals are going the other way,' said Mr Williams. 'They're trying to get *into* the country, not out of it. They hide inside containers or in the backs of lorries and they come in on the freight ferries, mostly. So we're not really organised to stop people getting *out* of the country. But my friend from the Border Agency is right. You can't just walk into this part of the port without someone stopping and asking you for ID.'

'So what would you do, if you were the man we're looking for?' asked Nick. 'How would you get to the ship?'

'On the water,' said Mr Williams simply. 'There are plenty of wharves and jetties and even a marina or two on this estuary. There's the offshore base upstream where they construct stuff for the oil and gas industry. There are always a few small boats on the river at most times of the day and even at night. If it were me, I'd get on to the river farther up, somewhere where there isn't much security. Then I'd sail downriver as quietly as I could, and bring my boat alongside the vessel I wanted to board. After that, I don't know. Would he have help on board?'

'Almost certainly,' said Nick. 'I guess he'd be passing himself off as a crew member. There must be someone in the crew who's in on it and will vouch for him.'

'They could drop a rope ladder over the seaward side of the vessel. He'd never be seen from the shore.'

'Thank you,' said Nick. 'That makes a lot of sense. So the answer is for some of us to wait for him in another boat on the lee of the vessel. Can we get one?'

'Yes,' said Mr Williams. 'We can use one of the Port Authority launches.'

So the plan was made. The police and the Border Agency would wait in the dock area where the vessel was berthed. Nick, his four helpers, Bas and me would join Mr Williams in the Port Authority launch. We would hide somewhere in the shadows, waiting for the sound of a boat coming downstream.

It was now getting dark, nearly six in the evening. Only six hours to go until the vessel sailed. A cold wind was coming in off the North Sea, biting through our clothing as we stood outside the Portakabin while Nick and the two policemen finalised arrangements. The man from the Port Authority drove off to organise the launch.

A few moments later the two policemen left in their car.

The UK Border Agency official came out and said, 'I'll drive you down to Berth Two so you can have a look at the vessel. She's the SS *Mamounia*, what they call a tramp. She carries general cargo, containers, just about anything she can get. A bit of a rust bucket.'

We drove down to the dock and parked on a wide strip of concrete, embedded with old railway lines. Overhead, arc lights were coming on as the night deepened. Down here, by the water's edge, it was even colder than it had been outside the Portakabins. I saw the bulk of the vessel looming above the quay. A few lights glimmered on board. There was not much sign of any human activity.

'That's her,' said the official. 'Our lads will be in the back of those sheds over there, together with whatever help the police can lend us. We should have everyone in position in the next hour.'

Half an hour later, Mr Williams returned with the launch. We met him on the dock, and climbed down a ladder to board the vessel. Nick, Bas and I were followed by Nick's four specialists. There was just room for three people in the small wheelhouse, so the other five had to sit outside.

'We'll take turns at sheltering from the wind,' said Mr Williams. 'It can get quite nippy when you're out on the water at night.'

The launch burbled out into the middle of the stream, then swung around and dropped into position behind the *Mamounia*. Above us, a few more lights now burned on the deck and from the superstructure, reflected in the oily water. The ship's engines had been started up and a low grumbling came from somewhere deep within her. There were other noises, too: voices from on deck, a metallic clang. The crew had started to board the vessel. We knew that each of them would be subjected to careful checks by Border Agency staff before they were allowed on the ship. The police were remaining out of sight.

'I hope to Christ we've got this right,' said Nick, shivering in the cold. 'It would be just our luck if Aseeb got away from Luton Airport.'

'Could that have happened?' I asked.

'Oh yes. We're good, but not that good. There are so many airports and ferries to watch. But Aseeb will be cautious about using the airports again, after the incident at Heathrow last year. That's why we're betting on him doing something different this time.' Nick paused, and looked out across the dark water and the reflections dancing on the waves. 'It's probably a total wild-goose chase. And yet – that phone call we traced yesterday came from here. And we think Aseeb has used this route before.'

From the wheelhouse, Mr Williams called softly. 'Keep the talking to essentials, Mr Davies, if you can. Sound travels a long way across water.'

Nick looked contrite. I pulled my jacket tighter around me in an effort to keep warm and looked at my watch. It was now after nine o'clock. Out at the Riverside Stadium, the football match would soon be coming to an end and then people would be spilling out on to the streets, causing even more distraction for the police.

More time passed. The motion of the launch was soporific and I could feel myself dozing off. Suddenly I sensed, rather than saw, a movement in the wheelhouse.

'There's a small craft coming down the river, in the middle

of the stream,' Mr Williams whispered to us. 'It might not be anything to do with us. Everybody keep still.'

I couldn't resist the temptation to peer forward. I couldn't see anything; then maybe the dimmest of shapes against the constellation of shore lights from Port Clarence on the north bank; the faintest phosphorescence of a wake.

'He's turned inshore,' said Mr Williams. 'This could be our man.' At once the slumped figures of Nick and his fire-arms specialists straightened up. I could hear the snick of gun slides. The craft was now clearly visible: a small boat with an outboard motor. It was impossible to see who was in it at this distance and in this gloom.

'I'm going to let him come in close,' whispered Mr Williams. 'Then try to cut him off. Keep absolutely still until we start moving.'

At that moment a police car came down the ramp that led on to the dock. Its blue light flashed once and there was the briefest whoop from its siren. The police on watch were doing a shift change but the timing was unfortunate.

At once the small craft accelerated into a tight turn, the snarl of its engine now clearly audible. It headed back up-river.

'Hold tight,' said Mr Williams. He opened the throttle and the launch surged after the fleeing motorboat.

'Where could he be going?' shouted Nick.

'I've no idea,' replied Mr Williams. 'It could be anywhere. We'll have to try to keep him in sight. He's travelling faster than us.'

The launch was now slapping up and down across the wake of the smaller boat. Then it settled into a parallel course, cutting through the water like a knife. A searchlight came on above the wheelhouse. After a minute it had picked up the smaller craft.

'He might be heading for the offshore base,' shouted Mr Williams above the noise of the engine.

Bas was talking into his radio. Looking back at the berth we had left, I could see three police cars, then a fourth, leaving the dock, their lights flashing and their sirens on. It would take them a while to catch up with us: they would have to go into Middlesbrough and fight their way through all the football traffic. Ahead, the craft we were pursuing started to turn towards the shore.

'He's heading for the offshore base, sure enough,' said Mr Williams.

'Any local security?' asked Nick.

'Not much,' replied Mr Williams. 'Not what you would want to put up against this fellow.'

The motorboat arrived at the dockside, and now we could see a dark figure scrambling out of the boat and on to the dock. He didn't bother tying it up, and the motorboat began to drift away into the stream. Moments later, we were landing ourselves. Nick and Bas were first up, then the four firearms specialists. I was last. Mr Williams remained on board. As we left he reversed the launch back out into the river and started sweeping the searchlight along the dock.

'That's him,' Nick said, pointing at a dark figure running out of the light and around the corner of a huge shed. 'Stay with me, Richard. I want you to confirm Aseeb's identity when we catch him. And that's all I want you to do. Have you got that?'

This last warning was delivered rather breathlessly because by that time we were running towards the building, Bas just behind us. The other four men went around the far side of the building, to head off Aseeb. We came to an enormous sliding door, big enough to admit a small ship, with a smaller door in one corner of it. This was open, so we went inside.

The internal space must have measured several acres. I could barely imagine what these sheds had once contained: perhaps ships had been built in here, monsters of iron and steel.

'Lights,' shouted Nick to Bas. 'Find the lights.' Bas was already flicking switches he had found beside the door. Floodlights came on far above us, the light glinting off metal: the enigmatic shape of a giant structure that was being constructed inside the building before being towed out to sea and lowered on to the ocean bed. In the shadows at the far end of the building, I could see four points of light: Nick's boys had got in and had switched on torches. There was no sign of Aseeb. Nick and Bas moved forward cautiously.

I looked around me. Aseeb could be hiding anywhere in this wilderness of metal and brick. There were piles of welding rods, metal plates and pipes, and stacks of flanges; at intervals were metal screens used to shield workers from the welding sparks, and machines of unguessable purpose. To my left I could see a doorway that appeared to lead into the outer wall of the building itself. Silently I went over to it and looked inside. A narrow stairway led upwards, but to what, I could not see. It looked as if this building had once had several floors, before they were torn out to make room for whatever oil platform was being built there at the time.

I climbed the stairs until I reached a narrow landing that appeared to run around the side of the building. Glassless windows peered down into the poorly lit space below, and looking through one of these I could see Nick and Bas moving carefully among the clutter on the floor. The four pinpoints of torchlight at the other end were moving closer, and if Aseeb was down there he would be caught between them, very soon.

But I didn't believe he was down there. A smell came to my nostrils – the faintest odour of sweat, and the scent of almond hair oil. After a moment I knew I wasn't imagining it. My desire to find Aseeb was very strong. I had not thought about what I would do when I found him. I wanted to ask him a question. But what that question was to be, I did not know. Whatever it was, I wanted an answer that would somehow comfort me, compensate for my overwhelming sense of loss. I knew I was unlikely to get an answer from Aseeb, but I had to try.

There was a movement at the end of the landing, twenty yards ahead of me. The light was very dim but I could see the figure of a man standing in the corridor. Why didn't he run? Then I realised that, beyond Aseeb, the corridor had been sliced away. Beyond where he stood there was nothing: only a drop of sixty feet or more down to the concrete floor below.

'You are a very persistent gentleman, Mr Gaunt,' he whispered.

I walked slowly towards him, as quietly as I could. I didn't want to alert Nick or Bas before I had had my chance to talk with Aseeb.

'Damned persistent,' repeated Aseeb, in a low voice. 'Unfortunately I have no gun, otherwise I would most certainly shoot you.'

I was only five yards away. My silence unsettled him.

'I surrender myself to Her Majesty the Queen and her authorised representatives,' he said suddenly, speaking out loud for the first time, his voice a little shrill. 'You are not an authorised person, Mr Gaunt. I want to surrender to the persons below. I demand to be taken into custody. I know my human rights.'

His voice caught the attention of Nick and Bas below. I heard Nick shout: 'Gaunt, where the hell are you? Who's that talking?'

They must have spotted the doorway, because I heard the sound of hurrying footsteps. I ignored them. I was now close enough to Aseeb to see that he was shaking. His dark brown eyes were fixed on mine and I could see the beads of perspiration running from his hairline down his face. He inched back so that he was standing on the edge of torn concrete. He spoke again, almost pleading:

'Please stay where you are, Mr Gaunt.'

'I have a question,' I told him. The words had come into my mind when I saw him. At last I knew what I wanted to ask. I wanted to ask what the last ten years of my life had been about. I wanted to ask why all those people had died in Baghdad; why Sergeant Hawke had been blown up in Afghanistan; why Adeena had to die. I just wanted to know what the point of it all was.

Aseeb looked past me, his eyes wide, the whites showing all the way around the dark brown irises. He was willing the other men to appear. I could hear them clattering up the stairs. As I looked into his eyes I knew he could never give me an answer to my question. So I asked him something else: 'Are you ready to die for what you believe in, like Adeena did? Are you ready?'

He did not answer. I think he was beyond speaking then. I pushed him lightly on the chest and he fell backwards into the gloom. A second later I heard the thud of his body landing on the concrete. I looked down. It didn't seem probable that he could have survived such a fall.

Nick and Bas arrived beside me so suddenly that for a moment I thought the three of us might follow Aseeb over the edge.

'What the hell happened here, Gaunt?' Nick said, steadying himself. 'Where's Aseeb?'

'I'm afraid he fell,' I said. 'He's down below.'

Twenty-Two

She wasn't even from Afghanistan.

She was ready to blow herself up for a country she didn't belong to. How could someone do that?

I asked Nick that question during one of the many debriefing sessions we had after our return from Middlesbrough. These took place in his offices above the parade of shops. This time there was no transport on offer: no black Audi, not even a minicab. I took the train and then walked.

The main office always seemed to have the same atmosphere of tension and irritation I had observed on my first visit. People sat with their heads down; phones kept ringing all the time. Nick seemed a little less tired on these subsequent visits and he had shaved and put on a clean shirt. Maybe his routine had quietened down since I last saw him.

On my last visit, he gave me a cup of coffee, watery as usual, and brought me up to date with events.

'You'll be relieved to hear that the inquiry into the death of Adeena Haq is now officially over,' he told me. 'We kept her married name out of the papers. She was shot by trained police officers in the course of their duties. As a result they prevented a second, very serious, terrorist outrage outside Lancaster House. You are not mentioned and officially you don't exist.'

So that was the end of that. No doubt Arthur and Martha would get a medal. Nick saw the relief on my face and added, 'The same goes for Aseeb. His accidental death while seeking to evade arrest is also a matter of record.'

He waited for me to comment. When I didn't, he continued, 'We wanted to *talk* to that guy, Richard. He could have told us a lot about who paid him, and where the money came from. You say it was an accident. That's what I'd do too: stick to my story. But no more chances, Richard. If someone drops dead from a heart attack on the other side of the street from you, we will assume it was you who did it and come after you.'

Nick paused to allow his point to sink in. Then he continued in a dispassionate tone: 'Of course, if we'd arrested Aseeb he'd have had his lawyers all over us and we'd have had one hell of a job proving anything. He was never caught near the action. It must have been Amir who collected Adeena and took her into central London. Aseeb was already far away. Still, we'd have liked the chance to talk to him.'

'Why was Adeena so ready to die for a country she didn't even belong to?'

'She never had a chance to think straight,' replied Nick. 'Her father was one of the original hard-core anarchists in the *événements* of 1968. Her mother had been brought up in the camps in south Beirut. Those camps were shelled and bombed by the Israelis, by the Christian militias, and sometimes by the Lebanese army. With parents like hers, what chance did she ever have of seeing the world any differently?'

He paused for a moment, then added, 'We see a lot of people like her in our files. In her late teens she was dragged around the tribal areas of Pakistan and the mountains of Afghanistan. She lived among al-Qaeda supporters and after the CIA killed her parents, they were the only family she had.'

'How come they let a woman do their dirty work for them?'

'The Taliban might not have allowed it, but AQ will use anyone they can get. Other fundamentalist groups have used women as bombers. Look at Hamas. There was even a woman who called herself Umm Osama Bin Laden and who started a woman's brigade for al-Qaeda.'

'What happened to her?'

'We haven't heard from her lately.'

'What about Aseeb?' I asked.

'We think he was a fixer: not al-Qaeda, not Taliban. He was in it for the money. The latest theory from our analysts – all their best work is explaining why something went wrong, rather then telling us what's going to happen – is that AQ wanted to make this attempt on the president in London because of the terrific propaganda. You've seen the papers since it happened?'

I hadn't. I'd been living the life of a recluse.

'Well, they're full of articles saying we should pull out of Afghanistan. Aseeb and his friends didn't really care whether they got their man or not. It was the publicity they wanted.'

'But Adeena said the Taliban were after her?'

'And they may have been,' said Nick. 'The Taliban don't want to get rid of the president. They think his government is doing a great job, doing their recruitment for them. The World Bank says Afghanistan is the fourth most corrupt country in the world. That's how the Taliban get their foot soldiers. They may well have been after Adeena.'

We both fell silent. As an explanation, this was barely

satisfactory, but it would have to be enough. All the people who could have told us more were dead.

'What are you going to do now, anyway?' asked Nick. He seemed to have given up trying to extract any further information about Adeena and Aseeb.

'I'm working at a jobcentre,' I told him. It was the only job I'd been able to get. Jobs were hard to find these days, even for those with qualifications. I had none: or at any rate, the qualifications I had were not valued in the civilian world. Nick laughed incredulously.

'Is that right? Is that really what you want to do with the rest of your life?'

'It's a job,' I told him. That was about all you could say for it. It was a job, and one in which my almost total lack of suitability for civilian life hadn't seemed to matter. It got me out of the flat, and paid me a wage. If I had sat around in the flat I wouldn't have been able to deal with the regret and the anger I still felt over Adeena's death: feelings made even worse because I still did not know quite what to believe. So I went to work and volunteered for all the overtime I could get, and came home and slumped in front of the television, then went to bed. The main thing was not to think.

At first I felt I had been betrayed by her. After a while I realised that whatever else she had done, Adeena had been true to her own beliefs. She had manipulated me, she and Aseeb between them, to give her the opportunity she had sought. I had been an accident. When they found the invitation to Lancaster House in my flat, the game plan had been changed. That was why she had come back to me: in order to use me.

In the manner of our times I sought to distance myself from what I had done. I attempted to look at the events of the last few weeks as I would once have looked at any other operation when things had gone wrong; not turned out quite as expected; or had, in fact, been a monumental disaster. We try to pretend that we can learn from our experience, with the irredeemable optimism of those who think some lesson can be distilled from the endless rehearsal of folly.

So what *had* I learned?

I had learned not to say yes, when someone offers you ten thousand pounds to marry someone you have never met. I had learned that it's a good idea to find out first what the catch is, when a good-looking girl turns up on your doorstep late at night asking for shelter.

So you could say that, as usual, I had learned nothing at all. The fact is I didn't care. I didn't care what she had been or what she had done. I wanted to remember her how she was during those two weeks we spent together. The rest of it I will try to forget.

In all of my life there has been only one true act of betrayal and it has nothing to do with Adeena. Nobody could have been truer to her beliefs, even though I know I shall never understand either her or them. What I have understood is that when Adeena turned to me in the courtyard outside Lancaster House, and smiled her smile at me, she was within seconds of what she believed to be martyrdom. So I too had no choice when it came to it.

I had grown used to the phone ringing and Nick's voice on the other end of the line, instructing me to go to his office. I hadn't really liked him, but he was company of a sort. He was my last link to Adeena, and the events of those weeks.

A week or two had passed since my last interview and I hadn't heard from Nick, so I took the trouble to walk down to the little street in Wandsworth. The office above the parade of shops was now empty. The venetian blinds had gone, and 'To Let' stickers were plastered across the windows. A day or two later I called Nick on the mobile number he had given me. All I got was a message saying the number was unobtainable.

The weeks passed, and became months. I worked away at my new career, but its anaesthetic powers began to fade. It was no longer enough to do a job that gave me no pleasure, and to divide my time between a desk, a television set and the sofa I dozed on at weekends. I began to wonder how I would conduct the rest of my life. There was a lot of time to kill before I grew old and died.

My thoughts began to turn from the dead to the living, and to the memory of my own act of treachery two years previously. It was not the worst thing I had done, only the most unforgivable. In between trying to forget about Adeena, and wondering how long I could stick at my new job, I found myself remembering Emma. At first it was just now and then; soon it was every day.

I wondered where she was now, and what she was doing. Only a few months ago someone had asked me at Freddie Meadowes' house whether Emma was now 'free' – free, that is, from my attentions. Free to be called up. Free to be wined and dined. Free to be taken into some stranger's bed. She might even be engaged or married by now, although I thought some kind soul such as Ed Hartlepool would have told me if that had happened.

For a while I simply accepted the idea that Emma would have moved on and met someone else, someone more suitable than I was. Occasionally I pictured her with the imaginary 'suitable' man. He might be a solicitor, like her father or mine. He might be a local farmer or landowner. Of course, her new husband would have given her a comfortable home and perhaps a baby or two. I would have heard, though, wouldn't I?

Why had I cut myself off from Emma? How had I managed to separate myself from my parents and my sister? What demon had possessed me so that I had lost touch with almost every single friend I had ever had? I knew that I had been damaged in some invisible way by my last few months in the army. I had read about so many other soldiers who had come home and gone off the rails. At least I hadn't been sent to prison yet – although God knows how I had avoided it. Maybe it wasn't my fault after all.

But in my heart I knew that I couldn't just blame it all on the wars I had been in. I wasn't even sure whether the fracture that had broken open deep within me was simply a consequence of the things I had seen; of the things I had heard; of the things I had done. When a stone shatters in the frost, is it because of the frost, or is it because the fault line was always there, deep inside the stone?

Maybe I should make an effort to get my life back, I thought. Maybe the scars – the psychic wounds of war – were fading. You never know. It could happen. Maybe I was going to be normal again one day. People got over things. If that was the case, then it was time to try to make something of my life instead of just drifting in and out on the tide.

One day a wholly unsurprising idea came into my head: 'Why not call Emma?'

What harm could there be in that?

At least then I could deal with all these images – Emma with a husband, Emma with a baby. I would know whether they were true or not. I might call her, just to find out how she was. Of course, once she knew who it was on the line she would probably refuse to take the call, or hang up. But we might speak for a moment. She would tell me about her new job, or the new man in her life. It would be painful at first but after a while I would become used to the fact that Emma had found a life without me. Once we had spoken, I too could move on.

That was what I told myself.

When I rang Emma's old number at her flat in Parliament Hill, there was of course no trace of her. The person who answered the phone had neither a forwarding address nor a phone number to give me. In the end I dug out her parents' number from an old address book. I didn't know whether her parents would even speak to me, let alone tell me how to get hold of Emma, but I couldn't think what else to do. It was Emma herself who answered the phone.

'Hello?'

Her voice was cool and distant: but the moment I heard it a picture of Em formed in my mind, as vivid as if she had been standing in front of me.

'It's me,' I told her; then realising it had been two years since she last heard my voice, I explained: 'It's Richard.'

There was an intake of breath, and then a silence.

'Don't hang up,' I said urgently. 'I just wanted to find out how you are.'

After a moment she said in a low voice: 'You ring up after two years to find out how I am? Why now? I can't believe you're doing this.'

'I've been thinking about you,' I said. 'I just wanted to pick up the phone and make sure you're all right.'

Another long silence, then: 'I'm all right. But I don't really want to talk to you.'

Then I said something that was quite unscripted: where the words came from I don't know, but they were out of my mouth before I could stop myself.

'Emma, I really want to see you again. Even if it's just for a cup of coffee.'

She thought about that for a while.

'I don't know how you dare say that. You betrayed me two years ago. I had to close the restaurant and I had to sell my flat to pay off the bank. Now I'm at home, living with Mummy and Daddy like some pathetic spinster. The best part of my life has gone by. Then you ring up out of the blue and invite me for a cup of coffee as if nothing had happened.'

'I'm sorry,' I said. 'I've been thinking about this call for weeks.'

'Well, the answer is no: I don't want to see *you* again, not even for a cup of coffee.'

So that was that. I thought she would hang up then, but she didn't. I could hear her breathing on the other end of the line.

'Em . . . I just wanted to say how sorry I am. I've never stopped regretting what I did, and how I behaved towards you. I was off my head in those days, but I'm better now. I have a steady job. Don't ask me what it is: you'd laugh if I told you. But I'm working. I'm trying to live like any normal person does. I guess that's all I've got to say: I'm sorry.'

Once again there was no answer, so I filled the silence.

'I'll hang up now. I can see how distressing this must be. I didn't want to upset you.'

Then a muffled voice: 'Richard – you can ring me again, if you like. Only not now: in a day or two.'

She sounded as if she was in tears, so I hung up. I stared at the phone, wondering whether she would ring back, but she didn't. Suddenly I was full of energy. I stood up and walked around the flat. What had I learned from the phone call? That she wasn't married, she wasn't engaged, she probably wasn't even seeing anyone. Her parents lived in a remote part of Dumfriesshire. She must be bored and lonely as hell. I wanted to see her again. This time I would get it right. I would see her again and we would talk.

Maybe there was a chance. There had to be a chance that she still felt something for me. I could hear it in her voice. And if there was a second chance, this time I wouldn't make such a mess of things.

The phone rang again and I picked it up almost before the second ring.

'Emma.'

'It's not Emma,' replied a familiar voice. 'Sorry to disappoint you, Leader. It's only me, Ed Hartlepool.'

'Oh,' I said. 'How are you, Ed?'

'Bored shitless. I'm in London for a few days. I'm thinking about going to the Diplomatic tonight, for a few hands of cards. Want to come?'

There were a thousand reasons why I didn't want to go to the Diplomatic. I disliked the memory of that smoky, dark and inauspicious room, full of the mingled odour of perspiration and cigar smoke. I didn't want to see the misanthropic Eric again, with his potato face and potato eyes. I didn't want to see Bernie, or Willi Falkenstein. I didn't really want to see Ed. I didn't have any money to spare, especially for gambling. I had turned away from that world for ever and the thought of going back to it filled me with revulsion. That was all part of my old existence, the life I had put behind me.

On the other hand . . . I was bored. The phone call with Emma had left me feeling restless and I needed to get out of the flat. I couldn't remember when I had last gone anywhere, or seen anyone outside work.

'Do you want to come?' repeated Ed.

'Why not?'

Acknowledgements

During my research for this book I read a number of books and in particular I would like to acknowledge the help I had from reading *Task Force Black* by Mark Urban, published by Little, Brown. I am also indebted to *The Circuit* by Bob Shepherd, published by Pan Macmillan.

I also had help from talking to a number of former serving soldiers in the British Army. I won't embarrass them by naming them, but would like to emphasise that any mistakes in this novel are all mine, and not the result of any advice I received.